The Tao of Laurenson

donated
Oct 2006

ALEXANDRA WRITERS' CENTRE LIBRARY

The Tao of Laurenson

R.F. Darion

© 2006, R.F. Darion

All rights reserved. No part of this book may be reproduced, for any reason, by any means, without the permission of the publisher.

Cover design by Terry Gallagher/Doowah Design.
Printed and bound in Canada by AGMV Marquis.
This book was printed on Ancient Forest Friendly paper

We acknowledge the support of The Canada Council for the Arts and the Manitoba Arts Council for our publishing program.

Library and Archives Canada Cataloguing in Publication

Darion, R. F., 1945–
    The Tao of Laurenson / R. F. Darion.

ISBN 1-897109-08-3

    I. Title.

PS8557.A5947T36 2006   C813'.6   C2006-902619-X

Signature Editions, P.O. Box 206, RPO Corydon
Winnipeg, Manitoba, R3M 3S7

For my father, George T. Smith,
who valued family above all
and met his death with great patience.

And with special love, for my grandson, Teio,
who joined us such a short time ago, and yet
is so far down the way that's known as The Tao.

CHAPTER ONE

The Glory Hills blazed with crimson and gold. It was September 24th and the temperature was an incongruous 28 degrees Celsius—more like summer than Indian summer. Dan Laurenson, commanding officer of the St. Michael RCMP, was painting the picket fence around his yard, hampered or assisted in varying degrees by his Chesapeake Bay retriever and by Christie Devenish, his... For Laurenson there was no appropriate word for what Christie was to him. All the traditional words like "lady friend," "lover," "mistress," and "flame" misrepresented their relationship; and he would have choked on the word "sweetheart." On the other hand, modern alternatives like "significant other" and "partner" were alien to him. Since Christie had entered his life six months earlier, he had very gradually (even for a forty-five-year-old) come to the conclusion that the only thing to be done with her was to make her his wife, whether her kids—or his—liked it or not. His were grown and scattered, but hers were very much on the scene and vocal about his increased presence.

In a rainstorm on a mountaintop, within a whisker of hypothermia in August, he had come close to asking her to marry him. There was something about the way she turned adversity into adventure that made proposing seem the only appropriate response. Still, sensing she would refuse, he had restrained himself; realizing how this frustrated him only later when he made love to her with such fierce passion that he frightened her a little.

Since these days Christie wanted to belong only to herself, it was ironic that, immediately upon her return to work in the fall, her concern had become focused on *not* belonging. In response to grant cutbacks from the government, her employer had resorted to an attempt at "creative dismissal," trying to nudge her into quitting her job so he could stretch his budget.

"Think of it as an adventure," Laurenson said suddenly, apropos of nothing. "Fewer paint spatters that way," he added, indicating her paint-flecked arms.

"Think of what as an adventure?"

"This whole thing with the school board. It's what you were thinking about, isn't it?"

"A pretty safe guess, I suppose, under the circumstances."

"No guess at all, considering you're going at the fence as though it were the chief superintendent."

"I'll never understand how you can take those kinds of dirty tricks so much in stride."

"This isn't the dirtiest trick I've seen in my time."

"He might as well have demoted me to janitor," she fumed. "Mick Rooney retired too. It's a wonder he didn't put me in *his* old job."

Laurenson chuckled.

"I don't see what's so funny."

"I know. And I never thought I'd see the day my sense of humour would be in better shape than yours. Staff sergeants aren't noted for their sense of humour, you know."

"So you think it's a real hoot making a facilitator into a secretary so she'll quit."

"You're leaving out the pretty pickle he got himself into with the union, trying to do that. And," he added with a ghost of a smile, "your own role in making sure they'd hang him out to dry for attempting it."

Reluctantly she smiled a little. "I guess he didn't think I'd be this hard to deal with." Her hazel eyes flashed, however, and she added, jabbing her paintbrush into the can of paint, "But it still burns me up that he'd do something this underhanded just to save a little severance pay. Haven't I said all along that it would make sense to cut my job in view of the tight budget? Isn't it bad enough that I have to start job-hunting again at forty-two? Do I have to be manipulated out of the money I have coming to me, too?"

"But think of all the good therapy you'd have missed if he'd suddenly changed his *modus operandi* after all these years."

"Therapy?"

"What else would you call having a chance to stand up to him—something to stand up to him *about*—as you head out the door?"

"I'm stressed out and *you're* calling it therapy!"

"You've been under stress for nine years. I thought the worm would enjoy turning."

"*Worm*," she sputtered. "That doesn't endear you to anyone, you know, you big lunk."

"No? I'll have to think of another way of making you feel better then. Something less *cerebral*," he added, with a gleam in his midnight blue eyes.

"Thanks," she said sarcastically. "Your good intentions are duly noted."

"And will be rewarded."

"Blat to that," she said with finality and, for the next few minutes, the only sound was the slapping of their paintbrushes interspersed with long yawns from the dog at their feet.

When the dog, Megan, flopped over onto her other side a little later, she knocked over the can of paint thinner. "Damn," Laurenson said, diving for the can a second too late.

It was on the resulting trip to Home Depot for more paint thinner that Laurenson first saw the old man. Gaunt and shabbily dressed in faded denim overalls that had worn through at the knees, the old man had a long weather-beaten face that was framed with wispy white hair at the the top and covered with white stubble at the bottom. From out of his sunburn, the man scanned each passerby with gentle brown eyes. At the same time, he absentmindedly patted the many pockets on his blue overalls with large gnarled hands.

When Laurenson passed back that way ten minutes later, the same man still stood on the same busy corner, patting his pockets and searching each passing face. Thinking he might be lost or in trouble, Laurenson pulled over within half a block and walked back toward him. He changed his mind and turned back to his car, however, when he saw with what scant interest those soulful brown eyes surveyed *him*. This wasn't, he decided, a demented person feeling lost and afraid; it was someone elderly but still alert who was waiting for a friend.

    The next time Laurenson saw the old man, he was sitting on a low wall surrounding the central fountain in St. Michael's largest mall. Still shabby and watchful, this time he lounged at his ease, idly swinging a big-booted foot and munching on an Oh Henry. This time, he showed some interest in Laurenson. This, Laurenson put down to the fact that he was in uniform and that St. Michael was still a small enough city that a resident would likely take note of each police officer serving there, even if those same officers stood no chance of mentally noting each resident. A second glance led him to amend his observation slightly. The man was more likely to have come from one of the surrounding farms than from the city itself. Certainly his boots were mud-caked in a way that didn't square with urban living; at least not on this dry fall day and among all these dry-shod mall customers.

    The third time he saw the old man, it was Christie who pointed him out. "Lately, every time I go downtown I see him," she said. "And each time I pass him, he looks at me long and hard. I'd worry if it weren't that I've seen him looking over *all* the women."

    In Laurenson's view it only made sense that men would look twice at Christie. Slender, pretty, and graced with shoulder-length honey-coloured hair, she was someone *he* loved to look at. If, however, the old man was looking at *all* the women—

    "Maybe he's not as old as I thought," he said.

    "It's hard to tell how old he is. Were those laugh lines or wrinkles?"

    "How old would you put him at?"

    "Over sixty at least," she replied.

    "*Sixty?* I was inclined to think he could be the far side of eighty."

    "You think he looks weak enough to be eighty? Every time I've seen him he's been on his feet."

    "Not bad for a civilian," Laurenson remarked. "If the college press doesn't come through with a job offer soon, I think the force would do well to snap you up."

She laughed and they walked on together. Had she not been with him, however, he would have stopped to talk with the old—possibly old—man. Someone who was becoming a bit of a public fixture made him curious.

At the office the next day, Laurenson again thought of the man and stopped by Corporal Val Tavarov's desk.

"Heard anything lately of an old man who's taken to standing around heavy traffic areas looking like a cross between a panhandler and an Alzheimer's wanderer?"

Tavarov looked up from a stack of paperwork. "Someone's finally complained about him?"

"You know about him?"

"I've heard of him, though I haven't seen him myself."

"What have you heard?"

Tavarov clasped his hands behind his head and stretched out his long legs. "As far as I know, he hasn't been bothering anyone, but we've been fielding a few calls since August—people wondering if this is a Dependent Adult in need of assistance."

"He looks pretty alert to me."

"That's what Darin was saying just the other day. Scott, though, has talking to this man high on his list of things to do."

"Figures," Laurenson replied. He had considerable respect for Darin Childe's good sense, whereas Scott McVicar, the oldest man serving under him, was constantly rubbing him the wrong way thanks to his rulebook mentality.

Tavarov shrugged. "The thing is, Todd pulled over and signaled to the man one day, only to have him start walking away. When he headed after him on foot, he lost him in the crowd."

"Really?"

"Yeah. Now I'm not saying accidents don't happen; but, if Todd Rainier wants to talk to some old guy on the street and loses him, it's got *me* just a little bit curious."

A thing like that made Laurenson curious too. Unlike some of his men, he wasn't a 911 cop, someone who responded to complaints by going through a few motions and then congratulated himself on doing a hell of a job. He was the sort of cop who, when he watched a prizefight on television, seized every opportunity to look the crowd over for hinky individuals…just for the fun of it. Like Val or Todd, he never went anywhere in uniform without being aware on some level of who tried to avoid him. In the States he knew it was the overly friendly individual who aroused police suspicion, but in a relatively benign environment like St. Michael, Alberta, it was still the person who looked away or tried to drift out of his purview who drew more than his fair share of attention.

"Still," Laurenson temporized, "Darin wasn't worried by him."

"No, but then Darin didn't try to talk to him."

"Maybe the Mafia has finally wised up to the advantages of using octogenarian hit men," Laurenson said with a grin.

"About time," Tavarov replied. "Just try loitering if you *don't* have white hair."

At that point the detachment short-wave radio came to life with a sudden screech and Laurenson started to walk toward his office. "Bravo three to Detachment," Ross Waring squawked through a steady rat-a-tat of static. Ten-twenty-three. EMR arriving. Looks like this is going to take awhile."

"I'll keep an eye out," Tavarov called out to Laurenson over the noise.

"Thanks. So will I," Laurenson called back.

―――

"I understand you're wondering about the old geezer who was hanging around the post office today," Ted Makarian said a few days later.

"Define 'geezer,'" Laurenson responded.

Makarian shifted uncomfortably, and began again. "Val said you'd want to know about an old man I saw watching the post office this morning. Not that he was bothering anybody."

"How old a man was he?"

"Beats me. Old as the hills, I'd say. Seventy anyway."

"Any idea who he might be?"

"Sorry. I saw him, but there wasn't any reason to *do* anything about him."

Constable Scott McVicar came into Laurenson's office warily.

"Something I can do for you, Staff?"

"Ah, Scott," Laurenson said, making an effort to sound cordial. "Sit down. I understand we've both become curious about an old man who seems to be becoming a bit of a local landmark these days."

"Everyone's seen him but me, it seems."

"You've never seen him? I heard you wanted to talk to him."

"I'd settle for seeing him, at least for starters. There was an old guy in here on a Saturday in July who fits the description. I'd be curious to see if he's the same fellow."

"Why was he in here?"

"It was a week or so after they dug up those bones south of here. Apparently he'd called the detachment in Spruce Grove trying to get some information, but no one would give him the time of day. At least, that's what he said. According to him, he filed a missing-persons report a long time ago and he wanted to know basically if the person he'd misplaced had turned up dead. Not that either of us put it that bluntly at the time. Naturally, I told him to contact K-Division Headquarters and gave him the number. Warned him that he probably wasn't going to be able to learn anything any time soon and then I got back to the phones. From what I hear the old man on the street could be the same fellow, but I can't for the life of me figure out what he's up to now."

"Did you get his name?"

"He signed the book, but I've gone back to it since then and—"

"Illegible?"

"Oh I could read it; that's not the problem. The problem is it was almost certainly an alias. M. Smith. It figures; he was checking on the identification of human remains after all. What else would you expect someone to be named who's inquiring into a wrongful death?"

Laurenson hesitated to ask the next question because he knew in advance that McVicar would pour forth a veritable flood of self-defense. It wasn't worth unleashing that flood just to elicit an answer that he could predict with considerable certainty. Still, it would be cowardly, he figured, to avoid asking the question in order to save himself the spiel.

"Any missing-persons reports on file that might fit?"

In the end, he figured it had been worthwhile asking after all. Not because asking had led to obtaining any information, but because McVicar had outdone himself in sanctimonious self-exculpation, providing more than a little entertainment.

Eventually the middle-aged constable concluded with, "I found it hard to justify going on a fishing expedition like that when we're short-handed and the chances of being able to find something that fit what little I knew were so slim. And anyway, what was I supposed to do with it if, by some miracle, I did find something?"

Laurenson bit his tongue but ended up saying anyway, "Nothing much, I suppose, unless you wanted to get a name off the report and track down this man so you could ask him what he's up to now."

McVicar paused, and Laurenson hurried on before he could launch another defense. "Though I can see why you would figure it made sense to just wait and see. Clearly you expected your paths were going to cross."

"Exactly. I'd have a hard time justifying putting my time into research like that when I could be out on the street doing some good *and* making it statistically impossible to avoid running into this man sooner or later."

"Exactly," Laurenson echoed. Privately, however, he was pretty sure of two things. One: it would have taken less than half an hour to have pulled the missing-persons reports for the last fifteen years. And, two, it was high time Scott McVicar got booted upstairs to a desk job or transferred to some nice little international airport somewhere. This was a man who had been passed over for promotion once too often, and it was about time his commanding officer did something about it.

Not agreeing with McVicar that being known by the name of Smith meant a person was living under an alias—there must be *some* Smiths, to judge from the number of people by that name in the telephone book—Laurenson did a DMV search of Smiths with driver's licences in the St. Michael area. When that didn't provide him with a male M. Smith, he looked for rural landowners. What was the use of having a hunch if you weren't willing to bet a bunch?

There was a Michaelangelo Smith living three kilometres south of town.

Laurenson took another five minutes and came up with a missing-person's report filed in 1989 by a Michaelangelo Smith of the address he had already obtained. A desk job was too good for McVicar; there must be some way of getting him assigned to visiting dignitaries and ceremonial occasions in Ottawa.

Laurenson examined with interest the information given on December 23rd, 1989 by the father of an eighteen-year-old named Rozilind Claire Smith. At that time, the daughter had been missing for forty-eight hours. True, she sometimes spent the night with friends, but her best friend, Brandy Heyden, had gone away to university in the fall and it had been at Brandy's house that Rozilind had most often stayed over. With Christmas only two days away, the father had been sure that something must have happened to his daughter. Why else wouldn't he have heard from her? He had called her place of employment, Lexilogic Data Systems of St. Michael, but they hadn't seen her since the 20th. There weren't many other places to check but he had called neighbours and a few of his daughter's friends, all with no result. Laurenson did the math on the father's birth date and came up with his age—fifty-six. That would make him sixty-one now.

The first thing an investigation had ascertained was that the daughter wasn't in any of the region's hospitals or morgues.

Next, it had been determined that her closet and drawers were emptier than they should have been. Still very full by anyone's standards, nevertheless, they no longer contained some of her favourite items: a white angora sweater, a grey cardigan with satin appliqué, some designer jeans, a spaghetti-strap dress with a seed-pearl trim, and a baby blue suede suit.

As far as anyone could tell, there had been no quarrel between Rozilind and her father, no trouble at work, no boyfriend problems, no financial or mental health difficulties…nothing that would explain a young woman's suddenly leaving without saying a word just days before Christmas. Neither was there any physical evidence to support a suspicion of foul play.

Eventually, the investigation had come to the conclusion many such investigations come to. When someone old enough to be on their own disappears without there being a reason to suspect foul play, it's logical to assume that the missing person disappeared of their own volition. When all the leads have been checked out, it only makes sense to move on to other more promising cases. If the family can't accept the absence of the missing person, they can try a private investigator, but chances are good that the object of their search doesn't want to be found and therefore won't be.

Laurenson himself was of the opinion that the police had better things to do than track down runaways who would only run away again once they'd been returned home, or to squander limited resources on custody disputes and other non-criminal matters. Still, he felt sorry for any parent left to face Christmas alone without the least idea of what had become of their only child. Since Michaelangelo Smith had been a widower for ten years by the time of his daughter's disappearance, Laurenson figured it must have been especially hard for him.

To make matters worse for the old man, he, as the missing person's nearest and dearest, had become a lightning rod for suspicion and innuendo. Regrettably so, it would appear, since his signature on Rozilind Smith's missing-persons report matched the "M. Smith" on the detachment's visitor register for July 15th. Who had ever heard of a killer searching for his victim years after the murder? Still, who could say with complete certainty that a person troubled with regret but grown confused and forgetful might not call attention to a previously overlooked homicide precisely by searching for a victim no one else even knew was dead?

Laurenson drove out to Michaelangelo Smith's farm on a beautiful warm day just before Thanksgiving. Stubble fields alternated with narrow plowed fields on either side of a long, tree-lined driveway. At the end of it, with its back up against a stand of tall pines, a small white house looked south over a large vegetable garden put to bed for the winter. He found Michaelangelo Smith changing the straw in a snug little hen house whose inhabitants were off foraging among some nearby raspberry canes. The ease with which Smith forked in clean bedding was a silent commentary on judging a man's age by his hair colour.

"Mr. Smith?"

At first, tunelessly humming, Smith didn't hear him. Laurenson watched unobserved, content to take his measure of the man for a moment before engaging him in conversation. The cleanliness of the hen house was striking, as was the friendliness of a little black hen that pecked quietly at the cuffs of the old man's overalls as he worked. The impression created by the scene was one of repose in action, and of a bond between the man and his chickens. The sweet smell of hay contrasted strikingly with the stench in which so many farmers expected their chickens to live. A fastidious man like Laurenson could not help being favorably impressed.

He was less positively affected by the way Smith's face hardened as he looked up and saw a Mountie in his doorway.

"Mr. Smith? My name is Dan Laurenson. I'm with the St. Michael RCM Police."

Suddenly Smith chuckled. "Old guard, I see."

"I beg your pardon?"

"The young ones refer to themselves as the RCMP. But no doubt you've noticed that yourself."

"Ah yes. Still, old habits die hard."

Smith examined Laurenson's sleeve and motioned toward the four stripes just below his shoulder. "Too many stripes," he said. "I can't imagine why anyone with that many stripes on his arm would be coming to see *me*."

"Do you remember having seen me before?"

"Should I?"

"Probably not. But I've passed you a few times lately in St. Michael. You were, I think, looking for someone."

The leathery face of the man said "not bad" but quickly resumed its poker-faced expression.

"And?" he prompted.

"And I wanted to know more."

"You must have gone to some trouble over me."

"Why do you say that?"

The man forked a little more straw over into a relatively bare corner. "I wasn't, as far as I know, wearing a sign with my name on it."

"No. Nor were you particularly well-known."

"I'm not even in the phone book, as you no doubt found out."

"I didn't even try the phone book," Laurenson said. "Too many non-pubs these days." This time he had no difficulty reading the timeworn face in front of him. "Too many numbers are unlisted these days. There are easier ways of tracing someone," he added.

"Still can't say I can see why you'd want to."

"Any word from your daughter?"

Smith forked a little more straw. "No. And no word from you folks either."

"Us, or K-Division Headquarters?"

"You're all a bunch of bastards in my book."

"Is that why you avoid cops who indicate they want to have a word with you?"

Smith frowned and then laughed. "Oh, I think I know what you're talking about. No. Well, maybe. But I'm sick of people asking if I'm all right; I figured it was just a matter of time before some busybody would sic the cops on me."

"No cop worth his salt is going to mistake you for a mental case. Not unless you're having one hell of a good day today."

Smith chuckled and leaned his pitchfork against a wall. "People are funny. One day they're out to make the world safe by getting you off the streets…without diddly in the way of a reason to think you're a menace, by the way. The next day they're sure you can't cross a street without their help. With about as much common sense behind their opinion, if you ask me."

"You're older now."

"Not a hell of a lot older. But I *look* older. My hair went white five years ago."

"It must have been a terrible time for you."

Smith looked searchingly into Laurenson's face and seemed satisfied with what he found there. "So, does that mean you've decided to help me?"

"Help you how?"

"Help me find out what you people have learned about the body they dug up south of Spruce Grove last summer."

"Of course I will. There's nobody who has a better right to know. But I want you to tell me one or two things too."

"Shoot."

"If you think your daughter may be dead, why have you been looking for her so much this fall? I gather that's what you've been doing, standing in public places known for their heavy pedestrian traffic, scanning every passing face."

"Someone thought they saw her. Com' on, I could do with a smoke. Want me to make you a cup of coffee?"

"No, that's fine."

"Well, then, let's sit down in the sun somewhere. I'm dying for a smoke."

They sat on a wooden swing a little downhill in a small stand of trees. Smith lit a cigarette and sighed contentedly.

"You were saying someone thought they had seen your daughter," Laurenson prompted.

"Yes, a neighbour who'd know her if anyone would. Not that it seemed likely. I *hope* she wouldn't come back to St. Michael and not even stop in to see me. But you never know; I would never have thought she'd have lit out the way she did either."

"It was totally unexpected?"

"Totally."

"No warning signs...even now that you've had more time to think about it?"

"Roz was never what you might call a contented person. The wonder was that she continued to live here with me once she got a job. She hated the farm. Through most of her teens she didn't seem to like me much either. But that's no reason to drop off the face of the earth, is it? I mean, kids leave home all the time. Why would I expect mine is going to do it differently? Without a word, taking practically nothing. She was eighteen, after all; she could do what she liked."

"What made you finally conclude she might have actually left of her own free will?"

"I don't know. No, I take that back. I think the light went on for me when they got me to go through her things to see if anything was missing. No daughter—that's one thing. But no blue suede suit...now that makes a person think. She loved that suit."

"So it was something you couldn't imagine her leaving home without."

"I can't imagine anyone being so attached to a piece of clothing that they would have to take it with them, no matter what. But Roz loved that suit and, though she liked nice clothes and had some choice items, she liked that particular suit more than any of the rest. The thing is—that suit didn't just walk out on its own."

"Maybe she tired of it without your being aware or noticing she'd gotten rid of it."

"I'd have noticed. She looked like a million dollars in it."

"So you say the light went on for you when you realized some of her favourite clothes were missing."

"For you people, too. Only you'd become attached to the notion that I'd bopped her over the head and buried her in the back forty or something."

"Not so easy to do in the dead of winter."

"Aw, the old well would have done nicely. I could have put her down it and shoveled snow over top. The thing is, I didn't."

Laurenson wasn't sure whether Smith was watching for his reaction with curiosity or defiance. "Apparently not. Why would you be in to see us five years later asking questions about a body we'd found, if you'd already disposed of her satisfactorily?"

"Exactly."

"So when was it the neighbour said she'd seen your daughter?"

"Early in August."

"Not so easy to stake out the entire city on your own during harvest time."

"Oh, I'm not still farming. I've rented both my quarter sections out. All I work now is my garden, the chickens and a few acres of tree farm."

"How do you get into town?"

"On my bike when weather permits. Sometimes I catch a ride, otherwise I walk."

"How long is it since you had a driver's licence?"

"A few years now. It's not a problem, living this close to town."

"Still, most people would keep their licence current if they could."

"I didn't renew it six years ago because I had a problem with cataracts. Since then I've had my eyes operated on and I could reapply, I suppose, but my old truck gave up the ghost about the time my eyes got bad, and since then the price of trucks has gone through the roof.

Even something with a couple hundred thousand klicks on it will go for three thousand if you can start it."

"Ever tried the auctions?"

"If I wanted to risk my money, I'd go to Vegas."

"How long do you plan to keep watching for your daughter in town?"

Smith looked away. "Well, winter's on its way. And, anyway, I guess I've given it about as good a shot as anyone could expect."

The loss of eye contact bothered Laurenson. The words being spoken were completely innocuous but it was as though a blip had suddenly appeared on a previously blank radar screen.

"Beginning to lose hope?"

"It was a harebrained thing to do in the first place," Smith said.

"Admittedly, it doesn't seem likely she'd return to St. Michael without contacting you."

Again a blip. This time, a moment's hesitation.

"Yeah, crazy idea, eh?" Smith laughed, and Laurenson's radar went blip, blip, blip.

"Well, in any case, I'll find out what I can for you about the remains found a few months ago."

"Great," Smith said. "I'd really appreciate that."

He sounded sincere and he'd stopped looking off toward a tumbledown section of ancient barbed wire fence. But still Laurenson wasn't satisfied. Was he getting fanciful in his old age, or had Smith sounded *too* sincere?

"By the way," he said, reluctant to leave just now. "I've been wondering about your name."

Smith laughed. "What about my name?"

"It's rather unusual."

"Exactly the reaction my mother was hoping for, apparently. Smith was my father's way of leaving the Old World behind when he moved to the new. My mother, however, wasn't big on total anonymity."

Now the man sounded natural again. Still, all the way back to his car, Laurenson's radar continued to go blip, blip, blip, blip.

Chapter Two

Laurenson waited for the door to open, steeling himself for the ordeal to follow. From the moment he'd expressed an interest in Christie, her two teens had shown nothing but hostility towards him. Teens could be prickly enough—even his own had had their moods—but Shaun and Angela seemed to be overdoing it—defending the status quo to the death. He smiled remembering how angry his own kids had been when he and Lisa had called it quits. Come to think of it, his kids hadn't even been living at home any more. *Let's face it*, he thought, *teens are ultra conservative...the world's most ardent rebels and greatest conservatives all rolled up in one hormone-drenched...torch*. He squared his shoulders as he heard the deadbolt being drawn back on the other side of the door. For the next few hours it was his job to keep the match from the torch. If he succeeded at that, maybe the kids would begin to see the potential benefits of his encroaching on their turf. Lord knew what those benefits would be; he didn't much like either the kids in question or the prospect of playing "Dad" again, but he would do his damnedest to make things good for Christie.

It was Christie who answered the door. She smiled but her face carried a heavy load of tension.

"How's it going?" he asked, handing her a box of truffles and a bottle of white wine.

"Supper's almost ready," she replied. It was an evasion that didn't escape him.

"Smells wonderful!"

"Come in, let me pour you a drink. I could do with one myself." Apart from the sound of steam escaping a pot, the house was oddly silent for 4:30 on Thanksgiving Day. As Laurenson stepped inside, Christie looked at the box and the bottle in her arms, blinked at them as though wondering where they'd come from, and then thanked him.

"What's wrong?" he asked.

"Nothing's wrong."

"You really hope to make that one fly?"

She gave him a wider, warmer smile. "Don't you ever go off duty?"

"You mean stop thinking? Why would I want to do that? Especially just as I enter the lion's den."

"Well, as it turns out, the lions are out at the moment. In fact, they're threatening to boycott the event."

"What, they absolutely refuse to eat me alive?"

"There's been a lot of snarling, but I think they're really not entirely sure who will be eating who, if they stick around."

"I could live with that."

"Live with what?"

"With a Thanksgiving dinner, alone with you. I know it doesn't do what you were hoping for; but, if two of us, at least, enjoy it… Well, that's more than most people manage with Thanksgiving dinners. At least in my experience."

She shook her head. "Thanksgiving is a time for family, not warfare and kids wandering the streets. Whoever heard of having a tête-à-tête over a turkey?"

"If wandering the streets doesn't make them happy you can be sure they'll come home by suppertime."

"You must have been dreading this more than you let on," she suggested shrewdly.

He shrugged. "Don't worry, I have no doubt whatsoever that dinner will go forward as scheduled. They've probably staked out the house, time is dragging like crazy, and they're getting hungrier by the minute."

She relaxed a little. "Sounds possible. Would you like a drink?"

He rolled his eyes at this second invitation, and she burst out laughing. "Okay. I feel like a rum and Coke, but I've also got—"

"Rum and Coke would be fine," he said, following her into the kitchen.

She poured drinks, took a sip of hers, and stirred a pot of gravy. Laurenson sat down on a high stool at a raised counter, taking a sip of his.

"Sometimes I wonder which one of us is conventional-minded," Christie remarked, peering into another pot and then giving it a shake.

"*Since when?*"

Right from the start he'd been aware that her preconceived notions about cops hadn't been flattering. And because he had successfully risen through the ranks of what she saw as a repressive organization, she was all the more convinced he must be narrow-minded and devoid of humour.

"You're sounding like Mr. Permissive or something," she complained with a twinkle. "Today I'm the one arguing for making the kids put on their company manners and 'do the right thing,' and you're advocating letting them run wild."

"All I'm doing is giving them permission to miss a family dinner." He refrained from saying, *one they're hell bent on ruining if they can.*

"You don't suppose they'll get the impression that I don't *care*, do you?"

"You've tried to be mother *and* father to them since your ex left. Far from giving the impression that you don't care, I think you've been giving the impression that you live only for them."

"The thing is, it doesn't seem to have sunk in. They always seem to feel deprived."

"Feel deprived, or act as though they feel deprived?"

"Admit it—you think I spoil them."

"You bet I do. But then I'm the one arm wrestling them for a bit of you."

She chuckled and Laurenson began to hope that she'd come around yet. The last thing he wanted was for the kids to succeed in poisoning the holiday she'd hoped would make peace among those she cared about.

Christie needn't have worried. When she finally served dinner—certainly within minutes of their beginning to relax and enjoy eating it—the back door slammed. Shaun and Angela sauntered in, looking more surprised than made sense in view of the fact that they must have passed by the dining room window just moments earlier.

"Hi," Laurenson said affably, "you're just in time."

Fourteen-year-old Angela looked to her older brother for guidance. When he appeared undecided, she gave Laurenson a tentative smile and sat down quickly at the table.

"Mmm. Smells good," she said. "Hope you left some for us."

The serving dishes heaped high with steaming food spoke for themselves, but Christie must have been feeling guilty. "We waited, but I was afraid the food would get cold."

Laurenson figured that was a bad move, not only because self-defense often invites attack but because kids who felt so cocksure, so *entitled*, struck him as way out of balance. These kids needed a dose of insensitivity. They'd had loving-kindness till hell wouldn't have it; to be disregarded for once would be healthier for them in the long run.

"You *never* have dinner ready on time. How were we supposed to guess this time it'd be different?" Shaun complained.

"Goes to show," Christie responded. "Miracles can happen."

Now that was more like it. Laurenson passed Shaun the turkey and resumed his interrupted conversation with Christie.

"So they won't let you work at your desk, eh? Why do you suppose that is?"

"Probably because of a legal technicality of some kind," she replied. "Sister Mary Clare says not to worry, their bark is worse than their bite."

"Sister Mary Clare is fomenting rebellion? What's this world coming to?"

"Ah well, she's always been a dear."

Shaun snorted.

"Pardon me?" Christie said, turning to him.

"I didn't say anything."

"I thought you wanted to say something."

"Not me. This conversation is boring."

"Feel free to jump in and save us from ourselves," Christie said.

Angela giggled and Shaun gave her a dirty look.

The silence drew out longer than was comfortable.

"You say they've contacted their lawyer?" Laurenson asked, drawing Christie back to the point she'd been making just as the children entered.

"Uh...yeah. I suspect they're hoping to nail me for refusing to accept re-assignment or something. I hear they've called a board meeting solely to talk about little old me."

"So what have they got you doing these days?"

"Lately I've been finishing off a high school unit I didn't get done before summer holidays. They were determined to stop me, until I started researching employer/employee legislation, then suddenly they didn't mind it so much."

"I'm surprised they didn't decide to fire you for doing private reading on company time."

"How could they when I was preparing a staff booklet on employer/employee legislation?"

"That's not what they're paying you for."

"It's not always easy to establish what they're paying me for. A facilitator can facilitate practically anything. In fact, the reason I didn't get this unit I'm working on finished last term was because they put me to work researching ways of improving communications with the schools."

They both laughed, remembering how she had come to him at the time complaining that she had found a solution to a problem and some colleagues had retaliated by making her draw up an action plan. Eventually they had made her draw up a whole series of action plans, each one of which they had then proceeded to reject for one reason or another.

"Hoist by their own petard!"

"What does *that* mean?" Angela asked.

"Probably, 'shafted by their own weapon,'" Laurenson said. "I have no idea what a petard would be. The thing is, your mom—"

Shaun yawned theatrically.

"Your mom," Laurenson went on blandly, "was forced to do some work that made her mad, but now that same work acts as a precedent, giving her a chance to get a little of her own back. Not only was she smart enough to think of a way of resisting an illegal ploy called 'creative dismissal' but she had the courage to do it."

"I don't see why you're laughing about it all," Angela protested. "It sounds awful."

"Awful things can be funny...especially when they turn out unexpectedly well."

"I don't get it," Angela said flatly. She turned to Shaun. "Pass the cranberry sauce."

"*You* get it, though," Laurenson said to Christie. "That's the important thing."

Angela turned her back on the cranberry sauce Shaun was now waving at her. "It's not that I don't *get* it," she said, "just that I don't *believe* it."

"Keep your eyes peeled," Laurenson replied amicably. "You'll be amazed how often people shaft themselves."

It was at that point that Shaun put a finger in his mashed potatoes, raised it to his mouth, and sucked on it. Slowly, with his eyes steadily on Laurenson, he repeated the maneuvre. It seemed like an odd thing to do, and Laurenson watched bemused. It wasn't until Ange began to giggle that it finally dawned on him what was happening. The finger at Shaun's lips was a middle finger; Shaun was surreptitiously giving him the finger. He watched, doubting his conclusion, and Shaun faltered, confirming it.

Ah shit. This kid was more of a jerk than he'd realized. Christie had spoiled him for so long it would take...who knew what it would take to straighten him out?

Angela put her napkin to her mouth in an attempt to cover up glee that seemed on the verge of exploding. Suddenly, Christie startled them all by standing up and pointing with a shaking finger.

"*Shaun. Leave the table. Now.*"

Shaun stared at her, his mouth slack with surprise and his middle finger up to its first joint in potatoes. Then his mouth snapped shut and his eyes smouldered. "What's *your* problem?"

"*You.* We'll talk about this later. Right now, I want you out of my sight."

Angela's eyes were round above the napkin she still held to her mouth.

Christie turned to her. "Would you mind bringing in the coffee, Ange?"

Shaun interrupted this on a rising note "I'm eating. Why should I leave?"

"Because I told you to."

"This is bullshit. I'm not done—"

"Oh yes, you are. I've had enough for one night."

"Mom! You're embarrassing him," Angela remonstrated under her breath.

"This is between your brother and me," Christie said. "Anyone who doesn't like how I'm dealing with this is welcome to leave the table."

Laurenson was as mesmerized as the teenagers. Christie turned to him. "Would you like some coffee?"

"I'd love some coffee," he murmured.

She turned one final scorching look on her kids and they rose as one and left the table silently, content to later relieve their feelings by each slamming a bedroom door.

"Well," Christie said with a shaky laugh. "Better late than never I guess."

"I knew you had it in you," Laurenson said.

"What a whopper!" she retorted, opening her lovely eyes very wide. "I know you thought I was letting them get away with murder."

"No I didn't. I knew you were giving them the benefit of the doubt."

"Do you think I overreacted?"

Laurenson laughed. "Do *you* think you overreacted?"

"No! I mean I know it's inconsistent to stomp on them now when I've taken a lot for a long time, but I don't care. They owe me something, even if they hate my guts for whatever reason—bad potty training skills...whatever—they owe me because I'm the only parent they've got who's been willing to keep them in my life. I don't deserve to be humiliated!"

"You? Wasn't I the one who was supposed to be humiliated?"

"Sure you were," she said, "but obviously you can take it. I, on the other hand—What suddenly got to me is how little kindness that boy feels for me. All that seems to matter to him is running the show. I don't understand."

"What don't you understand?"

"Why he doesn't love me. Don't I deserve to be loved?"

"Of course you do. Don't tell me you're going to start setting your value according to your opinion poll rating!"

She laughed tentatively. "Start? That's basically all I've done for the past ten years. Ever since Justin left."

"Well, as any staff sergeant could tell you, there *is* life after popularity."

"Even if there wasn't, I know perfectly well it's time I went ballistic."

"So you're not regretting it?"

She smiled, suddenly looking more relaxed than she had so far that day. "Someone once told me, the worm often feels better for turning."

Laurenson went into the office the next day feeling oddly relieved at how Thanksgiving had turned out. Not that it had been pleasant—though they'd gone for an enjoyable walk after supper—but he felt hopeful because Christie had finally confronted her children. In his experience, bullies required a certain amount of complicity from their victims if they were going to continue to dominate and manipulate. Although he doubted either Shaun or Christie thought of themselves as being part of a bully/victim relationship, he was pretty certain he recognized the signs.

"Morning, Staff," Miranda Cardinal said, looking up as he walked in. Miranda, a plump motherly woman with salt-and-pepper hair, handled the front counter at the detachment from 8:00 to 4:30 on weekdays. "There was a call for you after you left on Friday."

Laurenson glanced at the piece of paper she held out to him, "Good weekend, Miranda?"

"A very good weekend," she replied. "In fact, a family reunion of gigantic proportions."

"What do you consider 'gigantic proportions'?"

"Well, it took five turkeys to feed us all."

"I'm impressed."

"How about you?"

"Only two turkeys at our dinner," Laurenson said, "but it had its moments." He walked over to his office and dialed the number on the piece of paper he'd just been given.

"General Investigation Section, Runquist speaking."

"This is Dan Laurenson from St. Michael Detachment, returning your call."

"Ah yes. Sorry it took me so long to get back to you. I understand you want some information on an investigation of ours."

"That's right, the human remains found south of Spruce Grove. Is the lab finished with them? How'd it go?"

"Not bad. We lost less than half the bones to scavengers. We have the skull, so some facial reconstruction should be possible. Even got a femur, so it's no problem estimating height. Actually, I was hoping you might be of some help to us."

"I doubt it, I'm just following up on an inquiry you must have received last summer."

"There's no record—"

"Not from our office; from a Michaelangelo Smith of the County of Parkland."

"Yeah?" There was a pause. "I don't get it. What's your interest then?"

"The same as Smith's. I want to know if there's any chance the remains that turned up south of Spruce Grove could be the daughter he reported missing December 23, 1989."

There was the sound of papers being shuffled. "You think they might be?"

"You'd know that better than I would."

"But you *are* calling. You must have a reason."

With fast ebbing patience, Laurenson repeated his reason.

"What I mean is, you must have a reason for thinking this might be Rozilind Smith."

"I'm asking because her father wants to know."

"I don't see how—"

Apparently COs across Canada regularly promoted men like McVicar out of their detachments and into desk jobs at headquarters.

Laurenson interrupted with a trace of testiness. "I can see why you'd be wondering what it is about the father that would make following up seem like a—" He thought again of Scott McVicar.

"Like a productive thing to do. Put it down to public relations if you like."

"Public relations?"

"That's right. There's an old man thinks we're a bunch of assholes because we won't tell him if his missing daughter has been found."

"I wish we knew."

"You mean, there's a possibility it could be her?"

"Anything's possible."

"*Anything's possible?*"

"I mean, we can't rule out the possibility."

"Why is that?"

Runquist could be heard shuffling some papers. "Do you want this in detail?"

"I want this in *exhaustive* detail," Laurenson said, with an emphasis he felt sure Smith would have applauded.

"Well, the age would seem to be right."

"This was an eighteen-year-old?"

"Very likely."

If this was detail, Laurenson was glad he hadn't asked for a synopsis.

"What makes you put the age at eighteen?"

"Well, obviously *I* haven't; it was the forensic anthropologist who did. In this case, on the basis of how much the shafts of arms and legs had fused with the...the epiphyses."

"The what?"

"The knobby ends."

"So that's a pretty good indicator of age?"

"Apparently they begin to fuse around fourteen or fifteen and finish around eighteen or nineteen. A little earlier in females."

"You figure this was a female?"

"That would be easier to determine if the pelvic bones had been found. From the mandible, though, the answer would be yes. Probably. Most likely."

"Weren't there clothes? Wasn't there hair or jewelry or—"

"Both clothes and hair are biodegradable. And not everyone wears jewelry."

"So how long do you think the remains were— Where *were* they exactly?"

"A shallow grave in some trees just north of the Devonian Gardens. Clearly they'd been there more than a year."

"Why do you say 'clearly'?"

"Because all the flesh was off the bones. Because there was a web of cracks all over them indicating they'd been out in freezing temperatures. And because rodents had been gnawing on them."

"They only gnaw in the winter?"

"Apparently they won't touch them until they're at least a year old."

"Oh. Okay. So you can say for sure that they were at least a year in the ground, and that the person was at least eighteen years old. Do you know for sure they weren't ten years in the ground and the bones of a thirty-eight-year old?"

"The age is the easier thing to pinpoint. The fusing that's complete on, say, the femur isn't complete on the collarbone until twenty-two to twenty-five years of age. Top age for this particular individual was twenty to twenty-four."

"You said something about the femur making it easy to estimate height."

"I've been told it's the best bone for calculating height. There's even a formula for it. This femur was 49 centimetres long, which translates into a height of about five feet eight inches."

Now it was Laurenson's turn to shuffle through papers. Rozilind Smith had been reported at the time of her disappearance as 5'8", and 140 pounds.

"About right?" Runquist asked.

"About right. The only problem is, it's a fairly common height, for males as well as females."

"That's true. Too bad there wasn't a pelvis to be found. But that's about par for the course, I'm told."

"How so?"

"What I mean is that scavengers don't usually try to drag off skulls; there's not enough meat on them to make them appealing. As well, the larger heavier bones can be quite a job to drag away. A coyote with a human leg isn't likely to go far before settling down to feed. But there are some nice bones that make for good gnawing and are fairly portable once skeletonization has progressed. Which it will do, eventually. At the rate of nearly three pounds of flesh per day if the weather's warm enough and nearly a pound a day in cooler weather. The scavengers won't get much if they dawdle when the weather's warm enough for insects and bacteria to be feeding."

"Shoes!" Laurenson exclaimed. "Surely they don't eat the shoes too?"

"There were no shoes found."

"I wonder why."

"Well, I doubt very much they were removed to prevent identification, if that's what you're thinking. Nothing was used to speed up decomposition. Wouldn't that be the logical way to ensure anonymity? That or cutting off the head and the hands. Especially the head."

"Speaking of which, have you gotten anywhere with dental records?"

"Not yet."

"Not even with checking out just Rozilind Smith's dental records?"

There was a pause. "I'll look into it," Runquist said.

"Thanks." Laurenson thought a moment.

"That about do it?"

"Tell me more about where the body was found."

Runquist sighed. "What about where the body was found?"

"Is it an easy spot to reach?"

"If you have a truck or a four-wheel drive, I suppose. I wouldn't want to try to get in there with just any passenger car. It's a good three hundred metres off the road and fairly bumpy."

"Private?"

"Private enough. There are trees. No houses nearby. Yeah, it was a good spot."

"How did the bones come to be uncovered?"

"Some kids were out with their dog. The dog found a scapula and the kids went home hoping they had a dinosaur bone. Their teacher showed it to a vet a week or so later and called Spruce Grove Detachment on his advice. By that time, the kids had pretty much forgotten where they'd found the bone. Eventually, however, it was identified as definitely human and definitely modern and the kids took officers to all their favourite spots. An oblong patch of sunken ground ended up being the thing that made finding the grave possible.

It's not that easy making a grave blend into the landscape, even in cemeteries where they give the ground a few months to settle and then lay some sod."

"Far easier to put someone down a well."

"I can't imagine doing that but, with all the lakes you have in your area, I would think the perfect way of getting rid of a body would be to weigh it down and drop it in the middle of a lake."

"Or would be," Laurenson remarked dryly, "if it didn't take so much weight to keep a body down. Once the gases start building up in a decomposing body, even an anchor or a slot machine may not do it. So I've been told, at any rate."

"I'll keep that in mind the next time the wife maxes out her credit cards."

"Thanks for the information. If you like, I'll see about getting Rozilind Smith's dental records to the pathologist."

"Sure. Thanks. It's Dr. John Kaplan."

"Oh yes, I know him. Okay, I'll see to it."

Laurenson asked Todd Rainier, who was heading south of town, to stop in at Michaelangelo Smith's and get the name of Rozilind's dentist.

"Smith is the old man who's been staking out the city for a couple of months. I'd like to hear what you think of him."

"My pleasure. I've been wanting to talk with him."

"Yeah, I heard he gave you the slip a couple of weeks ago." Laurenson didn't want to say anything that might prejudice Rainier so he kept to himself the fact that he'd been talking with the old man and had come away feeling something wasn't quite right. "I'd like you to tell him as gently as you can that we can't rule out the possibility it was his daughter who was found in July. That's why we need her dental records—for identification purposes."

"There's finally a break in that case?"

"The age is about right. Since we have a skull, it should be easy to establish whether it *is* her. I can't understand why GIS hasn't done it already. When the body was found, Smith called them trying to find out if it could be the daughter he reported missing five years ago."

"Is it this man's character you want an opinion on, Staff?"

"That, his mental competence, and his state of mind. It would be great if you could chat with him for a while. I don't know if that'll be possible. He isn't very happy with us right now and bad news doesn't usually make a person feel better."

"It's not exactly easy to avoid chatting with the police if the police want to chat," Rainier remarked dryly.

"Well, don't push it, if he's really upset. I would appreciate it, however, if you could get the name and address of the neighbour who thought she saw his daughter in town."

"Sure, no problem."

The next time they saw each other it was the end of the watch and Rainier had just finished booking a bus driver for aggravated assault.

"I have the information you wanted, Staff," he said, looking up from his paperwork.

"How did it go?"

"You were right—he wasn't too happy with us."

"I gather he doesn't feel we've redeemed ourselves."

"Hell, no. According to him, we always respond exactly wrong where he's concerned. We dare to suspect him of killing his daughter; then we ignore him; then we *don't* ignore him; and then we jump to conclusions about some remains. When are we ever going to get it right?"

"What makes him think we're jumping to conclusions about the remains?"

Rainer grinned. "I asked him that and enjoyed watching him realize he'd just stepped off into thin air. The fact is, he doesn't know anything of the sort; he'd like to think we are."

"He asked a lot of questions about the investigation?"

"No. But when did that ever stop anyone from assuming we were making a mess of something?"

"What sorts of questions did he ask?"

Rainier thought a moment. "Actually, the only thing I can remember him asking is when we expect to get back to him about this."

"That's odd. A few months ago he was frustrated because he couldn't find anyone who would answer his questions. Now we've found out something and we're talking to him but he doesn't have any questions any more."

"Maybe it's taking a while for it all to sink in."

"You mean he may not have understood you?"

"Oh he understood me. There's nothing wrong with his mind that I can see. He gave me the information I wanted without the least hesitation or confusion...including the phone number of the neighbour and the location of the dentist." Rainier thumbed through his notebook. "By the way, she's Mary Grey, a widow who used to live next door but moved into the Trevere Apartments on Scotland Avenue three years ago. The dentist is Peter Stefanson and he has his office on the main floor of the Brownlee Building." He put his notebook away. "Anyway, Smith was out in his garage fixing a lawn mower...cannibalizing one old mower for parts for another...and I hate to admit it, Staff, but he was doing a better job of it than I could have. He looks doddery, but he isn't."

"Well then, presumably, he understood you."

"I thought he might be a little in shock because of the news."

"He seemed to be in shock?"

"No. I'm just giving him the benefit of the doubt."

"I overheard when you called in the 10-24. It was 11:50. That would indicate he's had four hours to pull himself together and start wondering about a few things, but he hasn't called asking me anything." He shrugged, "Maybe he's pretty sure we aren't about to solve the case after five years."

"I fail to see how he can be so sure we won't."

"I do too. Unless he's just remembered that he stuffed his daughter down a well."

"In that case, wouldn't he make more of an effort to look interested in what we're finding out for him? Such a sharp old guy has to know how suspicious it would look to give the impression that he thinks he knows more than we do. You don't go shouting 'wrong!' when the police think they may have found a clue. Jeez, that's the surest way to tip your hand if you've been stuffing bodies down wells."

"How long did you talk with him?"

"About fifteen minutes. He was actually nice enough in spite of not liking us very much. I got the impression he's lonely out there all by himself. Even that he appreciated having a little company."

"But not having us follow up on his inquiry."
"No. Not so's you'd notice."
"And he didn't even pretend to be thankful."
Rainier laughed. "Does that bother you?"
"Yeah, actually it does. It's not that I can't stand an ingrate; it's that I don't know what to make of someone who doesn't feel what you'd expect him to feel, and doesn't even pretend to."

Dr. Peter Stefanson provided the dental chart requested of him and Laurenson sent it to Kaplan by courier that same day. A few days later, Kaplan called.

"Staff Sergeant Laurenson? John Kaplan here. I'm afraid I've got some disappointing news for you."

"The dental work didn't match."

"It didn't."

"Conclusively?"

"Beyond any doubt. We had more than just her file to go on, you know. There were X-rays in her file."

"I gather that having X-rays makes a big difference."

"Oh yes. X-rays are a lot more reliable than written records. I've run into dentists who didn't even want us seeing their patients' charts... And for good reason."

"Why?"

"Because they've recorded more work than they did in the case of people with dental plans and less than they did in the case of privately paying customers," Kaplan snorted. "It's tough being in a high tax bracket, you know."

"Must be. Can you spare me another five minutes?"

"You mean right now?"

"Yeah. I was talking with Runquist and got the impression that you'd briefed him very thoroughly. Still, there are a few things I'd like to ask you directly."

"No problem."

"There's a formula for determining height from the length of the femur?"

"Yup. You multiply the length of the femur in centimetres by 2.38 and add 61.41."

"I understand sex isn't particularly easy to determine."

"Not as easy as race, believe it or not. Until puberty it's especially trying."

"But with a skull…"

"Haven't you ever seen a cross-dresser it took a third or fourth look to figure out? Haven't you ever wondered if you should pat someone down yourself or call in a matron and have her conduct the search? Take off the hair and the accessories *and* the skin… Well, I, for one, am not willing to stake my reputation on jaw bones and brow ridges. I spend half my life in court. I'd be dead if I ever lost my credibility."

Laurenson laughed, recalling how he'd infuriated a Kimberly matron once by calling her sir. "On the other hand, age is no problem?"

"Age is less of a problem. The bones are constantly changing. First the pieces of the cranium fuse. Then the shafts of bones fuse with the round ends. Then cartilage starts to ossify and bone to pit. There's always something going on. Up to the age of thirty-six you can be very accurate about age if you can lay your hands on a person's pubic symphysis."

"Their pubic *what*?"

"Symphysis. It looks like a piece of volcanic rock with three faces which change in strictly regular ways that have been noted and measured. Codified, if you like. Unfortunately, there was no pubic symphysis in the present case."

"So all you can be certain about is…?"

"That this was someone near twenty years of age. Likely a female: Caucasian. No signs of old disease or injuries. Five foot eight inches tall. And left handed."

"*Left handed*?"

"Yeah."

"Runquist didn't say anything about that."

"No? Well, handedness is another one of those no-brainers that make a difficult job a little easier. A person's dominant arm becomes a little longer, you know. And the shoulder joint wears down faster. This is visible even in someone the age of your Jane Doe."

"I understand you may be doing some facial reconstruction on the skull."

It was Kaplan's turn to sound surprised. "We are? It was my suggestion that we try what image enhancement can do. You can tell a lot by over-laying a photograph of the skull with the photograph of a possible match. You know, even an unconscious person can be hard to recognize sometimes, because muscle tension plays a major role in making us look like our old familiar selves."

Laurenson thought about that later when he saw Christie and wondered why she looked sort of strange.

"Are you all right?"

"Don't you start that too. That's all people have been asking me all day."

"In that case," he teased, "I'm lucky I thought to say it. Otherwise I'd have come across as unusually thick and insensitive."

Her eyes crinkled a little.

"Things haven't improved, I gather."

"We've taken to communicating through letters. At least I have. I wrote, suggesting he write to me if he found it too difficult to talk about this face to face."

"I take it he hasn't replied."

"Not yet."

"When did you write him?"

"Yesterday morning."

"Any ideas on why he hasn't responded?"

"It doesn't take a genius. He'd prefer to yell at me."

Laurenson put his arm around her and gave her a squeeze.

"I won't be able to stand it if you feel sorry for me," she said in a very low voice. "Right now, about all that seems to be keeping me going is the way warfare at home takes my mind off work, and warfare at work takes my mind off home."

"I don't feel sorry for you," Laurenson said briskly. "I think you're extremely lucky to be solving all your problems in one fell swoop. Some people insist on doing it in dribs and drabs. Or not at all. You don't go numb if you do it in dribs and drabs. And numb can be good."

Christie laughed. "Well you're right about one thing. I'm numb."

Laurenson slipped a hand down over one of her well-rounded buttocks.

"Not *that* numb," she said, jabbing him in the ribs with her elbow.

"Then there's only one thing to do. Come to my place and I'll give you a nice long massage. No ulterior motive. Scout's honour."

She made a point of checking for crossed fingers before laughingly accepting his offer. For his part, he made a point of giving her a sheet with which to cover herself when it came time to start the massage.

She raised her eyebrows as she took the sheet and he planted a quick kiss on the top of her head. "That's so neither of us will forget that this is a massage, a whole body massage, and nothing but a massage," he said.

"I'm sorry," she said. "I–I haven't been 'in the mood' much lately, have I?"

"Don't apologize. I think I could count on the fingers of one hand the number of times you've been in this house and we haven't made love. I'd hate for you to think of this as a kind of toll-booth or something."

"I probably would feel better, though, if we did. Make love, I mean. It's just that sex seems to need a certain base level of well-being even to get started."

"Right now it'd be about as appropriate as trying to have sex when you've got the flu."

She relaxed a little then but still felt like a block of wood under his hands. Patiently, he worked on all the tightness, stiffness, and resistance that was her body's way of saying no to what had been happening to her. Little by little she became more pliant, more at ease, softer, somehow reminiscent of grass in the wind.

He left her asleep on the bed and went for a good long run. She was gone when he returned.

Chapter Three

Miranda looked up as Laurenson walked in the next morning. "Weather's going to change," she said.

"You think so?"

"I *know* so." She held out her hands. "See?"

Even from where he stood, it was apparent that arthritic joints on Miranda's swollen hands had turned red.

"Does this happen every time the weather changes?" Laurenson asked with surprise.

"No. I think we're in for a really bad storm."

For an hour or so, it looked as though cloud cover would be about all the day would bring. As Laurenson pulled out of the parking lot on his way to Michaelangelo Smith's, however, a few flakes of snow began to fall lazily. The snow had become a veil of huge flakes by the time he cleared the city's newest, most expensive suburb and began looking for the old man's driveway.

Smith was at a window as Laurenson pulled up. He watched him step onto his sagging veranda before slowly opening the door. "I guess you might as well come in, since you're here."

Laurenson stepped in and looked around with interest. At the centre of the tiny living room of the small, plain house was a wood-burning stove with glass doors. Inside it, a fire was burning, brightening and warming the entire front of the house. Mullioned windows stretching halfway across both the east and south walls seemed to bring the falling snow very close; but the fire kept the chill of it far away, rendering it merely picturesque, maybe even comforting. The room smelt of pine logs and a little of wood smoke, too.

"I'm glad I came," Laurenson said.

"Well, sit down. I'll pour you some coffee." The old man gestured towards a worn but comfortable-looking overstuffed couch.

Laurenson settled into its soft blue cushions with pleasure and used his moment of privacy to study a series of pictures on the wall opposite him. He had already seen the graduation picture Smith had provided when filing his missing-person's report. The dark-haired girl with the thin face and green eyes peeping out from under a mortar board was familiar; not so the other Rozilinds as they had emerged down through the years: among them, a chubby curly-haired tot who laughed into the camera, a lanky pre-teen with troubled eyes, and an elegant young lady in a yellow prom dress, heaps of hair piled high on her head. She was a pretty girl, no question about that. She just didn't look… Laurenson tried to put his finger on what spoiled the girl's looks, but couldn't put it into words.

"Here." The old man was back with a big steaming white mug. "I take mine black, but I have fresh cream in the fridge. You can have sugar or honey too, whichever you prefer."

"I never get fresh cream," Laurenson said, handing back his mug. Alone again for a moment, he set aside the question of what it was about Rozilind that he had glimpsed through her picture, and turned to others, pictures that showed Michaelangelo Smith and his wife as an awkward bride and groom, as doting new parents, and the proud owners of a prize-winning black and white pig. Time had been kind to Smith, giving him a bit of the look of a Merlin or a beneficent old leprechaun; as a younger man he had looked simply earnest and graceless.

"Thanks," Laurenson said, taking the mug Smith handed him upon his return. "This is a very comfortable place you've got here."

The old man laughed. "Old-fashioned and worn, but I like it. I've lived here forty years now; wouldn't feel comfortable anywhere else."

"You were saying your daughter didn't like it here."

"No, this certainly wasn't her style. Poor Rozilind."

"Why do you say 'poor Rozilind'?"

"It can't have been easy for her. Motherless at a time when a girl needs her mother most. Different when a kid's greatest ambition is to fit in. I pinned my hopes on it building character."

"It probably did." Smith looked at him closely and seemed about to say something. "So," he said, obviously changing his mind. "What brings you out here this chilly day?"

"I thought you had already guessed."

"Why is that?"

"Because you don't seem at all impatient to hear my news," Laurenson said, watching closely as he drew out the moment of anticipation a little more.

"Well..." Smith paused to think. "I guess I've learned patience, all right, but I'm certainly all ears."

"I'm happy to be able to tell you that it wasn't your daughter who was found last summer."

"You're quite sure of that."

"The dental X-rays establish it beyond the shadow of a doubt."

"Good. Though I have to admit I never was inclined to believe she was dead. I always had a feeling she'd come back. I was just checking, like you give a door a tug, even though you know you've closed it."

"Interesting comparison," Laurenson remarked.

Smith thought about it. "Now that strikes me as uncalled for. I almost said, 'just as you check for mail every day, even though you haven't received any for a week.'"

"I didn't mean anything by it."

"Oh, I don't blame you for probing. It's your job. And you don't strike me as the sort who's in it just for the pension."

"You say you always felt she would come back. I guess you must have thought about what you'll do if she ever does."

Everything Smith had been saying to this point had been so reassuring that Laurenson was beginning to wonder why he was wasting his time on such a routine matter, but suddenly the old man seemed stuck for words. Laurenson didn't find that reassuring. He felt sure that he must know...ought to know...the answer to this question off by heart.

"I don't know," Smith began slowly. "I—I suppose I won't believe my eyes. Not for a minute or two anyway."

"I gather you're still looking for her on the streets of St. Michael," Laurenson said gently, noting that Smith had spoken as though he expected to catch sight of his daughter rather than hear from her.

"Oh, I haven't been looking for her for several weeks now. I figure I gave it a fair try."

"It can be hard to stop once you've gotten going." Laurenson was thinking mainly of how he had, himself, sometimes built an inertia of persistence, thinking, "Just one more day… I've put so much into this I might as well try just one more time."

"It was always an off chance at best," Smith said. "And I had to take into account the fact that so many people seemed to think it was an odd thing to do that it *must* have been an odd thing to do."

"The police sometimes go about finding people in pretty much the same way."

"But I'm not the police, am I?"

"Do you regret giving it a try?" Laurenson asked, surprised that Smith didn't seem to be taking comfort from the fact that one cop, at least, was saying it hadn't been a totally crazy thing to have done.

"With someone like Mary Grey saying she'd seen her, it seemed like a very sensible thing to do. But, even if Roz had come back, that doesn't mean she stayed. I had to put a time limit on it, you see."

"Did you ever try calling people who knew her to see if—" He never did get to finish the question.

"No! Well, yes, but nothing came of it."

"Who did you call?"

Smith's reluctance to answer was palpable. The more vague his answers, the more Laurenson pressed for specifics, and clarity in those specifics.

"Ah, this old memory of mine," Smith finally said. "I think it's safe to say I contacted everyone it made sense to contact. None of her friends had seen or heard from her since her disappearance. And most of them thought it was strange I was asking at all."

"Most of them," Laurenson said. "Who didn't?"

"I should have said 'all of them'," Smith said. "Though some were politer and more patient with me than others."

Okay, so now the old man sounded as though he'd found his way back to solid ground. Laurenson wondered if he could be led back out into the quagmire so its boundaries could be more easily traced.

"Where exactly did you set up watch?"

"Oh, well, you know...wherever there are lots of people—the malls, downtown, outside the library and the post office, outside banks." As Smith slowed down, Laurenson prompted him, "All banks? That must have been quite a job."

"The main branches of all of them, yes. How could I know where she'd be doing her banking these days?"

"With ATMs she could be doing it *anywhere*."

"Exactly. I never put much faith in the banks. But some of them were great locations for people-watching."

"You were very thorough. What about Lexilogic Data Systems?"

"What?"

"What about the place she worked for a few months after she graduated?"

"Oh. Yeah, I watched there too."

"Very much?"

Smith picked up his coffee cup and headed toward the kitchen. "Not a heck of a lot. I didn't think it likely she'd go back there."

"Why?"

"Why should she?"

"Why should she come back here at all?"

But Smith was in the kitchen by this time, and didn't answer.

When he returned, Laurenson picked up at almost the same spot in his line of inquiry. "If she were to come back, presumably it'd be to see you."

"Not necessarily," Smith said grimly.

"Five years is a long time to hold a grudge."

"Who says she's been holding a grudge against me?"

"Hasn't that always seemed a possibility?"

"I suppose."

"I don't quite understand. Are you saying she had no reason to hold a grudge, or that she wasn't the type to hold a grudge?"

Smith sighed. "I don't quite understand something myself— why you're asking so damned many questions. What are you after?"

"I get the feeling something is bothering you, and I wish I knew what."

Soulful brown eyes flew to his face and then fled to the safety of contemplating the fire.

"Mr. Smith? Isn't there some way I can help?"

"Life is sad," the old man said.

"Your life certainly hasn't been easy."

The old man waved away the comfort. "Not mine. Rozilind's. Poor Rozilind."

"You don't know for sure that she isn't happy," Laurenson started to suggest. But he didn't persist because he could see it wasn't helping.

It was only after he left that it struck him the interview had come unraveled on the subject of grudges. His last question had gone unanswered. He wondered if Mary Grey knew the answer to that last question.

———

It was some time before Laurenson was able to drop in on the little old lady who had lived next door to the Smiths. First, he stopped to call AMA for a car that had spun off into the ditch right before his eyes; then he stopped to deal with a collision a block off Chisholm; and, finally, he helped get a car moving that was spinning its wheels on one of the steeper ridge roads. He knew he had better not stop long at Mary Grey's; the good citizens of St. Michael were undoubtedly about to set a new record for smash-ups, just as they did every year when the first heavy snowfall made driving treacherous.

"Oh my," Mrs. Grey said, opening her apartment door to him. "You *have* chosen wicked weather to come out in, haven't you? Well, it's an ill wind that blows no one any good. I've had to cancel bridge for lack of a fourth, but see?" She pointed to a counter on which there stood two plates heaped high with fancy sandwiches, the kind his wife used to call "dainties."

"Mmm," he said, "Those certainly look good."

"Well, dig in," Mrs. Grey said. "Anything you can take off my hands will be a blessing. She poured him a glass of cranberry juice and waved him over to her dining room table.

Laurenson grabbed a couple of asparagus and Cheez Whiz roll-ups. "This is very kind of you."

"Not a bit of it. I understand you want to know something about Michaelangelo and Rozilind Smith. Maybe it will save time if you just ask me questions."

"You knew them well?"

"Both well and long. I still like to talk to Michaelangelo. He's a good man."

"What was Rozilind like?"

"I didn't, if truth be told, particularly like her a lot. But to give the girl her due—she was very bright, resourceful, and energetic."

"Someone who could take care of herself."

"In spades."

"Were you surprised when she disappeared?"

"Here, don't bypass the olives," Mrs. Grey said.

She topped up his drink as she continued talking. "Oddly enough, I suppose, I wasn't really surprised. Oh, I guess I was at first. But when it really began to look as though she'd engineered her own disappearance rather than being snatched off the street or something, then it seemed quite in keeping with what I knew of her."

"In keeping with what you knew of her? In what way?"

"She was ambitious and unsentimental; I could imagine her ditching whatever she thought might hold her back. In fact, her leaving home seemed less surprising than the fact that she'd stayed there even after getting a job."

"Even though she ran away without a word of goodbye?"

"She could have done it in anger, I suppose. I can't quite see why she wouldn't pack her bags and at least leave her father a note, but then I never did see things quite as she did. Here, try these." She passed him some small square sandwiches which looked to be made of Spam mashed with relish and, possibly, mayonnaise.

"What sorts of things didn't you see eye to eye with her on?"

"It's not that I argued with her, you know, it's just that I never did understand why she felt the way she did about some things. For example, her father bought her a gorgeous blue leather suit, which must have set him back a pretty penny, and she complained bitterly that he obviously thought she was as big as a house since he'd bought it a size too large. I couldn't imagine how a small mistake like that could overshadow how right the present was in every other way."

"She wore it a lot, though, didn't she? It couldn't have been too big."

"I suppose you'd have suggested it made it her look thinner like Michaelangelo did." She laughed. "Of course he returned it to the Bay and got one a size smaller."

Mrs. Grey took a sandwich, and nibbled daintily at one corner of it.

"Roz's best friend's father gave Roz a job at Lexilogic when she got out of high school, and she was really disappointed that he wasn't sending her off to university along with his own daughter. Again, I couldn't see what her problem was. Surely it wasn't his place to be sending her to college. And, anyway, she could have gotten one of those heritage fund scholarships if she'd worked just a bit harder. Lots of kids get them."

"I gather her father wasn't able to send her to college himself?"

"He went heavily into debt seeking a cure for his wife when she got cancer. He wouldn't sell his land but he did take her off to the States for a lot of expensive treatments. One thing I'll say for Roz is that she wouldn't hear of him going into debt for her so soon after finally getting clear of it. Anyway, she was certain—absolutely certain—Brandy Heyden's father wanted to send her to university. Lord knows why she would think that."

Laurenson reached for another asparagus Cheez Whiz roll-up. "What do you think would cause her to come back here?"

"I can't imagine. I've wondered if I didn't just dream up the whole thing."

"Maybe you did."

"No. I'll never forget the look on her face when she realized I'd seen her. It was really funny. So was the little dance she did. The moment she noticed me she did a weird kind of slide and sidle, rather like a dance."

"Where did you two run into each other?"

"She was right in front of the newsstand on Oriole, just about to cross to the south side of the street. I was crossing *from* the south side of the street. Jaywalking if you must know."

"Can you show me what a slide and sidle looks like?"

Mary Grey did a shy little glide consisting of two steps back, and one step over. Laurenson thought she looked as cute as a button. "Only more like this," she corrected herself. She jerked her head back like a chicken and then did a little jump and shuffle.

"You say she was just about to cross the street?"

"Yes, she was off the curb between two cars."

"Did she look like she was turning to avoid you?"

"She never turned for a moment. In fact, she practically burned holes in my face with her eyes."

"Did either of you say anything?"

"I called out her name, but she didn't reply. She just stood there a moment, and then she kind of ran across the street."

"And you're absolutely sure you couldn't be mistaken? It couldn't have been someone else?"

"Especially it couldn't have been someone else when she ran. Rozilind always did run like a fawn...you know, all legs and not very coordinated. I called out to her again, but, if anything, she sped up."

"How close did you get to her?"

"Close enough to see very well, thank you."

"No. I mean, was she making room for you to pass between the two cars?"

"I passed behind the car she was standing in front of."

"Apparently she didn't want to renew old acquaintances."

"No, and, as it turned out, not even with her father. It never crossed my mind that she wouldn't call *him*."

"What did he say to all this?"

"That I must have been mistaken. Of course, I didn't tell him about it in quite the detail I've told you. I think he thought I was getting fanciful in my old age."

"He just dismissed you out of hand?"

"Oh no, he asked me a lot of questions about what she looked like, how she was wearing her hair, what kind of clothes she had on...a lot of questions. But then he said, 'Mary, she wouldn't be wearing green, you must have been imagining things.' Now, I ask you, what kind of sense does that make—a girl with green eyes won't wear green? I don't buy it for a minute. And, anyway, neither did he. After that he started hanging around street corners hoping to catch a glimpse of her himself."

"That's going to a lot of trouble over a daughter who won't give you the time of day," Laurenson suggested, reaching for what he promised himself was definitely his last sandwich.

"You wouldn't find me doing it, that's for sure," Mrs. Grey said. "But you know what they say about old men and old women."

"What's that?"

"Well, when a baby boy is born there are ten devils for every angel around his head. When a baby girl is born, there are ten angels for every devil. But by the time they've both reached seventy-five, the numbers have been reversed."

"That sounds like something an old man would say."

She chuckled. "Just wait till you've known a few more old men and women."

"Has Michaelangelo Smith mellowed a lot?"

"Sometimes I think he was born mellow. That daughter of his could do with developing a few soft spots though."

Laurenson wondered if Mrs. Grey might be able to complete the thought he had been unable to finish earlier. "She's a nice-looking girl but..." he trailed off.

"I know just what you mean," she replied.

"I wish *I* did," he admitted. "I'm having trouble putting my finger on what it is that spoils her looks."

"It's the resentment," she said. "I think some men find it appealing, although I can't imagine why. As far as I'm concerned, there's nothing particularly attractive about a sourpuss."

Laurenson made a mental note to try fill-in-the-blanks more often, at least when talking with smart old cookies like Mrs. Grey.

"What do you suppose Rozilind resented so much?"

"Mainly stupidity, to hear her tell it. Even when she was a little girl, everything was dumb, especially the rules."

"Any idea what grudges, if any, she might have been holding?"

"'Grudges' sounds like someone did something to her. I don't think people treated her any worse than anyone else...though a person who expects friends' fathers to put them through college might disagree. No, I doubt she was carrying grudges, I think what bothered her was resentment...just the ordinary garden variety resentment that comes of being critical of everything. Of being disappointed by everything and everybody."

"Being overly critical."

"Yes, things aren't perfect, and neither are people. I think Roz had a hard time accepting that; I doubt she ever did accept it. Her life wasn't going the way she thought it should and people didn't live up to her expectations. She was the cutest, most charming little girl, but she grew into the most discontented teenager I've ever seen."

This certainly squared with the impression the graduation photo had created.

"I don't mean to be harsh," Mrs. Grey added after a pause. "She was devastated when her mother died and she must have been horribly lonely afterwards. She had to have been, because Michaelangelo became very depressed and turned into something of a hermit."

"Do you think she was anywhere near as fond of him as he seems to have been of her?"

Mrs. Grey thought about that for a minute. "As I mentioned, I was surprised that she continued to live with him after getting a job. Since I know she didn't like living way off in the boonies, I figure she did that because he couldn't drive and her having a car made things easier for him. That would count as love, wouldn't it?"

For Laurenson, it seemed like enough probable love to make Roz's subsequent leaving without a word just before Christmas seem very odd, indeed. Primarily, however, he was troubled by the strong feeling he had that Michaelangelo Smith had lied to him. It bothered him because he hadn't the slightest idea why the old man would need to or want to.

Laurenson started back toward the office at the earliest possible moment, but he found it difficult to make headway. Snow was coming down heavier than ever, the wind was picking up, and traffic was becoming hopelessly snarled. By now pedestrians were up to their ankles in light, fluffy snow, side streets were drifting in, and intersections had been spun into sheets of ice by the tires of many vehicles. The airwaves were busy as every officer on duty was either advising on conditions, updating a status report, or being sent to the scene of an accident. Barron needed the fire department's Jaws of Life and an ambulance. Waring was dealing with the mayhem that had been caused by a semi-trailer's jackknifing across all three lanes of traffic on highway 16X. McVicar was putting out a BOLF on a stolen vehicle that had just been involved in a hit and run.

Laurenson called in his location and asked where he could be of the greatest assistance.

"Here in the office," Tavarov said. "There's someone waiting to talk to you."

As Laurenson put down his handset, Keith Dayandan's voice broke through a burst of static. "Collisions R Us, here. I feel sorry for you guys stuck inside. Anyone want to swap jobs?"

Back at the detachment, Laurenson stopped at the front counter to tell Miranda he would never doubt her arthritis again.

"You didn't believe me?"

Darin Childe, searching for the correct form on which to make a use-of-force report, glanced over his shoulder with a gleam of mischief. "Well, that's one way of getting a Commissioner's Commendation, Staff. Frankly, though, I think there are easier ways."

Miranda's eyes narrowed. "A Commendation for Outstanding Service?"

Childe grinned. "Where's the outstanding service in admitting he doubted you?"

"What commendation would he be talking about then, Staff?"

At that moment, Laurenson noticed Christie Devenish on a bench by the front door. "Beats me," he said. "Unless he means the one for bravery."

Leaving Childe to his fate, he hurried away. "Christie! What are you doing here?"

She gave him a weak smile. "Making a nuisance of myself."

"Not at all. What's up?"

"The school called to ask why Shaun wasn't there. They do that automatically around ten o'clock unless they've already been told that the child won't be in. I tried calling the house and there was no answer so I drove home to roust Shaun out of bed. At least, that's what I thought I'd be doing. Sometimes he goes back to bed after I leave for work."

Something about Christie's face made Laurenson take her into his office at that point. As soon as he closed the door, she crept into his arms like a hurt child.

"Oh Dan, he was just heading out the door as I arrived. A knapsack on his back, an angry letter on the kitchen counter... I couldn't stop him. I tried. I really did. He shoved me and then he ran. I called after him but he only ran faster."

"Do you have the letter with you?"

She groped in a pocket, then pushed a crumpled sheet of loose-leaf paper toward him. Although clearly hovering on the verge of tears, she seemed determined not to give way to them. Laurenson cast his eye down a half dozen lines of nearly illegible penmanship that was as full of bad grammar as it was of bad manners.

"Well written," he said grimly.

She looked at him with surprise. "Well written? I thought it was remarkably childish. And," she added with a glimmer of mordant humour, "an indictment of our school system as well."

"Maybe that was for effect?"

"Effect? What kind of effect?"

"To convince a concerned mother he'll never last for a minute on the streets...at least, not if there's a letter that needs writing."

"That's not funny!"

"No. I know. I'm sorry."

She cut him off. "Oh don't go apologizing, I know you're only trying to cheer me up. Just find him for me. *Please*."

"Have you figured out what I'm supposed to do with him when I find him?"

"Bring him home, of course!"

"And tie him to his bed?"

She stared at him in silence a moment. "We'll get counseling."

"Has Shaun ever indicated he'd be willing to accept counseling?"

"He's just a kid—"

"He's five inches taller than you and outweighs you by about forty pounds."

'What's that supposed to mean?"

"You know what that means. He's—how old is he now?"

"He'll be seventeen on the 13th." Now she dissolved into tears.

"November 13th? He's three days short of seventeen?"

That struck Laurenson as a piece of remarkable timing. In fact, he'd be willing to lay odds that Shaun intended to be home again for his birthday.

"Hey," he said, gathering her back into his arms. "Hey. We'll do what we can."

She pulled away suspiciously. "Why? You obviously don't think it'll do a bit of good."

"I don't think you can make him stay, or talk to you, or become happy. I think, deep down inside, you know as well as I do that you can't. But there are a few things I can do, and I'll do them to the best of my ability."

"Thank you." She whispered it to his front pocket.

"There's just one thing; if I'm going to do my best, I expect you to do yours."

Her head came up with a jerk. "You think I haven't?"

"I know perfectly well you have. But I'm afraid you may be reluctant to do what I'm about to suggest. Before I waste my time and, maybe, irritate the heck out of Shaun to no good purpose, I want you to consider what you need to do to increase our chances of not just bringing him home but bringing him to stay."

"I'll do it," she said. "Whatever it is, I'll do it."

"You promise?"

"Yes, of course, I do."

"Good. I want you to call your ex and tell him what's happened."

"Why?"

"Because he has a right to know. And, he may just be able to help."

"He won't help. Trust me."

"Maybe not, but he still should be informed."

"You don't know what—"

"You promised."

"He'll only make things worse." She pulled away angrily. "Oh, don't worry—I'll do it. But, I'm warning you, we'll live to regret it."

"Good girl," he said.

"Don't patronize me."

She seemed to find comfort in filling out the missing-person's report. Laurenson knew that was because she felt she was doing something to bring her son back. She would have felt much less comforted had she realized the extent to which he harboured deep misgivings about finding Shaun; or, to be exact, about returning him home.

It didn't take a genius to see the boy had set things up so that Christie would feel his displeasure to the greatest degree possible. Although leaving in a snowstorm was likely just a piece of good luck, running away just days before his birthday was *not*. Had he not shoved Christie on his way out the door, his note might have seemed pathetic. Even as things stood, it had gone a long way toward making his mother forget that ever since Thanksgiving he'd turned a cold shoulder to her efforts at working things out with him. If the Mounties of St. Michael hauled Shaun home, as Laurenson believed the boy expected them to, Christie would be beautifully set up for manipulation and emotional blackmail.

The important thing wasn't to find Shaun, it was to make sure he stayed as safe as possible until he returned home. Laurenson knew a thing or two about putting the word out where it would do the most good among the low-lifes who posed the greatest threat to any young boy at odds with the world or on the run. If Shaun stayed in St. Michael and had any common sense at all, he should be okay.

Besides, if he stayed in St. Michael, even though Edmonton was so close, it meant he wanted to be found.

Laurenson put out a BOLF on Shaun. Next he made a few phone calls, a sort of black market Be On Lookout For. Then, having done all he could for Shaun for the moment, he went to help with the line-up which had formed at the front counter. Mainly it involved people who were reporting accidents too minor to warrant police attendance at the scene. One couple, however, was there because their landlord had refused to fix their lock properly and they were sure he was sneaking in to steal money from them. Laurenson tried to explain that this was a Landlord and Tenants Advisory Board matter, but the couple refused to believe it wasn't something the police could fix easily by going out and arresting their landlord.

"You don't even know he's the one who took your money. How can you be so sure someone else hasn't found out that your door doesn't lock properly?"

They went around in circles on that for nearly five minutes. Finally, Laurenson said, "Look, if you put a couple of twenties out in plain sight and rig up a video camera, you may get evidence we can act on. Right now, this isn't something we can do anything about. You'll have to complain to the Landlord and Tenants Advisory Board...or fix the door yourselves. You can probably sue him in small claims court for the cost involved, if you decide to do that."

When they tried to take him around the mulberry bush one more time, he declined the invitation. "You're not listening to me. I'll write it out for you."

He thought he had just caught himself sounding like a prick. The problem was, having seen so many things over and over again ad nauseam made what didn't look obvious to others look all too obvious to him. There came a point where the world seemed to be full, not just of scumbags, but even more so, of jerks, neurotics, and idiots.

He felt a twinge of sympathy for Rozilind Smith because he, too, found people exasperating. He felt another, however, for people like the couple before him who had reached adulthood still believing the police protected everybody from everything. And he was beginning to feel more than a little sympathy for those like himself who spent half their lives running around trying to put out other people's fires.

He'd become a mounted policeman because he'd felt there weren't enough white knights galloping around rescuing people, but, these days, he didn't want to saddle up unless reasonably sure those in distress had already tried to save themselves. This applied even with Christie. So far, he'd seen little indication that she had come to terms with the problem she was having with her kids. Until she did, he thought any help from him was likely to do more harm than good. Laurenson devoted the rest of his day to putting out small routine fires of no importance whatsoever while the city of St. Michael ground to a standstill under thousands of tonnes of snow. These weren't the best circumstances in which to be a runaway hoping for a quick capture, or a distraught mother wondering what had become of her runaway. They were, however, ideal for anyone who thought time would tell how best to proceed.

When Laurenson returned home, close to midnight, he found a message from Christie on his answering machine, begging him to call as soon as possible, no matter what time that might be. He looked regretfully at his watch but didn't hesitate for a moment.

Christie picked up her phone on the first ring. "Oh, Dan, I'm so glad!" she exclaimed, when she heard his voice.

He thought she didn't sound glad, she sounded desperate.

"Are you okay?"

She gave a shaky laugh.

"What's happened?"

"I hardly know where to begin."

When he waited for her to pull her thoughts together she said, "What's the matter? You're awfully quiet."

"Just giving the gerbil wheel a chance to slow down so you can jump off."

"You seem pretty darn sure I've been on one."

"I have a blood pressure gauge pointed at the phone."

She gave a short laugh, then said in a less strained voice, "You sound tired."

"It's no use trying to change the subject; you're the one we're talking about."

"Well, I won't ream you out after all," she replied, "though, believe me, I've been looking forward to it all evening."

"Yeah? What'd I do now?" Laurenson closed his eyes, because they simply wouldn't stay open another moment.

"You told me to call Justin. And I did. And I've been taking your name in vain ever since."

"Justin?"

"My *ex*."

"Oh. Good."

"Uh uh. Not good at all. He's on his way and he's furious."

"I don't see how he could be either."

"Well, you obviously don't know Justin. He's furious at me for being the worst mother west of the Great Lakes, and he's coming to see to it that I lose custody of both the kids."

"Coming how? By dog team?"

"How can you joke at a time like this?"

"Sorry. Still, I fail to see how he's to get here unless he has a dog team."

"That's not the important part," she protested. "Whether he gets here tomorrow or the next day…who cares? He's coming with an application for a change of custody." She added with a touch of her old wry humour, "With, he assures me, a lawyer-crafted, two-page, three-hundred-dollar application for a change of custody."

"So he says."

"I believe him. He sounded dead serious."

"I thought he wasn't interested in the kids these days."

"I did too. Apparently that's just another of the many things about which I know less than nothing. He's got a list as long as your arm."

"I'll bet. But, do you believe him about the custody? If so, this changes everything."

"What do you mean?"

"If he's shifted into father gear, and into *high* father gear at that, you're not facing the problem with Shaun alone any more."

"I don't know if you've got some kind of romanticized picture of our facing this thing shoulder to shoulder or something. But trust me on this, he's out to score points off me. He's not going to cooperate, he's going to try to *annihilate*. Me, that is."

"Granted, that's not good news from your point of view…will it be good news from Shaun's or Angela's?"

"What!" It came out sounding like a squawk more than a word.

"I mean… Well, let's face it, what's bad news for you may actually be good news for them. For all you know, their most cherished fantasy might be to have their dad ride in on a white charger someday, proving that—contrary to all appearances—he really does love them."

A long hesitation from Christie suggested he probably wasn't far off the mark.

"Is that what you really think?" she finally asked.

"As opposed to, 'is that what you're pretending to think?'"

"As opposed to, 'is that what you'd *like* to think?'"

"Christie," he said with quiet emphasis, "I've spent the last twenty years double-checking every damned thought I've had, for fear I might be blindsiding myself. The conclusions I'd like to come to are the ones I come to most slowly. I don't expect you to know this about me, or even to be willing to take my word on it…but I do expect you will know it by the time we've worked our way through this mess."

"I'm sorry," she said. "I didn't mean it."

"Don't apologize. It was a reasonable thing to think."

She sniffed audibly. "Better double-check every damned thought *I* think, Dan. I don't want my kids to want their father more than me. Not when I've put everything into them for so long."

"They know you love them, Christie. It's their dad they're not sure about. At least, that's how it looks from where I stand."

Now she was openly crying.

"Christie? Hey, it's okay. Everything's going to be all right."

"I know, I know. Just give me a moment. I haven't told you everything yet."

He waited, hoping he wouldn't fall asleep before she could finish what she had to tell him.

"I guess I'm a bit sensitive to my approval rating," she began.

"Approval rating?"

"They decided to fire me today," she explained in a rush. "After I left your office, I called work and said I wasn't feeling well, and Trenton Cockburn himself called to tell me he wanted to see me in his office right away. When I got there, he started to read me the riot act for absenteeism, which apparently means having left the building on personal business during working hours and having called in sick when anyone could see I wasn't sick. He then launched into a long complaint about my resisting transfer and being uncooperative and...and—" She stopped and blew her nose.

"And behaved like the complete jerk he has always been?" Laurenson supplied helpfully.

"And behaved like the total moron and utter creep he has always been," Christie amended in a much steadier voice.

"Please tell me, there's been another homicide at St. Michael Catholic Schools."

It was a risky joke but she took it in the spirit intended. "Like I'd be willing to do anything that would land me in the hands of St. Michael's brutal cops! No. But I did do something I think you may approve of."

"You're a good judge of what I'd approve of, I hope."

"Actually, I didn't plan it or even really intend it. It's not as though I thought anything through. It just kind of happened."

"What kind of happened?"

"Well, you know I've been under a lot of strain and this thing with Shaun has about brought me to the limit of what I can handle. I mean, it's been *months*—"

In a low, menacing voice, Laurenson said, "Christie, I'm holding a gun to the mouthpiece of this phone. I'm warning you—you'll tell me *now* if you know what's good for you."

She laughed. "You'd think twice about threatening me if you knew what I did in Cockburn's office when he threatened me."

"Brat! *Talk*. I'm warning you."

She laughed even more heartily. "Okay, okay, put the gun down, I'll tell you." She paused for effect, a kind of silent *ta dah!* "I had a nervous breakdown."

"You what?!"

"You heard me. I burst into tears; totally natural, completely genuine tears. And then I looked at Trenton's face and I thought *My God, he's scared* and I didn't make the least effort to stop crying. That was probably very bad of me but after how they'd dragged the uncertainty out so I'd be under stress, and then reassigned me to what they'd been sure would be a totally unacceptable job, and then waited till I was reeling from Shaun's leaving—though they had no way of knowing that—and ordered me in so they could fire me on a trumped-up charge of absenteeism. I mean, after I'd thought of all that, I doubt I could have stopped crying if I'd wanted to. But of course I didn't want to. I wanted to pick up my human resources file and shake it in Cockroach's face. And I thought *why not?* and did it. And, you know, you were right—it was therapeutic and the worm enjoyed turning."

"So what did Cockroach...er, Cockburn do?"

"What any normal male would under the circumstances, he got his secretary in there ASAP so there'd be a witness to the fact that he was behaving like a perfect gentleman...and then he began to behave like a perfect gentleman. But by that time, I'd had a chance to realize that I was doing much better than I had all through the months I'd been keeping a stiff upper lip. So I whispered something about having a nervous breakdown."

"My God! I mean, good!"

"It *was* good. He saw dismissal-with-cause flying out the window and months of stress leave walking in the door. When I said I couldn't take much more of this, what kind of severance package would they be willing to offer if I tendered my resignation? he offered me a fair, even a *handsome* package."

"Did you take it?"

"No."

"*No?*"

"Not till he added benefits which are to continue until such time as I find another job. It only makes sense, doesn't it, that someone in the middle of a nervous breakdown would need medical benefits?"

"So he added benefits?"

"It took him awhile. He had some trouble with Human Resources, I gather. But the tears weren't stopping—and, believe me, I wasn't trying to keep them going; they'd taken on a life of their own—so he wanted a memorandum of agreement signed before the office closed for the day. It probably wouldn't hold up in a court of law, considering the state I was in when I signed it; but, of course, I intend to honour it."

"So you're officially out of there?"

"With a Cockburn hug as I headed out the door."

CHAPTER FOUR

Justin Devenish did make it into town the next day in spite of the near paralysis of that part of Alberta which extends from Red Deer to the Peace River Country. Newly unemployed, Christie was able to devote much of her time to dealing with her ex-husband and his new taste for fatherhood. Since Laurenson was fully occupied with the aftermath of the storm, Christie was pretty much on her own.

Michaelangelo Smith had slipped out of sight and out of mind too, at least until a woman who worked at Lexilogic came in to report a case of mischief to auto and handed her complaint in to Laurenson. In small neat handwriting her statement described having parked in the company parking lot at 8:00 am the previous morning and having returned to her vehicle at 3:00 pm…the time when staff were told they should go home because of the weather.

"I would have reported it yesterday," she said, watching Laurenson read over what she had written, "but when I got here, there was a line-up that went out the front door."

"And one not much shorter today, I'll bet."

She shrugged. "I figured I'd have to forget about time and just get it over with if I ever expected to file a claim with my insurance company."

Laurenson read further.

"It looks as though it'll be a fair-sized claim."

"That's what my husband thinks. Isn't it something? I didn't know people around here did things like that." She gestured towards the damage she had just itemized: the driver's side window smashed, headlights smashed, the driver's side seat slashed, paint scratched all along the driver's side of the car...

Laurenson's pen hovered over the page. "One continuous scratch?"

The woman blushed. "Well, it's not just one scratch, it's more a series of scratches."

"What do you mean, a series of scratches?"

"It's a word. Do I have to put that down? I'd rather not."

"What word?"

"Bitch."

Laurenson couldn't imagine anyone less bitchy than the diffident young woman before him. Still, the offending term was gender-specific and had been carved into a car belonging to someone of the appropriate gender. It had taken more work than "slut," "fuck," or "shit" would have, all of which usually served vandals well. And, in any case, the weather had hardly been the sort that encourages vandals to linger over their handiwork.

"Has anything like this ever happened to you before?"

"No, never!"

"When you drove to work in the morning, Ms. Tilley, is it possible you cut someone off accidentally, or parked in the wrong stall, or—I don't know—scared a pedestrian who was about to cross the street?"

"You think I had to have done something or this wouldn't have been done to me?"

"No, of course not. But, as you say, this isn't the sort of thing we see much of around here. A bit of spray paint on a public building, done at night, is more what we're used to."

"Well," the woman said with a glimmer of a smile, "I guess I'll just have to stop giving the finger to everyone who drives too slow, won't I?"

"Considering how cold it is driving with a broken window, it might be a good idea. At least till spring."

They finished up the paperwork and Laurenson glanced at the clock. "A quick flash of the complaint form has been known to soothe irritated employers," he remarked, tearing off her copy for her.

"Good. Mr. Heyden's a dear, but my immediate superior is a bit...unforgiving."

"Oh, yes, Lexilogic," Laurenson said, thinking of Michaelangelo Smith. "Have you worked there long?"

"Ten years."

"I understand the company has grown tremendously in that time."

"By leaps and bounds ever since we patented the new virus-scan software."

"Oh? When was that?"

"Five years ago."

"Rozilind Smith worked there five years ago. Did you happen to know her?"

"Actually, it's six years ago now that she left. But, yes, I worked in the same department as her."

"As you've probably heard, her father's been making inquiries, wondering if she's returned."

"What makes you think I would have heard that?"

"He called Lexilogic, asking if anyone had seen her recently."

"Really? When was that?"

"Early in the fall."

Chantelle Tilley thought about that for a moment. Noting the little frown lines between her brows, Laurenson inquired further. "Is it important?"

"No, I just would have thought Mr. Heyden would have said something to me about it."

"Why? Was she a friend of yours?"

"Hardly! No."

"Was there a problem between you?"

"I don't know. I mean, I don't think there was, but I can't really be sure."

"Why is that?"

"I was the one who reported the money missing."

"There was money missing?"

"What I mean is, there were irregularities in our accounts payable. Six years ago."

"Do you think it's possible you were the reason Rozilind left town so suddenly?"

"What do *you* think? They start looking into bills we'd paid which we can't find the authorizations for and next thing you know Rozilind's disappeared."

"It could be a coincidence."

"Anything's possible, I guess."

"You sound doubtful. Do *you* think Rozilind could have been responsible for the irregularities?"

"If she wasn't, there was more than one coincidence. Our accounts payable didn't get screwed up any more after she left."

"Was she fired?"

"No. She left the day after they started investigating."

"Would she have connected you with their starting an investigation?"

"I don't know. It would depend on how much Mr. Heyden told her… He seemed to like her, so he might have told her a lot." She paused. "Whether she connected me with the inquiries or not, I would appreciate knowing if she's come back."

"Do you think she would be the sort to harbour a grudge?"

"Anyone who spotted the problem with the invoices would have been required to report it. It's not as though there was anything personal about it."

"Makes sense to me. But do you think Rozilind would have seen it that way?"

"If you ask me, she got off remarkably easy. Mr. Heyden is such a nice person, he never said a word against her, even when it looked pretty certain she'd been ripping him off."

"Maybe he couldn't bring himself to believe it. She *was* awfully young for an embezzler. He might have found it hard to believe she'd know how to, what, 'cook the books'?"

"All it takes is a crooked supplier and someone inside the company who'll process their invoices without checking that the figures on them are correct."

"Someone offering to split the take if she'd cooperate. Is that what you think it was?"

"Maybe."

"You don't, do you?"

"Of course I have no way of knowing, but I'm inclined to think it was the other way around—that she might have gone looking for people who could be talked into submitting false invoices and offered to split the take with *them*."

"Why would you think that?"

"Because she had a way of talking people into doing things."

"What kinds of things?"

Chantelle shrugged. "Iffy things, favours... I don't know. It's not for me to say."

"If they were illegal favours—"

"Oh, I wouldn't have done her illegal favours. No, but I covered for her a few times when she wasn't at her desk. Finally, I began to wonder why she was always off talking to guys in other departments, photocopying, using the fax machine...things that didn't go with her job."

"Was it a good one? Did she have a future with the company?"

"Yes. It was especially good, considering her qualifications. It's hard to imagine her risking a career with a company like Lexilogic just for a few thousand dollars."

There appeared to be a lot of things people didn't ordinarily do that Rozilind Smith did. Of all of them, the one that Laurenson found hardest to explain was returning to St. Michael without contacting anyone.

"How do you know she hasn't contacted anyone?" Val Tavarov asked, when Laurenson talked with him about it later.

"You mean, you think this bit of vandalism counts as contact?"

"Hell, no! I'm not convinced Rozilind Smith was involved. If it was her, why wasn't this Tilley woman targeted way back in August?"

"I have no idea why she wasn't," Laurenson admitted.

"Exactly. And, besides, what good would a bit of vandalism do Rozilind?"

"Do people carrying a grudge lash out to accomplish something, or to relieve a feeling?"

"Be that as it may, I still don't see how we can be sure Rozilind ever did come back to town. In fact, I don't see how we can even be sure she's *alive*."

"Oh well, as for that—the fact that both Mary Grey and her father were convinced goes a long way towards convincing *me*."

Tavarov's response was blunt, as it always was when they batted ideas around. "Well, I'm not convinced. I find it hard to believe an eighteen-year-old could successfully pull off a complete change of identity."

"Eighteen would be an ideal age for it. You apply for a social insurance number and a driver's licence and there's no reason for anyone to wonder why you haven't done so before."

"She'd need to have a birth certificate."

"You know as well as I do that running through obituaries or cemeteries will turn up more than enough kids who would've been eighteen in 1989 if they had lived long enough."

"Yeah, but would a teenager realize it was possible to apply for a birth certificate under the name of someone who had died?"

"We can't assume she wouldn't have—apparently she knew how to embezzle."

"I have a problem with that too," Tavarov said.

Laurenson suspected Tavarov's problem was an excess of chivalry. He checked out Genevieve Neve's views on the subject, the next time she came on duty.

"Men tend to underestimate women and kids," Genevieve said. "In my opinion, underdogs are the *most* likely to resort to fraud. It goes with seeing yourself as an underdog."

"Still, men commit more crimes than women do."

"Who needs to commit a crime if they've mastered subterfuge? But if it comes down to deciding to break the law, it only makes sense for women to use their brains and leave the muscle approach to the guys. And it's using muscle that gets reported most."

This reminded Laurenson that Christie had extricated herself from her situation at the school board more deftly than most men would've been able to. A man in the same situation would've declared war—or threatened to—Christie had, however, gotten what she wanted by dissolving into tears. The fact that she had taken so much abuse before resorting to such a stratagem struck him as evidence of what an extraordinary woman she was.

"I'm taking you out for dinner," he announced, calling Christie up a few minutes later.

"You are out of your mind," she declared.

"This isn't an option, like French; it's a requirement, like breathing."

"You know how things are for me right now."

"Exactly why I want to see you."

"Right now, it would be interpreted by just about everybody I know as a slap in their face."

"Right now, it wouldn't be a bad idea for everybody you know to see I'm not just a rumour or a tall tale...and that I don't *always* disappear when the going gets tough."

"I don't mean to give you a hard time—"

"Well, I mean to give you one."

She chuckled. Thus encouraged, he scrapped the idea of going to The Taj Mahal, and ordered takeout from them instead.

After supper, Christie curled up before Laurenson's fireplace and sipped on an Irish Cream liqueur while he got a roaring blaze going.

"Ooh, I'm stuffed," she moaned.

"Unzip your pants."

"I've got a better idea," she said, slipping out of them.

"Remember when it used to take me hours of concerted effort to get you to this point?" he teased. "Anyone who wants to be on *terra incognita* all the time is just plain crazy."

"Who's she?" Christie asked, almost succeeding in keeping a straight face.

With one last critical look at the fire Laurenson headed over to the couch. "Now," he said, slipping a hand up the inside of one of her long legs, "back to the soap opera."

She rolled her eyes.

"What else would you call it when he tries to make out you haven't been letting him see his kids?"

"Oh that."

"*This*," Laurenson said, inching further up her thigh, "is called something else."

"*This*," she said, "is taking my mind off *that*, much more than it should." She half-heartedly tried to remove his hand.

"You were starting to tell me about the reunion between your ex and little Miss Rapunzel," he prompted, resisting removal.

"Justin was sitting in the living room, having just thrown in my face the fact that I'd gotten cranky during Shaun's measles thirteen years ago. Suddenly, Ange was standing shyly in the doorway and he jumped to his feet and stood there with his arms out. Actually, I wasn't sure Ange was going to take him up on the invitation—I mean, just last week she was angry because he still hadn't called to wish her a happy birthday—but he said, 'Hey, kiddo, have you forgotten your old man?' and next thing I knew they were holding onto each other for dear life."

Laurenson made a move to put his arms around her, but Christie said resolutely, "Thank you, but I don't intend to cry. I thrashed that out with myself after our talk last night, and I've decided it would be sheer perversity to begrudge poor Ange a little fatherly affection."

"So you were okay with having them hold onto each other for dear life?"

"Of course I was okay with it. What I wasn't entirely okay with was the way they then both shot me a look and went away to talk privately…out of earshot of *me*."

"I, too, prefer having my ex grill the kids about me in front of me," Laurenson laughed.

"Maybe I'm getting paranoid, but Ange made a phone call last night and was awfully quiet about it. At the time, the thought crossed my mind that she was updating Shaun—"

"I wouldn't be surprised. Now aren't you glad that her dad's on the scene?"

"What's to be glad about?"

"One of Shaun's parents has access to information on where he is."

"I was hoping I'd be that parent."

"I know…and that you'd be that parent thanks to me. But as long as Shaun's safe—"

"I don't understand why he's still missing."

"He's still missing because, in his estimation, you haven't suffered enough yet."

She twitched. "Why's it up to him? You're trying, aren't you?"

"I'm trying. His timing turned out to be—"

"The pits," she put in. "Yes, I understand." She thought for a while then snuggled up against Laurenson's chest. "I have a sneaking suspicion they may end up ganging up on me."

"It's not what I had in mind when I suggested calling Justin but I, too, have a sneaking suspicion that they might. It's okay. Things have a way of working themselves out."

Laurenson had planned a bank robbery one lazy day while trolling for jackfish. A key element in that robbery had been disruption caused by a blizzard. He was grateful that the citizens of St. Michael did nothing more anti-social during blizzards than slide into each other with their vehicles. Nevertheless, by Shaun Devenish's birthday, he was getting tired of sorting out the vehicular crises that were still straining his resources. It was only the fact that the plate glass window the van had smashed through that morning was on Oriole that motivated him to respond to a call that would normally have been assigned to a constable. Oriole was just a block south of the Lexilogic offices.

Once he had dealt with damages, injuries, security (there was an elderly woman attempting to "loot" the premises), and the paperwork that would be the basis of at least two insurance claims, he stopped by Lexilogic's posh "Data Therapy" centre and asked to speak to Mr. Russell Heyden.

Heyden poked his head out of his office rather as though he expected someone to take a pot shot at his bald spot. Seeing Laurenson, he smoothed his vest over his round belly and gestured for him to come in.

"Staff Sergeant Laurenson? I'm pleased to meet you. Quite a week this has been, eh?"

"Fortunately, things are getting back to normal," Laurenson said, looking around him with interest. Heyden's overcrowded office looked a bit like an electronics store; it even contained four computers that were up and running.

Heyden watched Laurenson's face and gave a puckish grin. "Hard to keep my hands off the product, as you can see. Please sit down. I can't imagine what's brought you out here."

"I was in the neighbourhood," Laurenson said, still trying to absorb what was, for him, a welter of technological hardware and papers.

"Chantelle Tilley told me what happened to her car," Heyden ventured. "We'll be putting up surveillance cameras in the parking lot. It comes as a bit of a shock that they'd be needed, but there you have it. Apparently they are."

"You've never had any vandalism before?"

"Never. But young people these days…well, it's a changing world."

"Is that what you're inclined to take it as—juvenile vandalism?"

"What else could it be?"

Laurenson shrugged, "I hoped you might be able to tell *me*."

"Well, naturally, you'd know more about this sort of thing than I would; but I assumed some young rowdy was let out of school early and had nothing better to do. You know: everything's out of whack so anything goes. He—it would probably be a he, don't you think?—decides to create a little mayhem of his own."

"It's been known to happen, but not usually in this way. Kids who are out to create mayhem like to spread it around; they'll walk down an alley breaking windows as they go; they don't usually limit themselves to one vehicle. There's more bang for the buck hitting five targets lightly than there is in giving one target a thorough going-over."

"Oh, well, if you say so." Heyden again smoothed his vest down. "Well, all we can do is take preventative action so it doesn't happen again."

"I haven't totally given up hope of finding out who did it this time."

Heyden's eyes widened. "You think they might have left fingerprints?"

Laurenson didn't bother pointing out that the weather had been cold enough to warrant wearing gloves or that the car might well not have had an actual finger laid on it during the attack. "Let's go back to your theory of someone wanting to create mayhem and approach it by asking why they'd choose Chantelle Tilley's car as the place to do it."

"I can't imagine how we're supposed to do that," Heyden said, looking uncomfortable.

"Often we go through company employment records looking for disgruntled—"

"Over some broken glass and scratched paint?"

"Someone with a knife seems to have something of a grudge against one of your employees," Laurenson said solemnly. Not for a moment did he consider admitting that he would never have pursued this matter had he not become personally curious about another, possibly unrelated one.

"Oh. Oh well…"

Heyden again smoothed down his vest, and Laurenson decided the gesture might more accurately be interpreted as a wiping of hands. He noticed, as well, that Heyden, a mouth-breather who kept his mouth open slightly at all times, was now wheezing slightly.

"So," he went on smoothly, "I wonder what you can tell me of problem employees you have had in the past."

Heyden looked about him with what struck Laurenson as something close to alarm. "Well. Well! I suppose I'll have to look into this."

"Nobody comes to mind?" he asked blandly.

"I'm wondering if perhaps the answer might lie in applications for employment that we've turned down."

"Chantelle Tilley works in your personnel department?"

"No. Oh no, she doesn't."

"Where does she work?"

"Accounting."

"Perhaps this might be related to a billing matter then."

"I have a hard time imagining how that could be," Heyden said.

"No? Well, 'who' is more important than 'why,' and you'd be surprised how often we can find out 'who' by doing an employee check, by looking for anyone who's been having problems with other employees or has left the company under a cloud or for reasons unknown."

"Is it necessary to go to so much trouble when there's been so little damage done?"

"Upset at what had been done to her car and driving without headlights in a snow storm, Mrs. Tilley could have been injured."

"But she wasn't."

"Not this time."

"You really think there's danger she will be—could possibly be—bothered again...over some bad blood among co-workers or something of that sort?!"

"How do we know she's not being stalked?"

"Th-that's ridiculous."

"Admittedly, it seems unlikely, but we can't rule it out. Especially since there isn't any other trouble you're aware of among your employees."

Laurenson was enjoying himself. People complained continuously about police performance. Security-conscious businesses were especially critical of how the police responded to complaints, particularly minor complaints. It bordered on therapeutic to be taking a complaint "too seriously" for once. That, of course, wasn't why he was giving Heyden a hard time. Heyden had had ample opportunity to recall that he had had an employee who'd left the company under unusual circumstances, that that employee had worked with Chantelle Tilley, and that that employee might have suspected Tilley had gotten her into trouble. That he would keep downplaying the damage done to Tilley's car rather than "remember" the problem employee seemed odd, to say the least.

"I gather you weren't able to jog his memory," Val said, grinning.

"Not even when he said they'd check their files and I told him to be sure to go back at least five or six years. I couldn't have been more pointed if I'd tried."

"You didn't want to just out and out confront him with what he was doing?"

"I wish I knew what he was doing."

"Obstructing justice, for starters," Val said. "The investigation into Rozilind's disappearance sure as hell wasn't *helped* by his keeping quiet about the trouble at work."

"I may raise that matter with him some day," Laurenson said. Right now, though, I don't like to tip my hand because I can't for the life of me figure out why he's still being loyal to her. Until I can, I want to give him as much latitude as possible. Maybe he'll say something that'll actually help me make sense of all this."

Tavarov shook his head. "I hope it's worth all this trouble."

"Trouble? What trouble?"

"What do *you* call it then?"

Laurenson grinned. "Come to think of it, his hand *was* sweating when I shook it on my way out, so maybe 'trouble' is the right word after all."

Miranda poked her head into the coffee room just then. "There's a young lady to see you, Staff."

"About?"

"She wouldn't say. Her name is Angela Devenish and apparently that should be enough to clue you in to what she wants. Sorry."

"No, that's okay. I'll be right out."

Laurenson didn't at first recognize the girl who sat by the front door jiggling one booted foot. Whenever he'd seen Angela she'd had her hair in a ponytail and had been wearing jeans and a T-shirt; the Angela waiting to see him wore a short skirt, wet-look boots, and a crocheted top through which he could see more than made him comfortable. Her usually straight hair was a huge mass of curls and her usually fresh young face lay hidden under a lot of make-up applied with an apparently inexperienced hand. She looked like nothing quite so much as a raccoon with large red lips.

"Ange? What can I do for you?"

"I need to talk to you," she said.

"Certainly." Ordinarily he would have taken her to his office but her odd appearance made him somewhat wary. Until he knew what she was up to, he preferred her to be up to it in one of the interview rooms. "This way," he directed her.

She looked at his name stenciled across the frosted glass of his office door. "Um, aren't we—? I thought we'd go to your office."

"We're just going into an interview room."

"I'd rather talk to you in your office."

"Why is that?"

"Because...because an interview room is so official?"

"It may be official but it's quite comfortable, you know."

"Maybe, but I think your office would be better."

"It's just a matter of proper procedure," he assured her. "And, believe me, it's meant for your protection more than mine."

"Yours!" she laughed. "Like what would you need to be protected from?"

"Mainly," he said with a smile, "from accusations of having failed to follow proper procedure."

Reluctantly she allowed herself to be guided to the interview rooms outside the holding cells and directed into one of them. Very reluctantly she took a seat.

"I'll be right back," Laurenson said, slipping out to start the recording equipment.

When he returned a minute or two later, Angela glanced over at the unobtrusive one-way observation window. "Some mothers' boyfriends would actually invite a girl out for lunch."

"Aren't you supposed to be in school?"

"They gave me permission."

"To come see your mother's boyfriend? Why?"

"Because you're a Mountie, of course! It's about my missing brother."

"What about your brother?"

"It's his birthday," she said, in a suddenly sad voice. "I think it's just awful he's all alone on his birthday."

"Apparently he doesn't feel that way, or he'd have come home by now."

"What makes you think he can?"

"What makes you think he can't?"

"I get the impression you don't want him to come home."

"What matters right now is what Shaun wants. Do you have any idea what he wants?"

"It's cold in here," Angela said with a shiver.

"Perhaps you'd better put on your jacket." She didn't take his advice, and he went on. I was just asking what Shaun wants."

"Who knows what he wants? Maybe he wants to become a drug peddler or a bum boy."

"*I beg your pardon?*"

Angela blushed furiously. "Well, that's always the risk, isn't it? That kids like Shaun will sell drugs or sell themselves."

"You'd be doing him a favour, encouraging him to reconcile with his mother."

"Like she'd ever reconcile with him!"

"You think she wouldn't?"

"She can be a bitch sometimes."

"Do you have any influence with your brother?"

"I see you're not arguing about Mom being a bitch," she said.

"I fail to see what good it would do to argue. In fact, I fail to see what I'm supposed to do about any of this."

"Mom thought you'd be finding Shaun for her—that you'd have him home in a flash."

"What makes you think it's up to me?"

Her voice took on a cajoling tone. "I know you can find people when you want to."

"What makes you think Shaun is even in St. Michael?"

Angela appeared to be at a loss. Laurenson raised his eyebrows and waited.

"What does it matter where he is?" she finally asked.

"You know that we police only this area; we don't go trolling the streets of Edmonton looking for runaways."

"Well, anyway, I have a feeling he's here."

"Is that what you came to tell me?"

She stared at him, gaping a little.

"Why *did* you come to see me?"

She looked around her, as though expecting to find the answer to his question written on the bare white walls enclosing them. Again, Laurenson waited.

"I don't know how come you can't feel it, but it's absolutely freezing in here."

Laurenson got up, picked up her jacket and draped it over her shoulders. He found it reassuring that she shrank from him and pulled her jacket closed.

"I don't think Mom will like you any more if you don't bring Shaun home, you know."

"Have you any influence with Shaun?" he asked for the second time.

"Me? Like could I tell him what to do? No way! You could though."

"If he wouldn't listen to you, how likely do you think it is that he'd listen to me?"

She gestured toward his gun. "It looks to me as though you're much better equipped than I am for making him listen. I saw the cells out there. It wouldn't take much to have him bawling for his mom if you locked him up in one of those. You wouldn't even have to lay a hand on him...though it would probably speed things up a bit if you let him think you might not be able to resist."

"Is that what you came to suggest—that I put the boots to your brother?" Laurenson laughed. "*On his birthday?*"

Angela leaned forward, looking earnest. "Nobody said anything about hurting him. Or doing anything else you could get in trouble for. You're allowed to handcuff people, aren't you? To lock them up? To fingerprint them? I bet he'd resist arrest. You're allowed to subdue people who're resisting arrest, aren't you?"

"Well, thanks for the advice," Laurenson said levelly.

"And thank *you* for the help," she replied with more than a trace of sarcasm.

"Who was supposed to be helping who?" he asked. "I thought you had come to help me save my relationship with your mother. Who," he added with a gleam, "won't be reconciled with Shaun but won't speak to me ever again if I don't bring him home immediately."

"Well, don't say I didn't warn you," Angela said. "She's already beginning to doubt you."

"Speaking of doubting things, I doubt that having Shaun return to your mom is high on your agenda."

"What makes you think that?"

"Your dad is applying to get custody of you both."

She bit her lip, then stood up abruptly, and headed toward the door.

"Hey, Ange, care to tell me what it is you *really* came to get from me?"

She answered without turning around. "I'll tell Mom about this little chat," she said. She opened the door. "You can bet on it."

Laurenson thanked God he had it all down on tape.

On his way back to his office, he met Tavarov's inquiring look with a shrug. "Hard to say what someone wants when they come armed with everything from a slingshot to a harpoon."

"I'd have been happy to have sat in on the interview."

"I think she *thought* we had an observer. Don't worry, she fingered her weapons but that was about all." He took a step and added, "I look forward to the day that brother of hers runs into a female he *can't* wrap around his little finger."

Back in his office, Laurenson called Christie. "Thought you might want some company tonight, it being Shaun's birthday and a rather disappointing one."

"I haven't totally given up on hearing from him."

"I can always come over to your place."

"Maybe later. If he doesn't call by 8:00, I'll call you."

She called at 8:15. "How about coming over for some Black Forest cake?"

"Have you the makings for Black Russians?"

"'Fraid not."

"I'll bring them then. As I recall, Black Russians go well with Black Forest cake."

"I warn you, this is a homemade cake and already drizzled with kirsch."

"Okay, I'll bring coffee liqueur instead."

"Ange not home?" he asked.

"No. She left this morning dressed to the teeth. I figure she must have arranged to meet Shaun for supper."

"But still you cooked a roast?"

"How did you know?"

"I can still smell dinner."

"Oh. Would you like some?"

"No, cake and coffee will be great."

She cut him a huge slice of chocolate cake layered with heaps of whipped cream while he poured coffees and laced them liberally with Irish Cream liqueur.

As Christie took a sip of her coffee she smiled. "You're awfully good to me."

"Hardly. I'm the one sitting here enjoying your company and filling his face with the most delicious cake he's ever eaten. This isn't exactly an act of mercy."

"He must hate me a lot, if my own son won't come and do the same. I told Ange that I was going ahead with the birthday dinner; I thought it might be the nudge that would bring him home again."

"He's lucky to have a mother like you."

"Don't say that. I know you mean well, but all it does is draw attention to the fact that he doesn't think so. What does that leave me but self-pity or blame? Have you noticed how much of my life has been devoted to self-pity and blame lately?"

"You've been going through a bit of a rough patch, it's true."

"When a woman keeps marrying abusive men, they don't say, 'you've been going through a bit of a rough patch'; they say, 'what is it about you that makes you seek out abusive men?' I've gotten to the point, Dan, where I'm wondering why my life consists of dealing with one critical person after another. It's like being accident-prone. I overheard someone saying today that the storm three days ago was the last straw for her insurance company. They're canceling her car insurance because she's been involved in three no-fault accidents. No-fault! I gather they know that some people just keep attracting the same kind of mishaps forever."

Laurenson's first impulse was to try to reassure Christie, but he took a sip of coffee as a way of resisting the impulse. What good would reassurances do her? He was surprised himself by the amount of rejection she had experienced. She was warm-hearted, intelligent, and gutsy, but still things went badly for her.

"There are people who seem inexplicably unlucky," he said. "I guess nobody wants to insure an unlucky person, any more than they want to insure an unhealthy one."

"What is it about me that makes me such a loser?"

"You're not a loser. Do you really think being more like Shaun would make you more of a winner?"

"I must be a loser, I keep losing things." She put a forkful of cake in her mouth. "Right now I'm losing my kids. I can't deny it; I can see that they want their dad to get custody. I've been trying to write my response to his court application, and every sentence takes me an hour because I keep wondering how I can be claiming I've been a good mother and he's been an uninterested father when I have two nearly adult children writing letters telling the court I'm a slut and I've been keeping them from their loving dad."

"You know you're not a slut and he's not a fond father."

"Oh, yes; I'm not so far gone I can't see *that*. What I'm having trouble with is understanding why they're lying."

"If they had any justification for attacking you, they wouldn't have to lie."

"It's taking the easy way out to claim they're wrong and I'm being victimized. Why am I always being victimized?"

"There's a set of guidelines for avoiding being mugged. Have you heard of them? Things like walking purposefully and alertly, looking confident and unafraid…"

"You're telling me how not to be mugged by my kids?"

"It's our kids who know best every weakness we have and have spent years finding ways of exploiting the ones they can exploit."

Christie took another mouthful of cake. "No," she said, laying down her fork with a clatter. "I mean, I know that's true as far as it goes, but I refuse to think of it like that any more. I can't go through life like an old woman in a dark alley trying not to limp so I won't get mugged. I've got to—well I don't know what I've got to do, but I've got to do something different."

"I'm not sure what else you *can* do."

"Naturally. You're a policeman and see the world through a policeman's eyes." She reached out and squeezed his hand. "Believe me, I don't mean that as a criticism. Not like I would've a few months ago."

"How do you think I should see this?"

"I was brought up to see it as a matter of good versus evil," she said with a shake of her head, "but I'm trying to get over that." She laughed. "The educator in me saw abused women as people trying to find the right response to being abused."

"I think I recall hearing that from you once."

"But I was reading something—you can stop making faces, you know I read amazing things sometimes—I was reading something that keeps popping back into my mind…often just as I wake up in the morning. A psychiatrist, a Jungian, writing about synchronicity, told how she had a patient who spent some bad months battling a co-worker who was his shadow self—"

"His what?"

"You know, who was everything that he had just been trying to overcome himself. According to her it was part of his cure: synchronicity provided him with the darker side of himself to come to terms with. In coming to terms with the rejected aspects of himself in another person, he finally got free of them himself."

"Sorry, Christie, you lost me way back at 'shadow self.'"

"You know how people say we can't stand other people who remind us of what we reject in ourselves? Haven't you found it's true? Take me, for example. Weren't you once laughing at how I seethed about goody-goodies working for the school board but was afraid to get involved with you because being involved with a man brings out an old need in me to be perfect?"

Laurenson smiled ruefully. "About the same time, as I recall, that I was shocked at discovering I was a controller too, just like the rapist I was trying to track down."

"Well, maybe coming to grips with him helped you come to grips with the controller in yourself. And maybe, just maybe, spending nine years working at the school board helped me come to terms with the goody-goody in me. That's what the Jungian would have said; only she wasn't writing about that, she was writing about synchronicity—about how things come into our lives just when we need them. 'When the student is ready, the teacher will appear.'"

"I gather you've figured out some way this explains your ex's sudden appearance on the scene."

"I'm working on it."

"You say you're having a hard time writing your response to the accusations?"

"Yeah. I finally spent an hour writing a total confession, admitting everything they'd accused me of. Really hamming it up. Only then could I get it out of my system and go on to something a bit more sane. But I still had a hard time defending myself."

"Do you still have the confession?"

"Do you want to read it?"

"Sure, if you like; but that wasn't what I was thinking of. Something like that could, if it fell into the wrong hands, put an end to any hope you might have of successfully fighting the application for a change of custody."

"The wrong hands? Like Justin's...or the KGB's?"

"I was thinking of Angela, actually. She came in to see me today, ostensibly to get me to haul Shaun home for his birthday but—"

"To haul Shaun home? How?"

"We didn't get into that. We didn't get past 'why.'"

"Isn't the why of it obvious?"

"Not to me. I had a feeling I was being set up. There was nothing in her behaviour to indicate that she had her heart set on reconciling you two."

Christie sat sipping coffee and thinking. Eventually, Laurenson got up and brought them both more coffee.

"They don't know what they're doing," she said, as he returned. "They have no idea what they're getting themselves into. I wish I could..."

"Warn them? Tell them what he's like?"

"Do you think there's any chance he's changed?"

"You can always tell them they're welcome back if they find they've made a mistake," he suggested. "Maybe that's how your response to the application should be framed. Maybe you should suggest a trial period with the final decision on custody being Shaun's and Angela's."

Seeing Christie's face brighten, he knew he had come up with something that met her needs. He might even have stumbled across a way of getting around the fear of coercion that made teens so difficult to advise. His only regret was that he hadn't stumbled over it a few years earlier with his own kids.

After that, Christie brought him down her confession and they read it together. "It is true I uttered dire threats involving a cessation of visiting privileges. I admit I was unreasonably unwilling to drop off and pick up children once doing so entailed covering distances of three thousand kilometres. Likewise, I freely admit I limited correspondence between the children and their father, being tired of writing their letters for them and, eventually, becoming too lazy even to nag them about writing their letters for themselves."

"I guess I don't need to worry about this falling into the wrong hands," Laurenson laughed.

"Better read the part about my being a slut, before you decide that," Christie countered.

A page later, Laurenson was surprised to discover that he was still able to blush. "Have you ever considered writing bodice rippers?" he asked.

"Maybe I will, once I've gotten this respondent's response thing written. Do you mind giving me a hand? I mean with the response."

Together they crafted a short letter to the court. Christie expressed concern that communication had broken down to such an extent that her children were clearly angry with her and unhappy in her care. She praised her former husband for the concern that had brought him across the country on short notice and in difficult circumstances. She said she believed the question of custody ought to be left up to the children, and urged they be given ample time to make their decision. She assured everyone that she would continue to love her children and want to spend time with them, whatever they decided. And, finally, she promised to enter counseling with them, should they return home.

"Maybe they won't like the bit about counseling," Christie worried.

"If they don't, you need it for your protection," Laurenson warned.

Chapter Five

Rio Vanagas was down on the 1989 missing person's report as one of several boyfriends dating Rozilind Smith on a regular basis. He was also in the Lexilogic files as a computer programmer who had come to work for the company in June of 1994. Here was a chance to kill two birds with one stone. Three, actually, Laurenson figured. Talking to Vanagas would be one way of conveying to Heyden that he did intend to pursue his inquiries. In his experience, nothing was more effective at prompting secretive people to talk than knowing others were talking. Often, they were more afraid of the spin others might put on their stories than they were of people hearing the stories themselves.

Vanagas was definitely not a computer nerd type. Blond and built like a Nordic god, he looked handsome enough to have been a feather in an eighteen-year-old's cap. Presumably giving him up would have caused any girlfriend to have second thoughts about disappearing.

Vanagas was happy to talk with Laurenson. Like Mary Grey, he'd been puzzled by Rozilind, and he welcomed the opportunity to sift through memories of her once again.

"I thought we were pretty close. We saw a lot of each other through most of grade twelve; but all that came to an end shortly before grad."

"You two had a fight?"

"Not even a spat. But Roz stopped talking to me."

"Why? You must have asked her."

"I would have if I could have. I really mean it when I say she stopped talking to me. She literally wouldn't say one word to me. She turned and walked away every time I got close. She hung up when she heard my voice. It was crazy-making. I spent hours every day just running over what I could have said or done that would have made her react like that. I went to everybody we knew, trying to find out what people were saying about me...what Roz was saying about me. If I'd said or done anything she could have taken the wrong way, I think I'd have felt a whole lot better—at least I'd have understood—but I hadn't, and it was driving me nuts trying to figure out what was going on. I'd still like to hear her side of it. I mean, she must have had a reason, right? I'll be damned if I can figure out what it was."

"When exactly did she stop talking to you?"

"The end of May. May 1989. Just before grad."

"Were you planning to go to grad together?"

"Yeah. I even hoped it'd all blow over by then, but it didn't; she never actually *said* she wasn't going with me, but it was pretty plain even before she agreed to go with Trevor Winckler that it wasn't going to happen."

"So she didn't tell anybody what was bothering her. I thought she was best friends with Brandy Heyden."

"For what it was worth."

"You mean, you don't think they were close?"

"I don't think Roz liked Brandy nearly as much as Brandy liked her. Brandy thought Roz was the coolest person...everything she wanted to be. Let's face it—Roz was witty, sexy, high-powered, *interesting*. She had a charm about her, no question about that. Brandy was the one who kept the friendship going. In the end, they fell out of touch...naturally enough, I guess, since Brandy went off to college like I did."

"Where did you go to college?"

"The University of Toronto. I was going to settle for UBC, but Toronto accepted me at the last minute, just before grad." Vanagas corrected himself. "Not exactly just before grad. More like just before she broke up with me."

"Do you think there could have been a connection?"

"It's hard to see how there could've been. What skin would it've been off her nose that I got accepted?"

"So she hadn't applied there herself?"

Vanagas spoke gently, as one might who assumed Mounties hadn't been to university and so couldn't be expected to know anything about admissions procedures. "She was planning to get a Master of Business Administration. I was going into computer sciences. We weren't competing for a spot in the same program. My success or lack of it would have nothing to do with hers."

"Are you saying she'd applied at the University of Toronto, just not for the same program you applied for?"

"That's right."

"So it's possible she heard about the success of *her* application around the same time you heard about the success of *yours*."

"Probably."

"Presumably she wasn't accepted."

"It was a bit much for her to expect she would be. Her marks were mainly in the seventies. Marks like that weren't going to get her red carpet treatment anywhere, let alone at the U. of T."

"I was under the impression she was a very bright girl."

"Oh she was! Maybe too bright for her own good. She figured she knew how to maximize her marks while minimizing her effort. She had it all down to a fine science. In theory it made sense—because short-term memory is so short, you don't study until just before exams; because you want to save your effort for the big assignments, you don't bother with the ones that count for only two percent of the total mark...that sort of thing. As it turned out, when the assignments that counted for twenty percent were marked hard, she found her approach hadn't been as cost effective as expected. She was furious. I've got to admit that some of her grades were way out of line; the teachers were so pissed off with her that they marked her a lot harder than the rest of us. If her father hadn't been such a wuss, he'd have raised a ruckus and things might have turned out different. As it was, he didn't back her up and, by the time she complained to them all and fought with half of them, I doubt there was a single teacher who would've been willing to give her a favourable letter of recommendation."

"Recommendations are part of the application package these days?"

"Not always, but they count for a lot with the top programs and universities."

"So marks on the province-wide exams aren't enough."

"She thought they would be. Who knew? Apparently acceptance is conditional on how you do in June, but rejection isn't."

"If she'd done exceptionally well at the end, presumably she could've written to various Deans of Commerce asking to be reconsidered."

"I guess. So maybe it all took its toll and she didn't ace the exams as expected. On the other hand, Roz never did have much faith in people, in either their judgement or their good will. Wouldn't it take trust or optimism or something to do a thing like that?"

"She went to her teachers to get her marks changed."

"Yeah, and took quite a drubbing."

"I understand she expected Brandy's father to pay her way through university. That seems pretty optimistic to me."

Vanagas laughed. "Now what kind of crazy idea was that—that Russell Heyden would make her his protegé? I never understood why she was so sure he would."

"Could you have been mistaken? Maybe she wasn't as sure as you thought."

"She was less worried than I was about where the money was going to come from, and her dad's a dirt poor farmer. I still don't understand why she didn't just take out a student loan and go to the U. of A.; thousands of kids without money go to university on student loans every year."

"So maybe her marks weren't up to snuff after all."

"It wouldn't be the first time she did worse than she expected, I suppose," Vanagas said, sounding doubtful.

"You don't really think it was that, do you?"

"No. I don't think she could bring herself to apply for financial assistance."

"Too proud?"

"How should I know? All this came up after she froze me out."

"But you'd dated her for a year. You must have known her as well as anyone; well enough to make a guess, at any rate."

"I suppose." Vanagas shook his head. "Some people thought she was proud, but that wasn't my take on her. I took her for pissed off. Lots of things didn't seem fair to her, even before the teachers gave her a raw deal. I can imagine her thinking, *Like hell I'm going to go into debt for a second-rate degree*."

"So she preferred to go to work for the man who'd reneged on his promise to finance her education."

"She never actually said he promised, you know."

"So what makes you so sure he must have promised?"

"I told you she wasn't a trusting person. Now, I ask you, what does it take to make someone like that so sure they're going to be given something the rest of us would never dare hope for?"

"Beats me."

"Beats me too. I mean, for the Roz I knew, I can't imagine even a promise being enough."

"There's always a chance that a person who isn't inclined to depend on the good nature of others might be inclined to rely on their behaving badly," Laurenson suggested.

Vanagas took his meaning immediately. "That's just plain disgusting!"

"You're in a better position than I am for judging how likely it is."

"Roz and Russell Heyden?"

"Is that so very different from using her sex appeal to get what she wanted from a raft of admirers at school? Not that I'm saying she was using anybody; but the fact that she had a string of boyfriends makes it look like a possibility. As I recall, grade twelve girls usually set their sights on going steady with guys who look like you."

"There are advantages to playing the field."

"Not so much for girls. Girls tend to make a bad name for themselves playing the field."

"Roz thought too much of herself to be promiscuous," Vanagas replied stiffly.

"Then she ran the risk of being called a 'lez.' My kids were in high school around the same time you were, you know."

Vanagas grinned. "Okay, so she wasn't an iceberg. Still, she wasn't a slut by any means. I'm not the only one who respected her; the other guys did too."

Laurenson wondered how a young girl had managed to pull off a balancing act like that, but he decided not to pressure a good source of information who appeared to still have a bit of a thing for her.

"What did you think when you heard about her disappearing suddenly?" he asked.

"I couldn't believe it. I suppose anyone can be murdered, but Roz was hardly the sort to take candy from strangers. And then you guys figured it looked like she'd decided to vanish, and I couldn't understand that either. She wasn't the sort to back off, much less run away. What kind of trouble could make her want to totally disappear?"

"Can you imagine anything that would make her want to come back?"

"Come back to St. Michael?" Vanagas shook his head. "Maybe her dad's funeral. He was a nice old guy; I suppose she'd probably want to come back if he died."

"Other than her dad," Laurenson pressed. He wondered, however, why he bothered. Obviously Vanagas couldn't imagine her coming back at all.

"If you told me there was a place being haunted by her, I'd buy it in a minute. Whether there really are ghosts or not, she'd haunt something to settle an old score. But, to come back here unless she'd made it big. Naw. Never. Kids in our class were pitying her by the time it was all over." He seemed struck by a thought. "Imagine you guys still looking into her disappearance after all this time."

"Someone thought they saw her."

"I wonder if I'd recognize her if I saw her. It's been a long time."

"Hardly seems likely she'd come back." Laurenson rose to leave, wondering which was more improbable—that Roz would return, or that her father would drop his determined vigil and lose all interest in her whereabouts. As for Russell Heyden's slight case of amnesia, he was beginning to think there was nothing so surprising about that, after all.

"By the way," he said, pausing at the door. "Am I correct in assuming no one mentioned to you that she'd been seen in town?"

"Roz? For sure not. But then I'm really not in touch with anybody from school any more. I see a guy from my class pumping gas at the Co-op sometimes but we don't ever talk. Not that I don't want to or anything but, actually, I don't even remember his name."

"Roz's father called Lexilogic asking if anyone had seen her. I thought someone might have mentioned it to you."

"Who here would know I once knew Roz?"

"Russell Heyden would, wouldn't he? I assumed her father must have talked to him."

"Oh, yeah, I didn't think of that. Well, anyway, I doubt he'd have taken the old man seriously. He's been going through a bit of a hard time. Heyden has, I mean. He's got lots of his own worries occupying his mind these days."

"That's the impression I got. Not business troubles, surely."

"I'm sure he's not in financial trouble; he's launching several great new products in the spring. More likely it's health problems. Every time I see him he seems to be taking one pill or another."

"Well, thanks for your time," Laurenson said. "And, if you do see Rozilind Smith—"

"No use giving me instructions," Vanagas laughed. "I'd drop dead of surprise if I saw her."

"What makes you so sure Mary Grey really did see Rozilind Smith?" Tavarov asked. "Sure she may be a smart lady, but so's Tasha, and *she* makes mistakes."

Laurenson set down his cup of coffee and stood up. "These are cars parked on Oriole," he said, positioning two chairs in the coffee room. "And this is the reaction of the woman with green eyes when she realized Mary Grey was looking at her."

He stood between the chairs, jerked his head back, did the little step sidle dance Mrs. Grey had demonstrated, stared hard at Tavarov and forged determinedly ahead, breaking into a run. Tavarov doubled up with laughter.

"Maybe I'm doing the fawn-like run a little too accurately," Laurenson suggested.

"The whole thing is preposterous," Tavarov said.

"Unusual," Laurenson corrected him. "So unusual that I have no difficulty believing Mrs. Grey did see something like this on Oriole in August. Who'd make stuff like this up?"

"Who'd jump and jerk around like that? Are you trying to tell me a sexy sophisticate in her mid-twenties would?"

"It's not the sort of response I think a person would dream up, or forget if they did see it."

"How old did you say this Mrs. Grey of yours is?"

"What you haven't noticed is the sense it makes if you look at the parts rather than the whole. There's the double take; that's surprise. There's the hard stare; I don't know, maybe it's not being sure who this person is, maybe myopia, maybe glaring because you don't like running into this person, maybe wariness, or maybe even trying to hold their gaze. Then there's the getting the hell out of there—"

"That's not all there was."

"No, not by a long shot. There's the fancy footwork." Laurenson did the routine again. "Anything about it strike you?"

"Nothing I'd care to share with you, Staff."

"Well, of course, a chair is a poor stand-in for a car. But if a person is standing back of a left tail-light and then takes two steps back and one over, it's my considered opinion that that would likely put them pretty much right smack dab in front of the licence plate on the vehicle they're standing behind. Combined with holding the person's eye and then darting out into the street—not the safest maneuvre, if you ask me—then what, at first, seemed too grotesque to be real, actually begins to make sense."

Tavarov got it. "First impulse is to hide the licence plate because you ran into this person while standing behind your own car. Final impulse is to get the hell out of there, probably as quickly as possible, and heading in a direction that you looked to have been heading anyway."

"Either that or away from what is significant about the place...in this case, away from the Lexilogic offices. And maybe, throughout you carefully watch their reaction."

"You figure she was at Lexilogic?"

"I'm almost certain she was. Maybe not inside the building, but there watching it or looking for someone or something. Something brought her back, and it wasn't her father."

"I take it Heyden made quite an impression on you."

"He's hiding something. Apparently he was hiding something six years ago when Roz disappeared. Since when does one of these CEO's want *less* police service than we're willing to offer?"

"If Mary Grey really did see Roz, Heyden can't have killed her. I mean, though having an affair with his daughter's best friend might have made him a suspect six years ago, it can't hurt him now, if she's still alive." Tavarov took a long pull at his coffee. "Well, it can't, can it?"

"The hell of it is, I don't see how it can. Though blackmail is always a possibility, I guess."

"What? You mean this dirty-old-man-drooling-over-his-daughter's-best-friend thing?"

"Who'd want something like that coming out if it didn't have to?"

"She wasn't a minor."

"Maybe she was at the beginning."

"Even so, it's more of an embarrassment than a threat. It wouldn't be hard for him to make a case for having been seduced by a dishonest young tramp whose whole purpose was to get him to give her a job so she could systematically embezzle from his company. You do time for embezzling, not having an affair...even if it *is* with a seventeen-year-old."

"Maybe there are pictures that would knock your socks off."

"Uh uh. She wouldn't have left town when the billing irregularities turned up if there had been."

"Well, then, maybe he fell head over heels in love with her, even if she didn't fall for him. Maybe he's still trying to protect her good name."

"You really think it's possible?"

"Possible, maybe. Likely? I don't think so. Roz's old boyfriend, now a programmer with the company, says Heyden has problems. He thinks they're health problems because Heyden's always taking pills. Now I got the impression, too, that Heyden had problems but I don't see why we've got to assume they're health problems. His popping pills may simply mean he's got problems which are so serious they're affecting his health. By the same token, I'm not inclined to think his health would suffer because Roz needed his protection; it strikes me as more likely he'd be worried sick because he's got a problem with *her.*"

"Well, he can always call us if he wants help with his problem."

"Isn't it ironic? Nobody wants help from us."

"Well, why should they? Her father has adjusted to her loss and he was the only one who really cared all that much about her."

"Her father was single-handedly staking out the entire city just a few weeks ago."

"Granted. Note, he wasn't asking *us* to keep an eye out for her."

"Well, that's hardly surprising. He couldn't get anyone to give him the time of day when he asked about the unidentified remains found in the area; why should he expect we'd help him check out something as unlikely sounding as her having come back on the sly?"

"Admittedly he probably wouldn't. But then you came along. And from where I stand, it looks as though he must have known he'd found a sympathetic ear, at last."

"Yes," Laurenson said, suddenly struck by something. "Yes, he had." He got up and poured what remained of his cold coffee down the sink. With great deliberation, he filled another cup with fresh coffee and turned back to Tavarov. "*But by then it was too late.*"

Tavarov was watching him with amusement. "How'd you learn to do that? A light bulb has suddenly materialized over your head."

Laurenson hardly noticed he was being ribbed. "Yeah, well, I tried my damnedest to put my finger on what felt wrong about the first talk I had with Smith but I got nowhere. Finally, it makes sense. Sure, he was still pissed off at us because he hadn't gotten any answers regarding the unidentified human remains; but he wasn't showing the interest you'd expect. When I got back to him later, he didn't even ask what I'd come out to tell him. There was no suspense, no curiosity. He said he'd learned patience. He said he'd never really believed she was dead. But that wasn't it. By then he *knew*."

"Knew she wasn't dead?"

"Right. By the time I first talked to him, his interest in the remains was minimal. I'd be willing to bet he'd already abandoned his stakeout. But he was such a polite, philosophical old fellow, that it was hard to see what was going on. Everything that rang false about his reaction makes sense if by then he had obtained new information that made all his previous inquiries outdated."

"What kind of information could he possibly have—?" Tavarov snapped his fingers. "He must have seen her!"

"That's the only thing I can think of that would be so compelling it would leave nothing of interest for me to tell him."

"But, then, why didn't he tell you he had already found his daughter, thank-you-very-much? Most people would be only too happy to."

"Yeah, I know. He must have had a good reason not to. And it certainly wasn't that he wanted to spare my feelings."

"I gather that, all in all, you think he's an okay sort of person."

"That's how he struck me. Not that I'm an infallible judge of character."

"The daughter, on the other hand, isn't exactly anybody's choice for citizen-of-the-year."

"Neither is she public-enemy-number-one. Maybe Heyden has been so loyal to her because he had good reason to think she was falsely accused. Have you ever known anyone who was always getting a raw deal? You know, the sort of person who ends up bitter because it feels like they've been a magnet for trouble their whole lives?"

"I've known a lot of people who have *claimed* that was what they were."

"Never anyone who *was* just plain unlucky?"

"Well, maybe my brother-in-law. The family saying is that, 'if it weren't for bad luck, he'd have no luck at all.' If a guy can't keep a job, I'm inclined to assume that that says something about him. But I really don't get it in the case of Simon. He's a damned hard worker, obliging as hell, smart, honest, and funny; at least he *was*. Last time I saw him he was on anti-depressants."

"So why do you suppose he can't keep a job?"

"If you ever find out, maybe you can tell *me*."

"Well, I guess there's always a chance that Rozilind Smith has had your brother-in-law's luck. Her mother died when she was eight. Her grade twelve teachers seem to have ganged up on her. Who knows what else happened that we're never going to hear about? It could even be she got framed for embezzling and ran into a serial killer we still don't know about. They say, luck breeds luck; you start to expect people to be stand-offish so you hang back and people get the impression *you* don't like *them*. You stew over how things are going and you end up getting sick. You lose your health and you lose your job."

Tavarov threw in his own example. "You figure the world's constantly short-changing you so you try to balance things out a little more in your favour and next thing you know, you're charged with theft and things have really taken a turn for the worse."

"The thing that gets me about Rozilind Smith is that I can see myself in her, sort of. How critical am I? Not suffering fools gladly isn't exactly the failing of the dregs of humanity. The dregs are still out there picking pockets and mugging little old ladies."

"Ever seen *Planes, Trains and Automobiles?*"

"Have I? I love that movie. I can relate to the stiff-necked guy who's trying to get home for Thanksgiving."

"Ever noticed that the slob he's stuck with as a traveling companion breezes through most of the disasters they run into, while *he* keeps making things worse through his attitude? Maybe that's how it works. I don't see how this can apply to my brother-in-law but, then, who knows what kind of attitude he's got when he's not with us?"

"I can see how it would apply to Rozilind Smith. From what I heard, she tried to 'work smart, not hard' and set her teachers against her; she complained about the marks they gave her, and only made things worse. To make things better, she ditched a boyfriend 'to die for' when he got accepted at the U. of T. and she didn't. And, finally, it looks as though she wouldn't apply for a student loan because getting financial assistance hadn't been part of her original plan. I can imagine a person like that deciding to build an education fund out of what she could skim off the accounts-payable of someone who gave her a job instead of the tuition money she thought he was going to give."

"Maybe she still thinks she has the money coming to her and— What the fuck?!"

For nearly a minute there'd been a clinking sound growing in volume. Now suddenly there was shouting in the corridor down by the holding cells. Of one accord, both Tavarov and Laurenson jumped to their feet and headed for the door. At just that moment, a prisoner in leg irons launched himself at Constable Keith Dayandan with such force that he knocked his hat off. Under the bemused scrutiny of four cops—Genevieve Neve being there, opening a cell door—he leapt at the fallen hat and began to jump on it.

"Shit," Dayandan said.

Laurenson, struck by the oddity of seeing a well-dressed middle-aged man behaving like a cartoon character, stood taking in the scene for close to a second. Tavarov, however, was instantly on the move, and had almost reached the prisoner by the time Genevieve grabbed the chain on the leg irons and yanked the heavy-set man off his feet. He landed hard, the wind knocked out of him and a stunned look on his face. It had all happened so fast, he was probably wondering why he was on the floor.

"And now, sir, *into the cell*, if you please," Genevieve snapped.

Dayandan and Tavarov lifted the man to his feet with one smooth motion and propelled him through the cell door.

"Fuck you," the man gasped, largely drowned out by the sound the door made as metal hit metal.

Ruefully Dayandan picked up his hat and tried to restore it to its proper shape.

Genevieve grinned. "Working traffic just ain't what it used to be."

"What happened?" Laurenson asked.

"A man called 911 saying there was an attack on a Volkswagen Beetle in progress in front of his house. When Keith got there, the suspect was still trying to overturn a car containing a woman and her three-year-old son. He caught her at a red light after chasing her through traffic for several blocks. Apparently she had honked her horn at him as she passed him."

The man sat down heavily on the bunk in his cell and scowled at the floor.

"I guess this is officially St. Michael's first case of road rage," Dayandan said. "And, wouldn't you know it?—it turns out to be a lawyer."

Laurenson studied the jowly face with greater interest, but he didn't recognize the man. By tacit agreement, he and his officers walked back toward the coffee room before saying anything more.

"Local?" Tavarov asked.

"Edmonton," Dayandan said. "What's its name...the firm that represents that big insurance company. You know, the one with the reputation for never settling out of court. God, I hate lawyers."

"Are the mother and son okay?"

"Shaken," Genevieve said. "No pun intended. It was terrifying while it lasted. Keith got me to come talk with the woman till she felt better. Somehow he came up with a centennial pin for the little boy and had him smiling even before I got there."

"Too bad nobody got a picture; there's nothing like a picture when you're dealing with guys who lie for a living," Dayandan said.

"Of him jumping on your hat?" Laurenson asked, laughing. "I'd give a lot for a picture of that." He turned to Tavarov, "Speaking of attitude…"

"This guy kind of makes you look like Mr. Tolerance, doesn't he?" Tavarov said.

"Gotta love a guy who can do that. Nevertheless," Laurenson turned back to the two constables, "take particular care to dot the i's and cross the t's on this one."

Upon returning to his desk, Laurenson found a message asking him to call a Veronica Ralston of Social Services as soon as possible.

"Any idea what it's about?" he asked Miranda Cardinal.

Miranda made a face. "She may deign to tell you. She certainly wouldn't tell me."

"Staff Sargeant Laurenson, here," he said when Ms. Ralston answered her phone.

"Oh, yes. We've had a complaint. The caller said you knew the family. The Christie Devenish family."

"I do. What's the nature of the complaint?"

"I'd rather not say."

"I beg your pardon?"

"It's confidential."

"Even when we simply go out with you people on a call, we always ask…and find out, what the complaint is. Do you really intend to ask me questions about a family *and* keep the nature of the complaint a secret?"

"As you know, I'm sure, we get a lot of complaints. They're not always what you might call 'rock solid.' Especially not the anonymous ones. I'd hate to say anything that might constitute prejudice."

"Very well, go ahead."

"I'm pleased to see you understand my position."

"The pleasure's all mine. I'm more than a little curious to see how you'll question me without letting the cat out of the bag."

Her voice became colder and harder. "How long have you known the family?"

"Less than a year."

"Do you know them well?"

"I know Christie Devenish quite well. I've seen very little of her children."

"Do you know why her son ran away from home?"

"It would be hearsay if I told you what I'd been told and conjecture if I told you what I thought. Surely you don't want hearsay or conjecture."

"I never get anything but. Try me."

"The impression I get is that the kids have gotten in the habit of calling the shots with their mother. Lately, she's asked for a little more consideration and they haven't taken it well."

"You've a reason for saying this? You've seen them together as a family?"

"I had dinner with them on Thanksgiving."

"Did you notice anything strange about how the mother and son related to each other?"

Laurenson had been grilled on the witness stand too often not to see that this question was loaded with potential for abuse.

"Strange in what way?"

"Strange. Just strange."

"Well, then, yes I did."

She jumped all over his reply. "So you did. What, in your opinion, was strange about the way they related to each other?"

"Shaun seemed pretty sulky and rude."

"Yes. And?"

"That's about it. I got the impression he was rather spoiled."

"But I asked you if you'd noticed something *strange* about their relationship."

"I know. But if you're not willing to define strange for me, I'm forced to go by my own ideas on what's strange when it comes to the parent-child relationship. For me, it's strange to see a kid getting away with such bad attitude and behaviour."

"You really think a teenager would run away because his mother's too soft?"

"Not because she's too soft maybe, but certainly if she tried to tighten up on discipline after having been soft, yes."

"So that's all? You didn't think there was anything unhealthy about—"

"Unless you can clarify for me what the difference is between 'strange' and 'unhealthy,' I'm afraid I may not be able to help you much."

"Well then let me ask you this. Do you have any reason to feel it would be unwise to force Shaun Devenish to return home to his mother at this time?"

"Yes, I most certainly do."

"Well, you might have said so sooner."

"I thought I'd made my position quite clear. Until Shaun's mother can convince him to enter family counseling, I think it would be very unwise to return him home. It would be particularly unwise to put him in a position where he might feel forced to return home. He's hostile enough now. Why give him a grievance?"

"You seem determined not to consider the possibility that he might have a grievance already."

"That's what counseling seems to be designed for…airing grievances. If he had any, you'd think he'd want a chance to have them heard and dealt with."

"Have you ever considered the possibility that the boy's mother may have reasons for not wanting the family's dirty linen aired in public?"

"Counseling is hardly public."

"No it's not, but it's public enough to pose a problem if someone has been doing something she knows she shouldn't have been."

"Or something *he* knows he shouldn't have been. Yes, I think Shaun's a bit of a bully, and you know what they say about bullies thriving on privacy."

"Obviously you're totally on the mother's side."

"You seem to want, not so much to ask me my opinion, but to argue with me about my opinion. I'm puzzled. Didn't you tell me to start with that all you had to go on was an anonymous complaint?"

"We get good information from anonymous tips sometimes."

"So do we. We also get quite a few crank calls."

"Will you send an officer with me on this investigation?"

"Do you think you need one?"

"If I thought I needed one, would you send one?"

"Of course."

"Well, then, I want one...as a witness, if nothing else."

"It sounds like an excellent idea. I'm sure Christie Devenish will appreciate having an impartial witness...if nothing else."

Ms. Ralston's click followed remarkably quickly on her thank-you.

Laurenson hoped Christie's sense of humour would be up to what lay ahead. Somehow he had a hard time imagining her being serene about coming under investigation. Particularly investigation for sexual abuse. And especially when his own staff would be involved.

Chapter Six

Laurenson wasn't sure what he wanted to say to Christie about the pending investigation so he decided to put the matter out of his mind for a while. He chose to do this, not by burying himself in paper work as he told himself a better man would have, but by driving out to talk with Michaelangelo Smith. He didn't flatter himself that Smith would be pleased to see him, but he looked forward to having fewer unanswered questions rattling around in his head.

Smith stood in front of a metre-high mound of snow. "Speak of the devil," he said. "I was just thinking of you."

Laurenson stared at a cleared area which was the size of the parking lot in front of the detachment. "You did all of this by hand?"

"More like half. Just enlarging on what a neighbour ploughed for me yesterday."

"Still, it's one hell of a lot of snow."

"It's not like I'm too old or decrepit to shovel snow. Exercise keeps a man healthy."

"You said you were thinking of me. Why is that?"

"Because I never did thank you for checking out about the body."

"I'm pretty sure you did."

"Not as I ought to have. The one cop willing to help... I could've shown more appreciation."

"If there's one thing I can't stand, it's somebody who does his job reluctantly and expects eternal gratitude for doing it at all."

"Any of your men enjoy serving under you?"

Laurenson laughed. "Some more than others, I'm sure."

Smith drove his shovel hard into the pile of snow at his feet. "You keep coming back. I can't help wondering what makes you keep coming back. What crime has been committed that calls for so much investigating?"

"No crime. That's the hell of it; this is the first time I've let investigating a mystery take precedence over dealing with a crime."

"There's no mystery here."

"That you would say that is just one out of a whole cluster of mysteries."

Smith pulled a cigarette out of a pocket and lit it. "If you're still wondering why Rozilind left home—left home the *way* she did—it's because of the kind of father I was. Times have changed since I was a kid."

"Yeah? How?"

"When I was five, my father threatened to cut off my little finger. He said Arabs cut off a person's hand if they steal; that, being merciful, he wouldn't do that, but he'd have to cut off my little finger if he didn't want to have a thief for a son. I'd taken a dime from his pocket. What does a five-year-old know? I really believed he was going to cut off my finger. I believed that, but I never stopped loving him. These days, a kid will hold it against you forever if you yell at them."

"Depends on the kid, doesn't it?"

"Does it? I only ever had one. Still, I got the impression there might be a lot of them that would feel that way."

"Was Roz less than favourably impressed with your fathering skills?"

"She didn't need fathering, she needed mothering. I did a piss-poor job, especially when it came to dealing with the way we felt after her mother died."

"I'm sure you did much better than you think you did."

"I'm telling you, *I didn't*. I was so broken up, I couldn't stand to see her cry."

"I don't think there's anyone who doesn't have *some* regrets about—"

"I yelled at her for crying. Once I even hit her."

"But you apologized afterward, till hell wouldn't have it."

"Intuition isn't becoming in a man. Least of all in a Mountie."

They both burst out laughing; then Laurenson noticed that Smith's hands were shaking and he said, "You're worn to a frazzle and I stand here talking to you. So much for intuition!"

"Don't worry about me—I'm fine—but I *have* moved a ton of snow today. I can finish this up tomorrow."

"Finish what up? You don't even own a car, but you've got enough space cleared for ten."

"I get a discount on my insurance premiums by providing ambulance access," Smith said with a grin.

"Well, you're going to need every cent of insurance you've got if you keep this up," Laurenson retorted.

"Aw, I'll be attending *your* funeral. We're a long-lived bunch, our family."

But the old man was holding himself oddly, almost as though holding his breath.

"What's the matter?"

"Nothing. Just a touch of indigestion. Like any man who's batching it, I get my fair share."

It occurred to Laurenson that the storm could have made getting fresh groceries difficult. "Is there anything you'd like me to pick up for you at the store?" Seeing the answer was going to be negative he added quickly, "I'll be back this way tomorrow, it won't be any trouble at all."

"There's no need. No need to check on me, or to stop by the store for me. Not that I don't appreciate the thought. Just that there's no need."

"Well, now that we have that established to everybody's satisfaction, what would you tell an incurable busybody to pick up for you, if they simply couldn't resist picking up something?"

Smith smiled. "Well, I suppose I wouldn't have to throw it out if you did happen to buy a loaf of bread or a can of orange juice."

"Good. I'll keep that in mind, just in case."

"And maybe some sugar and margarine and a tube of toothpaste."

"Okay. Now let's get you up to the house. You can try for the *Guinness Book of World Records* again tomorrow."

"Don't think I won't."

"There isn't anything I'd put past you."

After a moment's hesitation, Smith took his first step toward the house.

"Hell of a case of indigestion," Laurenson remarked cryptically.

"Fat lot you know. It's my hemorrhoids that're bothering me. I was just trying to be polite…treating you like company."

He never actually winced, but his face became smoother and pinker once Laurenson got him onto the living room couch in front of a blazing fire. His relief was palpable.

"See you tomorrow then," Laurenson said.

The old man muttered something and Laurenson smiled. He could have sworn he'd heard "appreciate," "Nosey Parker," and "son" in there somewhere.

By the time he returned to the office, Laurenson decided he shouldn't warn Christie about the interview Family and Social Services was planning. He had never forewarned anybody before; to do so now would look bad. And anyway, Christie's natural reaction to hearing of the accusation for the first time would probably do more to clear her than anything else she could offer by way of a defense. If he did anything to take away her spontaneity or make her self-conscious, she could end up unnecessarily disadvantaged. About all he could do—and most definitely *would* do—was make sure she had Genevieve Neve as the official police presence at her interview. Genevieve would put her at her ease more than anyone else…and would show good judgement in evaluating the case Social Services thought they had.

With this decided, he had no difficulty inviting Christie to go cross-country skiing the next day or, indeed, *going* skiing with her, without making the slightest reference to the matter. Christie, who had received her severance cheque from the school board just hours before being given a book to edit by the College Press, was feeling more optimistic than he had seen her for months.

"I really do believe I see light at the end of the tunnel," she said, herring-boning up a steep little hill. "And if this job thing could turn out so amazingly well, it *all* will. Give Shaun two weeks with his father, and I'll hardly recognize him. Why, he'll be offering to wash the dishes for me! You know, I ran into Sister Mary Clare yesterday and she was asking me how it'd gone with Human Resources. When I told her they'd been most generous...well, she knows their reputation as well as anybody does... I just wish you could have seen her face! It was—I don't know. She looked as surprised as if I'd just walked out of the bedroom of an infamous drug lord, smiling."

"Sister Mary Clare knows how people usually look when they leave the bedrooms of drug lords?"

"My comparison. Sister Mary Clare knows how people usually look when they leave the offices of Human Resources."

"*You* know how people usually look when they leave the bedrooms of drug lords?"

Christie laughed and poled away from him with energy.

After two hours of skiing they headed back to his place to shower. When she left two hours later, she pointed to her own face. "See. For future reference. That's the look I was talking about."

"Are you saying people usually emerge from the bedrooms of staff sergeants looking as though they've just been screwed over by Human Resources?"

"Hardly!"

"Then your point is that there's not much difference between a staff sergeant and a drug lord?"

"That's exactly my point. They're both demanding, conscienceless, hard, scary—"

He stopped her with a kiss. But as she left to "be there for" the one chick remaining under her wing, he thought ahead to Social Services' investigation and wondered to what extent she would blame him for it. He could do without her seeing him as some kind of cross between a drug dealer and Human Resources.

One concern replaced another as Laurenson returned to Michaelangelo Smith's and got no response to his knocking. He could see snow boots inside the front entranceway so it seemed unlikely the old man had left the house; still, he didn't answer even when Laurenson banged on the door. Finding everything outside pretty much as he'd left it the night before, Laurenson returned to the house to check the windows and try the doors. Finally, he opened the front door using the time-honoured device of a credit card. He found Smith on the bedroom floor, clearly agitated, his pupils dilated and his breathing laboured.

"Got dizzy and went down," he gasped. "Must have fainted."

"I'm calling an ambulance," Laurenson said. "Let's just get you back in bed, first."

Waiting for the ambulance to arrive, Smith seemed excited and anxious to talk. "You're a damned nuisance but your heart's in the right place. Wouldn't want you to think I don't appreciate it."

"Stop trying to talk," Laurenson ordered.

The old man smiled. "Bet you don't say that often."

"Shh. I mean it. You'll be all right, but why put more of a strain on your heart than—"

"It's not *my* heart that's the problem. Poor kid! Nothing ever went right for her. Watched her begging her mother not to go, watched the light go out of her eyes after she died. Never knew what to do, always did the wrong thing."

"You did what you could."

"I couldn't protect her. Had no power over anything."

"You did your best."

Smith's eyes, soulful at the best of times, were the eyes of a kicked spaniel. "I was just one of the many idiots who made her life hell. She hated idiots."

"You weren't an idiot."

"Like you would know."

"I do know. You're too smart now to have been an idiot five years ago."

"One day she came home looking so happy, I couldn't imagine what would make her that happy. She'd rear-ended somebody with her little car." He held up a hand to indicate he hadn't finished with his story. When a spasm of pain had passed, he resumed. "She was happy because she'd done something dumb. It was a *relief* to have 'boobed' something herself. That's because her life was full of idiots."

It struck Laurenson that the only way of stopping the old man from rambling was to talk more himself. "Ever seen someone walk against a red light, bringing all the cars to a screeching halt and giving them the finger? Never mind answering; that was a rhetorical question. Everybody's seen somebody doing that sometime. It's the same sort of thing as Roz feeling relief at having rear-ended somebody. A person like that, it seems to me, is probably sick of playing by the rules and getting shafted. One day, they get so mad they break a traffic law so they can be wrong for a change. 'I never get to be wrong. It's my turn to be wrong!' It's not because their life is full of idiots."

"All her life she's been shafted. Even Heyden shafted her, the bastard."

The ambulance arrived at that moment, saving Laurenson from greater temptation than he could reasonably have been expected to resist.

"I'll see to your chickens and close up the house," he said to Smith as they carried him out on a stretcher.

"Tell the Babishes to the south of me. They'll look after the place for me."

"Will do. Now take care. You're in good hands now."

Laurenson did as he'd promised and then headed over to the hospital. By that time they had Smith in the cardiac unit, in intensive care. Laurenson was asked to wait for a few minutes so Smith's doctor could talk to him. Eventually, a tall thin man with sandy hair sought him out.

"I understand you're a friend of the family."

Laurenson hesitated. "He told you that?"

"I just don't get it," the doctor complained. "He's been asymptomatic for years. I saw him just last week and he looked great."

"He's not in any danger, is he?"

"We'll get him stabilized, then we'll run some tests. I'd never have predicted this would have happened; I'm not going to try making predictions now."

It took days to stabilize the old man, but eventually Laurenson walked into his room and found him eating pureed vegetables with a look of keen distaste on his face.

"Now that's more like it," Laurenson said bracingly.

Smith made a face at him. "I won't dignify that with a response."

"Cheer up. If you've achieved the goopy green stuff, can steak be far behind?"

"Well, yes, actually it can. You're as bad as the nurses who come in chirping, 'My, we're looking fine today.'"

"Well we are," Laurenson teased. "Present company excluded."

Something must have started down the wrong tube as Smith laughed, for he went off into a coughing fit.

"Easy; easy does it," Laurenson said, thumping him on his back. It was just this sort of thing that made him hate visiting sick people. Hung round with mortality, they seemed too fragile to be approached.

"Jeez," Smith said as he got his breath back. "I've heard of dying laughing, but I never thought I'd do it."

"I'm sorry," Laurenson said, contritely. "I'm a bull in a china shop."

"You're not the one who tried to breathe in his lunch."

"I always say or do the wrong thing when I visit sick people."

"You don't say. Well, you're a damned sight more enjoyable than most of my visitors."

Laurenson had assumed there'd be few visitors. His surprise must have shown on his face, he figured, for Smith went on.

"What'd you expect—that they'd let me spoil their precious recovery statistics?"

"I knew cardiac units were big on visitors; I just didn't…" Laurenson trailed off in embarrassment.

"Think they'd be able to conjure some up for an old cuss like me? Hell, they've got volunteers just for visiting old geezers. Isn't that rich? They send strangers in to be your friend. I don't think you can possibly imagine how tiring that can be."

"I assume it does more good than harm, or they wouldn't do it."

"I guess. Makes you look good even though I know you're here just in hopes I'll let something drop in a moment of weakness."

"Good thing for you I like sarcastic old curmudgeons."

"Hah! You saying you haven't got questions?"

"Now that you mention it, I do have one question. *Why'd you do it?*"

"Why'd I do what?"

"Why'd you shovel snow like hell and tell me you didn't have health problems, when you've got a heart problem?"

"I didn't have a heart problem."

"Since when do they treat hemorrhoids in a cardiac unit?"

"I can see why you like sarcasm so much; you're the most sarcastic SOB I've ever met. Well, for your information, I've never had anything but a mild arrhythmia and it's never even required medication. As for why I shoveled snow, I did it because I felt like it. I enjoyed doing it. It felt good. Better than good. It felt wonderful!"

"It didn't feel so good toward the end there. If you'd admitted that, we could have gotten you some help before you had a full-blown episode on your hands."

Smith was watching him closely. "How come you know so much about it? You got heart problems?"

"I don't know beans about arrhythmia, but my dad died of congestive heart failure."

"Oh." Smith pushed his lunch tray away. "Well, I'm not going to die. Actually, they're very pleased with my progress. I'll probably be able to go home before the week's out."

"They were surprised as hell that you ended up in such trouble."

"Somebody should show them a picture of how much snow I shoveled before biting the dust."

"Yeah," Laurenson deadpanned. "The ambulance driver was duly impressed; though five will get you ten your premiums are going to go up anyway."

"My premiums?" Smith chuckled. "Oh hell, I've never had insurance. Not *life* insurance. Never felt like betting on dying. As I told you, living long is in my genes."

Genevieve summed up the Social Services interview with, "They gave her a pretty hard time."

"Were they fair?"

"The older social worker was. And she knew how to build rapport. But then the younger one—your Veronica Ralston—took over, and things went downhill from there. In my opinion, Christie made a good witness on her own behalf. The Ralston woman seemed to have her mind made up and, as far as I could tell, ignored everything Christie said. Since you warned me they might be expecting favouritism on our part, I tried to stay out of it as much as possible, but I had to object eventually...it was turning into thinly disguised abuse."

"What happened when you objected?"

"The interview came to an end. I reminded Christie she could demand to have a lawyer present before continuing, and she stopped the session."

"Do you think there'll be another?"

"It's hard to say. But, if there is, I trust it'll be an entirely different kettle of fish...as long as Christie finds a lawyer with the guts to fight for her rights."

"How did Christie take the ordeal?"

"She was madder than hell."

"Good. Or, at least, that's better than the alternative."

"At the end of the session I asked for the name of Ralston's superior. I was hoping Christie would sit up and take notice. But I think she came to the interview thinking they were going to help her with her son and...well, how clearly would you be thinking right after finding out you weren't going to be rescued, you were going to be attacked?"

"Thanks, Genevieve," Laurenson said. "I'll see to it that Christie gets the superior's name."

Christie didn't call Laurenson; neither did she answer the phone when he called. After several attempts at reaching her, including leaving a message on her answering machine, Laurenson finally took a squad car and drove over to her house. Her green Dodge truck was pulled up behind the garage but she didn't answer the door.

He came back half an hour later and knocked longer and harder.

At 4:00 in the afternoon, he returned and sat parked in front of the house. That brought her out to complain.

"You can't seem to get enough of embarrassing me."

"Embarrassing you? I'm *concerned* about you."

"Hah!" She turned on her heel and began walking back toward the house.

Laurenson got out of the car, and Christie spun around. "Where do you think you're going?"

"I don't think you want to stand in the street discussing this."

"I don't. But I don't want to stand inside discussing it either."

"If you won't discuss it, how am I to know—?"

"You have the gall to pretend you don't know—?"

"—what it is you think I've done to make you so mad?"

"Do you have a search warrant?"

"Of course I don't have a search warrant. Why on earth would I?"

"Well, if you don't have a search warrant, you can't make me let you in."

"I wouldn't dream of making you do anything," Laurenson snapped. "I came here to help."

"Yeah? Then help. Go away."

"And just how do you think that'll help?"

"It'll spare me more annoyance than you can possibly imagine."

"No, it won't. Not any more than shutting you out made things better for Shaun."

"How dare you compare me to Shaun?!"

"Maybe now isn't the best time to talk. Fine. I'll come back."

"There is no best time. I don't foresee there being a best time ever again."

"Christie."

"How could you do it? How could you leave me without a shred of dignity left and then come here offering to help? I didn't think you were that low."

"Christie, it was Social Services—"

"Liar! She wore your uniform."

"She tried to help you."

"*Liar*! How can you tell such a barefaced lie?"

"Damn it, Christie, she was appalled at how they treated you."

"Well, she had a funny way of showing it."

"She held back so there wouldn't be any complaints of bias and interference."

"She told me to get a lawyer!"

"Yes. Of course she did. You didn't need to take abuse like that. Listen, no one has less love for lawyers than I do, but even I would have suggested you get one. You needed someone to rein in Veronica Ralston."

"You're twisting it. That's not what the police mean when they advise you to get a lawyer."

Laurenson began to laugh.

"Damn you, Dan Laurenson." Christie turned away again.

"Wait." He grabbed her arm. "Just a minute. You thought she was reading you your rights or something?"

"I'm not stupid. I know it wasn't reading me my rights. But I also know it's not a good sign when they advise you to get a lawyer."

Again Laurenson laughed. "Would you listen to me, Christie? If we advise you to get a lawyer, we're not after you for anything. If we were, the last thing we'd want you getting is a lawyer."

"I don't believe you."

"Well, now you're being just plain contrary. It put an end to the session, didn't it? It made the Ralston woman mad, didn't it? Genevieve Neve was looking out for your best interests. I picked her expressly because I knew she would."

"That wasn't how it looked to me."

"Apparently not. And to Ralston it probably looked like she was subverting the whole investigation. The truth lies somewhere in between."

"There's something very wrong with all this, but I'm too tired to put my finger on it right now. I'm clear on one thing though—only a snake would compare me to Shaun after what he's just done. So there you have it—you're a snake. And I don't believe you, because...because you're a snake. And, anyway, I'm not stupid; I'd have known it if I hadn't been all alone."

"I'll come back when you've had a chance to think about this."

"You haven't been listening to me. I don't want you to come back. Not when I've had a chance to think. *Not ever.*"

"I know you. You're fair-minded to a fault."

"You think you can flatter me."

"I think I can trust you to hear me out when you're more yourself. When you've had a chance to put your finger on what's wrong with this, me, or whatever it is that's bothering you, we'll talk about it. That done, we'll take it from there."

"No we won't," she said through gritted teeth. "Because there's no way you can talk your way out of this one."

"I wish you'd let me stay with you till you're feeling a bit better."

"You jerk. You total and complete jerk. 'Let me help you. I want to help you.' If you wanted so much to help me, why didn't you tell me what I was walking into? Why did you let me go in there blindly trusting everything was okay? Try to explain *that*."

"Not when you're feeling like this," Laurenson said.

"Not ever." She stalked off toward the house.

Against all his instincts, Laurenson made one more attempt. "I was sure your natural reaction to the accusation would clear you. I didn't want you going in there apprehensive and self-conscious."

She didn't slow her stride. If anything, she walked away more quickly.

CHAPTER SEVEN

Laurenson had visited Michaelangelo Smith twice already without having asked him what Heyden had done. He felt reasonably confident he had the self-restraint to continue visiting him without questioning him for as long as his condition warranted it. That the old man was glad to see him and had even begun to think of him as a friend was evident from how relaxed in Laurenson's presence he now was.

"Keeping the peace, that's all you guys talk about," he joked at one point during the third visit. "You should stop keeping it and start doling it out. It's scarcer than hen's teeth."

"I can see they're going to have to let you go soon," Laurenson responded. "You're getting too feisty to put up with hospital food much longer."

"I'm well on my way, they tell me. My doctor's as much as said I'd be home by the weekend if that didn't mean being out of the city on my own."

"Ever thought of—"

"I know what you're going to say. I told you before that this wasn't normal for me. Sure, I've had a bit of a hitch in my git-along. Even had to lay off the cigarettes and coffee for a while a few years back when Roz was going through a particularly rough spot but, hell, I'm never sick, never even get a cold worth mentioning."

"I've been amazed by your energy."

"Have you?" Smith looked inordinately pleased. "Now that's the one area where I *haven't* been completely satisfied. These days, there never seems to be enough energy for all I want to do, but still I get my work done."

"To say the least," Laurenson put in. "One of the things that struck me about you when I kept running into you on the streets of St. Michael was how often you were on your feet." He didn't attribute the observation to Christie, who had been the one to make it, but he did find his thoughts snagged on her as soon as he thought of her. "That's one of the reasons I came to the conclusion you weren't in trouble," he went on, trying to pull his thoughts loose. "You had the energy of a much younger man."

But his thoughts wouldn't come loose. They became even more tangled up with how wrong he'd been when he'd thought Christie would soon soften or want to tell him exactly why she wouldn't accept his reasons for having left her in the dark about the complaint against her. He had been sure they would talk, maybe even fight, but that they would make up. He would never have predicted they would get to Thursday without seeing or speaking to each other.

"And what's wrong with that?"

"Pardon me?"

"What's wrong with me having the energy of a much younger man? You said I did, just before you went off into your little trance there."

"Sorry. Nothing's wrong with it…as long as you don't try to move mountains of snow."

"Yeah, I guess I overdid it. Just felt so damn good…but of course I went too far. Won't do that again."

"It's not just a question of how hard you work. You're isolated out there. It could be a long cold winter."

"I appreciate your concern."

It sounded more like *mind your own business*.

Laurenson backed off a little. "Of course I know how much your place means to you. When you've lived somewhere for forty years it can be hard to imagine living anywhere else."

"Neither of you get it. You think I'm being sentimental about the place… Aw, forget it; I'm done arguing about it."

"I gather he's already said more than you care to hear on the subject."

Smith looked blank. "Who?"

"Your doctor."

It took him a moment. "Oh yeah," he said, finally. "We've been to the point of nauseam and back."

Whoa, Laurenson thought, *who did you think I was talking about? Who else could I have been talking about?*

"I suppose, being so close to town, you've had developers knocking on your door regularly..."

"Oh, so now I'm close to town! I thought I was isolated."

"It's all relative, isn't it? Close to town now that St. Michael has grown...still a bit isolated for someone without a car."

"It's not too far to walk or ride a bike and it's too damn close to town for *my* comfort. New subdivisions, they're like cancer. The richer people become, the farther out in the country they want to live. These days, that is...it was just the opposite when Roz was breaking her heart because she didn't live in town. Man, *then* she was just part of the majority." Smith shook his head. "They don't realize that they're not moving out of the city, they're bringing it with them. Well, not onto my land, thank you very much!"

"No, of course not," Laurenson said.

Smith shot him a look. "You think I don't know when I'm being humoured?"

"I'm not just humouring you. My favourite posting of all was a small hamlet early on, where my eldest could toddle out of the yard without danger...even from cars. He was everybody's son and there wasn't so much as a mean dog to keep an eye out for; Main Street was gravel and had a wooden sidewalk. At the age of three, my son would clutch a quarter in his chubby little hand and go down to the A&P to buy himself jelly beans. Man, I hated to leave that place! My wife didn't like it, though; she thought it was a bit *too* quiet."

"Yeah, Roz would too." Smith soon turned the talk to other things, and Laurenson let him. He made a mental note, however, of what it was he thought odd about what Smith had just said. He wondered if it would be stretching things too far to ask Christie for her expert opinion on the implications of it from a grammatical point of view. His father had always maintained that the best thing a person could do to mend fences with someone who was mad at them was to ask them for a favour.

"By the way," Smith said as Laurenson stood up to leave. "You used to drop by early in the afternoon. Isn't this after hours for you?"

"How can I justify coming here when I'm on duty, if I'm not going to ask you questions?" Laurenson teased.

"Does that mean you'll be coming after 4:00 from now on?"

"I gather evenings aren't convenient for you."

"Evenings are fine. It's just that Mary Grey wanted to know when *she* should come and since you were coming during the day, I told her to come evenings."

"Well, I can come during the day, I suppose, as long as you're willing to pay the price."

Smith took his measure with a long look. "I can almost believe you mean that."

"Why wouldn't I mean it? Mounties have to pass an integrity test. In fact, they have to pass it before they're even accepted as recruits. I aced it."

Smith snorted.

"What's so funny about that?" Laurenson complained so convincingly that the old man went off into a spurt of laughter.

"My my, aren't we having a good time!" a nurse chirped from the doorway.

"We are actually," Smith said; "though my friend here is a very dry stick indeed."

Tavarov didn't get it.

"So what do you think he meant?"

"Pretty much what he said. Or are you asking what I think he meant to say?"

"Aren't they the same thing?"

"Not by a long shot! I think he meant to say much less than he did."

"All right, then; what did he *say*?"

"Well, I think the really important part is: 'Neither of you get it. You think I'm being sentimental about the place.' But I think it was another telling slip of the tongue when he said, 'Yeah, Roz would too.'"

"You already said that, Staff. What I don't get is— I don't know what I don't get."

"Never mind," Laurenson said, "I know someone who'll understand exactly what I'm talking about. If, that is, she'll let me run it by her."

"I take it you mean Christie."

No secrets around this work place.

"Yeah. What do you think? Worth a shot?"

"'If not now, when? If not you, who?' to steal a quote from Ronald Reagan."

"Really? What was he talking about?"

"Changing the economy. Offhand, I'd say he had it easier than you will."

Tavarov was right.

The third message Laurenson left on Christie's answering machine said, "Look, I'm willing to pay for the information. It *is* a police matter. And I'd appreciate it if you'd refer me to someone who can help with it, if you won't."

That message got a reply.

"Sister Mary Clare."

"I beg your pardon."

"Sister Mary Clare should be able to help you out. Not that you didn't already know that."

"Oh. Yes, I guess it was pretty silly of me to think of *you*. Just force of habit, I suppose."

"I know you. I know what you were hoping."

"Really. Well, I'm sorry to say I called reluctantly and only on the advice of one of my officers. And, I might add, only after being assured that you would undoubtedly be willing to keep the meeting short, and hold it in a public place."

"Why?"

"Why, what?"

"Why so reluctantly and based on so many conditions?"

"Because I knew you'd think I was up to something low and despicable. I still haven't forgotten that jibe about the warrant, you know."

"What jibe— Oh!"

"Yeah. And as you can imagine, it hurt."

"I can't do this over the phone," Christie said.

"Can't do what, turn me down?"

"Can't figure you out."

"What's to figure out?"

"Whether you're laughing up your sleeve or not. Look, I'll give you my take on the...whatever it is. But I do want to ask something in return. I can't get my truck started. If I help you with this 'English usage' thing, will you see if you can get it started for me?"

Now that was more like it.

"I'll either get it started or figure out why I can't."

"Okay. So that means both your conditions just went down the tube—it won't be in a public place, and it probably won't take a matter of minutes. It'd probably be a good idea if you came over in your oldest clothes too."

"See you in ten minutes."

"I knew it!" she said when she saw him.

"Knew what?"

"That you'd come dressed to the teeth."

Good old Christie, bloody but unbowed. He wanted to gather her into his arms, but figured that would only confirm all her worst suspicions, so he shook his head. "*Armed* to the teeth," he said; "as befits a T-bone come to repair the cheetah's truck. How long's it been acting up?"

She gave him all the relevant recent history and accompanied him out to the windswept driveway to watch him work on her frost-rimed old Dodge half-ton. Unlike its owner, it wasn't a tough nut to crack; given a boost, the engine roared to life.

"Better leave it running at least twenty minutes to be sure it's fully charged."

"Come on inside while it's charging. I'll put on the coffee and you can ask away about whatever-it-is you think I'll understand better than anybody else."

There was no sign of Angela anywhere. Laurenson would have liked to have asked after her, but decided that discretion was the better part of valour.

"Okay, here it is," he said, scrubbing his hands at the kitchen sink. "I want you to analyze the verb tense in the following sentence: 'Neither of you get it. You think I'm just being sentimental.' Is there another tense I could have used?"

"What are the circumstances?"

"That's what I want to figure out. Naturally, since this was said to me, that part of it makes sense to me. I don't get it. But that's not what was said. What was said was, 'Neither of you get it.'"

"That hasn't got anything to do with the verb tense. Why aren't you asking me about the subject of the verb?"

"Because, about the only thing that doesn't make sense to me is how there could be two subjects, one standing there now and one long gone, and yet it could sound like it's all happening in the present. I *think* what I need to know about is the use of the present tense."

"Ah," she said, looking as though this was beginning to interest her. "The present tense is a funny thing. I doubt you could ask a hundred adults when they should use the simple present, and find one who could tell you."

"You mean most people don't know?"

"I'm not saying they don't use it correctly; just that they don't know why they use it that way. It's like the conditional. '*If you were as sick as you say you are, you wouldn't be running all over the house.*' Everybody has heard their mother say something like that and will even say stuff like that themselves, but probably they wouldn't know what you were talking about if you told them to make up a conditional sentence."

"So tell me about the present tense."

Christie thought a moment. "Okay. I guess it boils down to the fact that there are two forms of the present. You use one to emphasize that something's going on right now. 'You're shouting.' You have to say, 'You're shouting' if you want to stress that you're shouting *now*. If you don't, if you say 'You shout,' you're simply being matter-of-fact. Probably you're indicating that the other person shouts on a regular basis."

"What if the action occurred in the past?"

"The past would be, 'you shouted' if the action is over, and 'you have been shouting,' if it's continued right up to the present moment. The thing about 'you shout' is that it says shouting is typical of you; you have shouted in the past, you shout these days (though you're not shouting *right* now) and you'll probably shout in the future. It's like 'You ski;' it's a fact about you. It's kind of...global, if you get what I mean."

"So does 'Neither of you get it" indicate you guys didn't get it in the past, you don't get it now, and you probably won't ever get it?"

"Bingo."

"How do you link what one person is doing now with what was once typical of another person? Can you say, 'Both of you shout'?"

She looked as though she thought he must be losing his mind.

"Not if you hope to be understood. You'd have to say something like, 'You shout just like he used to.'"

"What if you're not particularly well educated?"

"What about it? It doesn't take a university education to do this right, all it takes is enough contact with the language as it's spoken. Being a native speaker should do it."

"But still, people get sloppy in their habits."

"Sure, they do, but generally it's the perfect tenses they murder. Is this really a police matter, or were you just pulling my leg?"

"You know what they say about slips of the tongue."

"I know they used to say, 'loose lips sink ships.' What do you have in mind?"

"Freudian slips, like 'Dead Dad'...that sort of thing can be very revealing."

"And you think 'Neither of you get it' is a Freudian slip?"

"I suppose to be truly Freudian, the 'it' in question would have to be sex," Laurenson said with a smile. "Still, if one person is the one standing in front of you talking to you, and the other is someone you supposedly haven't seen for five years, 'Neither of you get it' could be quite..." he paused, searching for the right word.

"Thought provoking?"

"That's it exactly."

"Speaking of provoking thought...or anything else... You do your fair share."

"More than my fair share," Laurenson said, putting his faith in the power soft answers were reputed to have when it came to turning away wrath.

He immediately regretted having said that, however, when he saw how Christie's face closed down. To someone as afraid of being manipulated as she could be, that almost certainly had sounded like an attempt at manipulation.

"But, that's beside the point," he said briskly. "Let me just see if I've got this correct—you can't let two subjects share a verb unless the time frame is the same in both cases?"

Christie seemed thrown off by the reversion to business. "Unless? Oh, of course. Well, you *can* of course; but you won't be saying what you want to say."

"But, still, most people don't go around saying 'you shout' if they mean 'one of you was always shouting when I was a kid' and 'the other one shouts at me the same way these days'?"

She seemed to be getting annoyed. "Not unless they're foreign. Foreign *and* newcomers. As I said, this isn't rocket science."

"That's great!" he said standing up. "Well, that about does it." He took two steps toward the door. "Oh, except I've been meaning to give you this. It's the name and contact information for Veronica Ralston's supervisor. Constable Neve felt you had every right to lodge a complaint about how you were treated during your interview." He set a piece of paper down on the table. "Naturally, she meant you should complain about Ralston. Not me."

He left Christie sitting speechless at the table staring at the contact information.

He drove away, lost in thought. When, at the corner of Chisholm and Century, he realized that he was thinking about verb tenses instead of Christie, he decided Michaelangelo Smith was therapeutic. Since he was therapeutic, it made perfect sense to detour a few blocks and stop in for an impromptu visit. Besides, Laurenson had just thought of an ingenious way of raising the matter of why Heyden was a bastard, without actually asking a single question.

He chatted with the old man for nearly half an hour before he got an opportunity to lead into the subject naturally. "It depends," he replied to something the old man had just said. "Some people would say, 'Curse God and die.'" He knew where he hoped this would lead, but Smith didn't go there.

"Are you a religious man?" he asked.

"Pardon me?"

"Are you religious?"

"That's not the adjective that leaps first to people's minds."

"Funny, I figured you came from a very righteous, maybe even severe family. What was your father like?"

Laurenson thought for a moment. "A lot like you, actually."

"Really? Did you at least go to Sunday school when you were a kid?"

"Sure I did."

"I thought so. Do you remember where 'Curse God and die' comes from?"

"From the Bible?" Laurenson hazarded half-heartedly, anxious to get back on track.

"That's a guess," Smith laughed. "What part of the Bible?"

If he couldn't answer the question, at least he could entertain the old man. "*Song of Songs*?"

Smith laughed till he began to wheeze. "And I'll bet that's the *only* part of the Bible you ever read willingly. No, it's from *The Book of Job*."

"Damn. I could've answered that one if I'd just thought a minute. It's what Job's wife said to him as he sat on an ash heap, scratching himself."

"Not bad for a pagan," the old man said.

"Give me a break. *Job* isn't exactly anybody's idea of a good time."

"I find *Job* enormously interesting," the old man said. "Imagine some poor old sod, about my age, loses his kids, his wealth, his health and the respect of his friends. Finally, his own wife says to him, 'Curse God and die.' Still he maintains that God's not punishing him...something we know is true, because a few pages back God was boasting about Job's goodness and agreeing to let Satan test his resolve."

"Yeah, I remember the general outline of the story."
"Do you remember the end?" Smith asked.
"God speaks to Job from out of a whirlwind."
"Saying what?"
"Basically bawling him out, as I recall," Laurenson answered without enthusiasm.
"Now, isn't that interesting?"

It was the wrong question to ask a man who'd just started a gambit he had hoped would provide something really interesting. Especially when the gambit now seemed irretrievably lost. But Laurenson was no Joe Friday, after "the facts, just the facts, Ma'am." His curiosity was piqued by Smith's identifying with Job. In a roundabout way, he might be talking about losing Rozilind. "I find it insulting," he said.

"You do?" The old man's eyes were bright. "Why?"

"Because He bawled Job out for not knowing how His own mind worked—I mean how God's mind worked—when there was no way for Job to know." He thought, but didn't bother to say, that a case could be made for Job's being more admirable than God since he held his temper, even in distress, while God, who lived in perpetual bliss, lost His.

"What sticks in my craw," Smith said, "is that He bawled Job out for saying what He'd just been saying to Satan Himself, but then He perpetuated the notion that life is easy for God's friends, by restoring to Job everything that had been taken away."

"How could He restore the dead sons and daughters?" Laurenson asked.

"That's the sixty-four-thousand-dollar question, isn't it?"

"He didn't restore them, He replaced them. It's not the same thing."

"I'm with you on that."

"Maybe the new family was better than the old."

Smith made a face. "It seems to me the wife could've done with replacing. With kids, though, there's always hope."

Laurenson was diverted by the thought of Job getting his unpleasant wife pregnant again another couple of dozen times. "They had more than twenty kids, didn't they?"

Smith chuckled silently. "You wondering how one woman was going to have fifty kids? She wasn't. *Concubines!* Remember, they had concubines in those days."

"Oh well, I guess it was all right then. Not that I was worried about her; it was Job I was feeling sorry for."

"You're awfully quick to forgive God. You think people are interchangeable?"

"No. Just that sometimes a person has to let go."

"No argument there. And it's easy enough to do when you're hurt and angry. But time has a way of wiping away the memory of all that, and saying you're sorry makes all the difference in the world."

"Saying you're sorry to who?"

"That's not what I meant. I mean you forget all the bad stuff when someone says they're sorry."

"Oh." Laurenson sighed. "Yes, of course. Except that, sometimes, it's hard to see what you're supposed to be sorry for."

"In the doghouse?" Smith asked gently after a moment.

Laurenson wasn't totally averse to sympathy, but neither was he used to accepting it. Having just noticed what looked like Chinese food containers in Smith's wastebasket, he tried for a light touch. "Nowhere near as much as you will be if that annoying nurse of yours spots those. How'd you get takeout in the hospital anyway?"

"Chinese food is good for you."

Laurenson glanced at the dietary instructions on a board over Smith's bed.

"Well, it *is*," Smith insisted. "It's good for the morale."

"No doubt. Would you like me to take those with me anyway?"

"Would you? I'd appreciate it."

Laurenson left with the contraband food containers a few minutes later. The thought of food made him notice how hungry he was, so he hurried home to thaw out some leftover beef short ribs he'd put in the freezer a few weeks earlier. It was just after eating these that he received a phone call saying Michaelangelo Smith was back in intensive care and doing very badly.

"Is there anything I can do?" he asked.

"Doctor Drissel thought you would want to be with him," the caller replied rather sharply.

"*Family friend*" must have found its way into the chart, Laurenson thought. *Well, who better to sit with him while he goes through this?* "I'll be there in fifteen minutes," he said.

Smith's doctor was with him when Laurenson arrived. "I'm glad you could come," he said. "His vital signs are way out in the stratosphere. He's not stabilizing well."

"Do you have any idea why something like this would happen, when he was doing so well just a few hours ago?"

"No idea. I wish I did."

"I saw him at 7:30. He looked ready to go home."

"I know. He was recovering beautifully."

"Is there any chance Chinese food could have done this? I mean, the MSG or something like that in Chinese food? He had some today."

"You should have checked before bringing him anything like that. Was he eating deep-fried food?"

"I wasn't the one who brought it. I don't know what was in it."

"Well, in any case, this isn't indigestion. Indigestion would be my biggest concern with the local Chinese food."

Laurenson looked at the old man lying twitching on the bed. His face was flushed and bathed in sweat. His eyes were closed and he seemed to be focusing on riding the waves of a stormy sea. Laurenson wondered if his pain was like that. Was it like huge waves threatening to engulf him? He wanted to take the old man's restless hand and give him something solid to hold onto. He had no doubt whatsoever that Smith was conscious and would appreciate a hand right now.

Smith opened his eyes when Laurenson sat down by his bed. "I told you so," he said.

"What did you tell me?"

"Nothing. Just saving you the trouble of saying it," Smith said, shifting uncomfortably.

"Well, it wasn't the Chinese food, if that's what you mean. Even if it gave you indigestion, it shouldn't have affected you like this." Laurenson looked around at all the monitors attached to the old man. *Shit!* His pulse rate was tracing its jagged course incredibly close to the top of the monitor, his breathing was irregular, and he seemed unable to find a comfortable position.

A nurse approached a minute or two later and Laurenson watched for her reaction to the heartbeat. She remained poker-faced, however, and wouldn't make eye contact. Laurenson decided the key to her reaction lay in her unwillingness to make eye contact.

"Is there anything you can do to make him more comfortable?" he asked.

"No." She nodded toward his hand, enveloping Smith's. "What you're doing is helping, though. Keep it up."

Keeping it up meant a stiff, sore vigil through the long hours of the night. Smith wrestled in silence with his pain, and Laurenson didn't try to make small talk, or even to coach him. He thought at first that it might help if he said something like, "Breathe. Focus on your breath," as he had when Lisa had been in labour all those many years ago. He couldn't assume, however, that this was like giving birth or that an old man would take kindly to that sort of support the way young women did.

For the first three hours, he wouldn't have been willing to bet the old man would live. He sought comfort in the thought that life had been hard for Smith and there might be something to the belief that people like him rested in peace when they died; but, as he watched Smith fight for his life, he realized that, hard as it had been, his life must have held consolation. His wife's dying had left him to raise a young daughter, and that daughter hadn't been what you'd call a joy, but apparently the old man had always hoped she'd come around. That was, he supposed, what he had meant by "with kids there's always hope."

And, of course, Roz might not have been as bad as she seemed to outsiders. Hadn't her father spoken as though she had reconciled with him from time to time? In his own experience, nothing wiped out an ugly incident quite like a simple "I'm sorry."

But then, there hadn't been much indication of reconciliation between Roz and her father. If there had been, would he have felt so haunted by a sense that he'd done everything wrong, had failed utterly, had been an idiot in her eyes? Apologies were not only the kind of soft answer suited to turning away wrath, they also reassured a person that there was a bond that endured even through hard times, even when tempers flared up and a person did or said the inexcusable.

Besides, Smith had spelled it out for him—his point had been that you forget all the bad things that have happened when the other person says they're sorry.

Laurenson kept coming back to this. Or more correctly, it kept coming back to him. He'd be watching the monitors, or listening to the squeak of rubber-soled shoes on linoleum, or following the pattern of bizarre movements Smith made with his limbs and suddenly he'd find himself thinking it again: "*But time has a way of wiping away the memory of all that, and saying you're sorry makes all the difference in the world.*"

It struck him that "time" isn't fifteen minutes, or even a day. The time that has a way of wiping away memories is a long time. At the very least, it's months or years.

Had the old man inadvertently referred to an apology he'd received from Rozilind *recently*? Was that what made life worth living right now?

Finally the old man drifted off into sleep and Laurenson took the opportunity to shift position. As Smith's sleep deepened, he stood up and stretched, then walked around. He needed a bathroom and wanted a cup of coffee.

I'll bet, he thought as he went in search of a vending machine, *Roz must still be around. Someone brought him takeout Chinese food, and it sure as hell wasn't me.*

CHAPTER EIGHT

In the early hours of the dawn, Michaelangelo Smith began to wake up. His odd jerks and twitches reminded Laurenson of a thin young man he had arrested some ten or fifteen years earlier. The memory snatched him out of a near doze.

The young man, caught cowering behind some raspberry canes in a widow's backyard, had just tripped her burglar alarm. Whether he'd entered her yard by accident, as he claimed, was impossible to determine beyond a reasonable doubt. What *was* established to everyone's satisfaction was that the man was high on amphetamines.

Laurenson waylaid the poker-faced nurse, the next time she came through.

"What are the symptoms associated with arrhythmia?" he asked her.

She hesitated. "With arrhythmia or atrial fibrillation?"

"Atrial fibrillation," Laurenson answered promptly, figuring the term he didn't know would probably provide more pertinent information than the term he did know.

"Rapid irregular heart beat, chest pain, weakness, faintness, and breathlessness. Why?"

"What about muscle spasms?"

"Oh."

"Oh?"

"Maybe you should talk to Mr. Smith's doctor."

"Why him? Why not you?"

"He's probably more familiar with spasms like these."

"You haven't seen spasms like these?"

"Not in connection with fibrillation or tachycardia."

"But you have seen them. In connection with what?"

"Doctor Drissel could answer your questions better than I can."

"Okay, I won't ask you in connection with what. Just tell me one thing: was it on a cardiac unit?"

She shook her head reluctantly.

"No? Where then?"

"In emergency."

"Amphetamine intoxication." Laurenson put it as a statement rather than a question.

"I didn't say that."

"I know you didn't. I did. I've seen it before."

"I'm not the best person to give you information; you'd better talk to a doctor. There'll be doctors starting rounds in an hour or two. Or would you rather I called the resident right now?"

"Don't bother the resident. I can wait to talk to Doctor Drissel."

The nurse hurried away as soon as she could, and Laurenson turned back to the old man. He'd not only seen amphetamine intoxication before, *he'd seen it before with Smith.* What else would the dilated pupils and agitation have been? Hell, even before then. Since when did old men shovel a ton of snow and then explain it away with "I just felt so damn good!"?

Laurenson felt good. So many things fit. The old man's complaint about never having enough energy these days, the energy he did have... *No. Wait a minute. If this was an overdose, how'd he get it here in the hospital?* Before long, Laurenson began to wonder, as well, how someone with a bad heart could have taken amphetamines for any length of time without having precisely the reaction he'd just had. If the old man had had to stop drinking coffee and smoking cigarettes because of his heart a few years back, did it make sense that he'd not only gone back to caffeine and nicotine but had graduated to amphetamines? It didn't seem likely.

Michaelangelo Smith opened his eyes, and Laurenson put his musings aside. There would be time to think later; he suspected that, in any case, he was too tired to think straight right now. Although he hadn't slept in over twenty-four hours, he didn't want to leave the hospital until he could decently call the Babishes and Mary Grey...perhaps around 8:30. If unable to arrange for someone to sit with Smith, he would talk to Doctor Drissel about finding a volunteer.

Fortunately, that didn't prove necessary. After a short—and with Mary Grey, a very interesting—chat, Laurenson had his replacement visitors. He didn't wait for Drissel to show up for rounds, but made a beeline for home as soon as he got off the phone. At home he found his long-suffering dog waiting at the door, torn between delight at seeing him and shame over a mess she had made.

"Ah, Megan, old girl," Laurenson said, "It's okay. I know you tried to hold it."

Old age is a shipwreck, he thought, as he cleaned up after her. He reminded himself that Megan wasn't old, but let the adage stand anyway. *Old age is a shipwreck.*

When he'd let Megan back in, he called the detachment to tell Tavarov he wouldn't be in for a few hours.

"You okay?" Tavarov asked.

"Bone tired. I didn't get to bed last night."

"Linguistic research?" Tavarov asked dryly.

"Very little of that, mainly watching Michaelangelo Smith fight for his life in the cardiac unit."

"Another heart attack? Son of a bitch!"

"Talk to you later."

"Take your time. Everything's under control here."

The receiver more or less fell into its cradle and Laurenson began the long trek upstairs to his bed. Megan followed him and stood watching him crawl between the covers without taking off his clothes. The last thing Laurenson heard before falling asleep was the thump of her elbow hitting the floor as she lay down beside the bed.

The first thing he did when he woke up was check the clock. *Two o'clock. 2:00 pm*, he reminded himself. He'd have to hurry.

Again he let Megan out. Forgot about her, actually, as he scrambled some eggs and made some toast. She came in the back door, as he headed out it.

"Damn! I'm sorry!" he said. He grabbed a plastic bag full of takeout food containers that he'd set on a kitchen counter near the back door. "If it weren't so cold, I'd take you with me."

He was in a hurry because he wanted to deliver the containers himself, and the lab he wanted to deliver them to was in Edmonton, thirty kilometres away. Driving rather over the speed limit, he got to the lab and then back to the detachment, arriving a couple of minutes after 4:00.

Tavarov was just shrugging into his coat as Laurenson came through the door. He looked up in surprise.

"Neither," Laurenson said.

"Neither what?"

"I'm not crazy and I'm not checking on you. In fact, I hope to be back in bed in...oh, let's say—" Laurenson looked at his watch. "Six hours at the latest."

"So why're you here?"

"To get one of the pictures of Rozilind Smith from her missing-persons file."

"And that would be because...?" Tavarov prompted him.

"Because Smith isn't about to answer any of my questions—not for quite a while, at least—and I'm dying to find out why his daughter has come back."

"So you know for sure she's come back?"

"I'm convinced of it."

"And the picture's for...?"

"Posting at the desk on the cardiac unit. If she comes in to see her father, I want to be called immediately."

"What makes you think she'll come to see her father?"

"A couple of things he said. The way he talked, I got the impression she'd mended fences with him. And he asked me recently why I'd taken to visiting him in the evenings. He said he'd told Mary Grey to visit him evenings, but I think he was trying to clear a time slot so Roz could come by without risking running into me."

"Another one of your famous hunches?"

"I talked with Mary Grey this morning. I was hoping she'd be able to come by to spend some time with the old man today."

"So you asked her about her visiting arrangements?"

"Didn't have to. She told me herself right off the bat that she'd been coming to see him mornings before bridge. She has a bridge game every afternoon."

Tavarov grinned. "How interesting!"

"You can imagine how much I look forward to asking Roz a question or two."

"Well, good luck. This is one fish I'd love to see you land."

"The Mounties always get their fish."

Driving over to the hospital a few minutes later, Laurenson chuckled as he remembered a line from the Gospels. "For I will make you a fisher of men." Christ! Here he was practically an apostle and he'd always thought of himself as irreligious.

The old man glared as soon as he saw Laurenson. "I'm tired. Go away."

"What's the matter?"

"I just told you. I'm tired. In fact, I'm exhausted. I don't want to be entertaining tonight."

"I didn't come here to be *entertained*—"

"Maybe not, but I'll feel like I have to talk. I want to sleep. Let me sleep."

"Something's happened to make you angry."

"I've had company all day. The nurses are in every fifteen minutes. The intercom never shuts up. This is crazy. A hospital is no place for a sick man."

"I thought you'd sleep through most of it."

"What's the good of having people come to see you if you're going to sleep through it?"

Since he wasn't willing to say being watched over was supposed to reassure people who were afraid, Laurenson simply agreed that it would be worse than useless for him to stay. "Have them call me if you want me. Don't worry about why you want me, or when, just have them call."

"Thanks," Smith said in a much gentler tone. "Get some sleep too. You look like hell."

Laurenson tousled the old man's hair. "I think you'll do fine, after all."

"Better than you," Smith called out as Laurenson headed toward the door.

He turned around and saw the old man was smiling weakly. With a thumbs-up he headed once more for the comforts of home. It was nice not to be needed.

A chinook blew in during the night, and Laurenson awoke to the sound of water dripping from the eaves. When he remembered that it was Saturday, he bounded out of bed. The sun was shining brightly; immediately, all thoughts of paying a duty call to either the detachment or the hospital were replaced by ones of cross-country skiing and taking Megan with him onto the trails west of town. Christie Devenish he put firmly out of mind; he'd have to give her time. What else could he do but give her time?

The snow was still dry but no longer crunchy. The sun was so warm on Laurenson's back that he was soon skiing in shirtsleeves, his fleece jacket tied around his waist. Miles out on a remote trail, he shared a large lunch of chicken sandwiches with Megan and basked in the sun. It struck him that this would be a bad time for his beeper to go off, signaling either an emergency at work or a call from the hospital, but for once in his steadfast, responsible life, he trusted to the universe to spare him. The universe spared him, and he finally returned home just before dusk, treated himself to a hot soak, and then broiled a celebratory steak. He and Megan dined on top sirloin and baked potato in front of a blazing fire.

Man, it was amazing! Why was this one of the best days of his life?

When Sunday was every bit as bright and warm as Saturday had been, Laurenson went skiing again, this time to a remote bay on a nearby lake for some ice fishing. He stopped in at the hospital on his way home, but left when he found Smith sound asleep and, by all reports, recovering well.

Monday saw Laurenson whistling as he walked into work. For some reason, he welcomed the sight of his in-basket overflowing, and he tackled the stacks of paperwork with relish. Late that afternoon, Miranda Cardinal finally brought him a coffee saying, "Coffee breaks aren't just for wimps, you know."

Laurenson tossed down his pen. "You're a dear, Miranda. Thanks."

A moment or two after Miranda left his office, Tavarov stuck his head in the door. "The word is out: you're in a good mood. Naturally, that has us all curious as hell."

"Go to hell," Laurenson said with a laugh. "Or, better yet, sit down."

Miranda came back just then with a lab report in her hand. "This just arrived by courier, to the attention of you, Staff."

Laurenson took it eagerly, and scanned it quickly. He then read it over more slowly and handed it to Tavarov. "Here. Take a look."

Tavarov read the report and looked up inquiringly. "I'm not familiar with—"

"Just before his heart attack in the hospital, someone brought Michaelangelo Smith some takeout Chinese food." Laurenson explained.

"This is about that?"

"I took the containers in to Dimas Friday afternoon. Yes, this is about that."

"Amphetamines," Tavarov said under his breath. "I don't get it. You suspected—?"

"The thought never crossed my mind till I'd sat watching the old man twitch and jerk for nearly eight hours. But when I finally twigged to it, I had to wonder how he'd gotten amphetamines in the hospital."

"You didn't assume it had to be a mix-up in medications?"

"No. Because the episode that landed him in the hospital in the first place had 'amphetamines' written all over it. Once I thought about it, that is."

"Are you telling me that instead of being home sleeping after you called me Friday morning, you were at the hospital tracking down takeout containers?"

"Sounds like something I'd do? Not on your life! I'd have called to have a couple of my men come down to search the bins for me. I took the containers earlier, when I left the hospital."

Laurenson added after a moment's reflection, "Which goes to show what harm a person could do by trying to save a patient from the consequences of cheating on their diet."

"Who do you think brought Smith the Chinese food?"

Laurenson shrugged. "Who do *you* think?"

Tavarov shook his head. "Roz? Naw. Why would she want to—?" He paused a moment. "You mean you think she came back to St. Michael to kill her father?"

"That was my first thought, but then I remembered that she hadn't sought him out; *he*'d been the one to seek *her* out. It didn't make much sense that she'd come back here to kill him but stick around for a month or so without doing anything."

"It doesn't make much sense either way. Unless, possibly, she has an extremely compelling reason to want to keep her return a secret."

"Mary Grey saw her, and told people she'd seen her. Her dad saw her, but wouldn't tell a soul. Why would she want to kill her dad instead of Mary Grey?"

"Why would she want to kill her dad, period? Maybe she wasn't the one who brought him the food."

"Thanks loads," Laurenson said sarcastically. "You're telling me this attempted murder I've got on my hands has nothing to do with any of the suspicious, not to mention just plain weird, stuff that's had me puzzled for more than a month. Well then, *you* solve it. Clearly it's beyond *me*."

"There goes the good mood," Tavarov remarked placidly. "Knew it'd never last."

"Not if you're going to talk coincidence!" The way he said it, he might just as well have said "Not if you're going to talk crap!" "Sure, sometimes a serial killer will come along just when a person's life is coming to a boil, but...not on my shift."

Tavarov laughed. "Okay. Admittedly it looks suspicious. And lately, who's aroused more suspicion than Roz? But what's the motive? You know as well as I do that it's almost impossible to solve—or prosecute—murder if there doesn't seem to be any motive."

"I'd settle right now just for preventing murder."

Laurenson corrected himself before Tavarov could. "Well, of course that isn't true. But solving comes second, and you know as well as I do that prosecuting often doesn't come at all."

"Want me to post a watch at the hospital?"

Laurenson sighed; this sort of thing wreaked havoc with a CO's budget...or, more accurately, with the efficient deployment of his all-too-limited resources. "Better safe than sorry. But not just yet. First I want another visit with the old man."

"Think you can get him to tell you something?"

"No. But I'd like to get him to ask me for something. And I think I'll have a better chance of doing that if he isn't as mad as hell at me."

"You figure getting protection is going to make him mad?"

"If he knows about it. I don't think this is the best time to spring it on him that we think his prodigal daughter just made an attempt on his life. Whether he believed she did or not, it could still affect his health; but I'm pretty sure he wouldn't believe me."

"He doesn't have to know about the watch."

"And I'll try to arrange it so he won't, but first I'm going to see if there's anything he'd like from home." Laurenson forestalled the question he saw coming. "If he'll ask me to bring him something, I can go into his house and look around. I don't know about you, but I sure wouldn't want to ask a judge for a search warrant without more than we have now."

"A lab report, a lot of suspicions, and a victim who won't tell you diddly. I can't say I blame you." Tavarov smiled. "Any idea what you're looking for?"

"If I had any idea, I'd stand a much better chance of getting a search warrant. No. This is a fishing expedition, pure and simple."

Laurenson suspected that it would be easier to accomplish his objective if he showed up about half an hour before evening visiting hours. So far, there'd been no reported sighting of Roz; the old man must be getting anxious. He'd want Laurenson out of his hair in case Roz was on her way over.

Sure enough, Smith jumped at Laurenson's offer of help. "There *are* a few things I've been wishing I had with me—a book I was reading, my watch, my shaving gear...actually, a *couple* of books, and a transistor radio. Would you mind driving by my place tonight?"

"Tonight?"

"Not that I'm asking you to come right back with the things, just that it's been on my mind. The Babishes are good people, but I'd appreciate having someone look in on the place for me to make sure everything's okay."

"No problem."

"And I'd like you to bring me the clothes I'll need to go home in. Not that I expect I'll need them for a while, just that it'd feel good knowing they were here. And pajamas. Lord, I'd give my right arm to be in a pair of pajamas again."

"I'll see what I can do. Maybe you'd better write me up a list...put down what colour pajamas, the names of the books, that sort of thing."

Smith wrote up the list with obvious enthusiasm.

"The Babishes have your key, right?"

"They should be home, but don't let it stop you if they aren't. You got in before without a key."

"Better sign the list, then," Laurenson said with a smile. "It'll put their minds at ease if they catch me in mid B&E."

The old man chuckled.

"Good to see you on the mend," Laurenson said.

"Can't keep a good man down," Smith said, scribbling away. "I must be a good man."

The best, Laurenson thought.

When the list was ready, he took it with an exaggerated show of nonchalance, said goodnight, and headed for the door. The hunt was on.

The chickens clucked sleepily when he looked in on them. Everything outside lay perfectly white under undisturbed snow. Laurenson let himself into the house, turned on the lights, and stepped out of his boots. It was cold! He wondered if it was cold enough to put the pipes at risk of freezing. He pulled on a pair of rubber gloves, turned the thermostat up five degrees and picked up item number three from Smith's written list—a beat-up old transistor radio that was sitting on a shelf next to the thermostat. The radio was dead, so

Laurenson went looking for batteries before doing anything else. Then he got together the shaving gear. There; if anyone came by, he had already made a start on the list.

After a close survey of the medicine cabinet, Laurenson closed the cabinet door and headed to the bedroom dresser. The dresser took time, not only because Smith wanted so many clothing items, but because he had other odds and ends tucked in there. There was a letter, for example. It turned out to be just some news from a third cousin in Belarus, but Laurenson read it with interest. Buried in a paragraph near the end there was a passing reference to Smith's refusal to accept the finality of Roz's disappearance. Laurenson checked the date, again. December 1st, 1994. *I know this is hard time of year for you. Our thoughts are with you especially at this time of year. I think you are right to not to give up hope. We keep your Rozie in our prayers as well as you. Perhaps, someday, who knows what is going to happen? May be it will be as you say.*

There were other odds and ends as well—matches, a roll of quarters, a package of cold medication, a decorated box holding some pins, buttons, tie clips and similar odds and ends. It looked as though a child had lacquered fall leaves onto a painted cigar box and then sprinkled glitter all over. It was a beautiful box.

Still holding it, Laurenson looked back at the cold medication. *I never even get a cold worth mentioning.* He put down the box and picked up the package. Opened it. Counted the clear capsules filled with small, brightly coloured pellets. Five remaining out of a package of ten. How many times had he asked a pharmacist to identify capsules like these? Usually they turned out to be cold medication. Sometimes they didn't.

Laurenson dropped the package into a bag and refocused. He didn't want to be interrupted before he could give the house a reasonable once-over. He was cutting down on the danger of that, not only by having a police cruiser parked outside but also, by going over all the usually productive areas first. Still, it was important to work as fast as he could.

When he was done with Smith's bedroom, he moved on to Roz's room. It looked to have been kept just as she had left it, all chintz, knick-knacks, mementos and stuffed animals. Going through it was time-consuming. He was especially careful with the mementos, because he believed they were likely to give him the best insight into Roz. He worked fast but carefully; in fact, he was so careful that he drew a rough diagram of the room and numbered the position of each item of note. On another sheet of paper, he listed these items numerically.

Numbers 15, 40, 72, 103, and 199 were particularly interesting, he thought. Respectively, they were a collection of framed certificates, diplomas, and awards; a pleading letter from Rio Vanagas; a list of New Year's resolutions written in a child's best penmanship; the obituary for Rose Lynne Smith, beloved wife and mother; and a child's painting…all dark skies brooding over a lone tire swing hanging from a dead tree.

When, however, he took one last look at the room from the doorway before turning off the light, he stopped and stared. The room in its entirety was, he thought, even more revealing than it was in its details. It looked complete. There were no visible gaps. When Rozilind Smith had left home, she'd taken her suede suit but not one of the pictures of herself and her mother, of her mother and father, or of her and her classmates. One of the latter now attracted Laurenson's attention. In it, Roz stood on stage, resplendent in a Victorian costume, caught in some dramatic confrontation with a heavily made-up boy sporting side-whiskers. Wouldn't she have been tempted to take this? She'd dried and saved at least a dozen roses down through the years; was it easy to walk away from this irreplaceable memento of a moment at centre stage?

There was no time to stand there pondering the vagaries of runaways. There was still the living room and kitchen to do. Laurenson found the books Smith wanted in the living room. On the bookshelf there, he also found a dog-eared volume of *The Complete Fairy Tales of the Brothers Grimm*. He took a moment to lay the book of fairy tales open, face up on a table. From the way the pages parted he was able to find the story that had been reread the most—"The Robber Bridegroom." Presumably this had been Roz's favourite. Something to read when he got the time.

Next, Laurenson looked through Smith's business papers and checked for things like bank account activity and investments. He glanced at his watch as he headed into the kitchen, the only room he hadn't checked out. 10:30. Why hadn't his beeper gone off? Either the nurses on the cardiac unit weren't keeping an eye out for Roz, or Roz was steering clear of her father. Which was more likely? He should stop by the hospital on his way home.

Although he hadn't expected to find anything of interest in the kitchen, the dish cupboard did hold something that excited him. Seven of the mugs in it were stored brim up, but two had been put back brim down. That was all the kitchen had to offer but it was more than enough. Slipping a pencil through the handles, Laurenson picked up the upside-down mugs and put them into plastic bags he found in one of the kitchen drawers. If there were any useable prints on these, they could be Roz's. The old man didn't store his mugs that way, and he probably didn't let many of his guests put his dishes away for him.

It was a little past 11:00 when he finally reached the nurses' desk on the cardiac unit. He showed his badge and explained his concern, concluding with, "Your shift change is at 11:00, isn't it? I'm afraid it's rather late to find out anything tonight, but I thought I'd look in on Mr. Smith anyway."

The nurse, a petite brunette with a husky voice, smiled up at him. "If you'll wait just a moment, I'll check the chart. I have something I have to take care of first, but I shouldn't be long."

From where he stood, Laurenson could see where the patient charts were. "Is this something you can find out from his chart?" he asked incredulously.

"You'd be surprised what we have to chart—whether the patient is ambulatory, how they're feeling emotionally, the questions they ask, if they have visitors..."

Yahoo! He felt only the slightest twinge of conscience at snagging Smith's chart and scanning it quickly while the nurse was gone.

When she returned, she flipped through it herself. He's had quite a few visitors, but only one tonight. That would have been you, I think."

"Yes. It was me."

"I'm sorry I can't help you more. Since I'm on night shift, I don't really know anything about visitors. Just what's written here."

Laurenson drew her attention to the photograph of Roz which was no longer on the bulletin board but was now taped to Smith's chart. "What about this particular person?"

She shrugged. "The niece? She wouldn't be coming in on the graveyard shift."

"What makes you think she's a niece?"

"Isn't she? A niece, I mean." She pointed to a scrawled entry on the chart that he hadn't been able to decipher earlier. Written during the weekend, it noted that the woman in the police photo was the niece whose visits always perked up the patient the most.

Laurenson knew from his own foray into the chart that his visits were also noted as favourably affecting Smith's mood. So, okay, apparently visitors were noted, and the staff was aware of Roz and of the request to contact the RCMP should she be seen on the unit. He thanked the nurse for her assistance and headed for home.

He felt disinclined to leave Smith unguarded any longer, but didn't want to rush to establish a police presence that would make it unlikely Roz would dare show her face anywhere near her father. He could, he supposed, post a practical nurse who worked as a police matron when needed, but she wouldn't be a cost-effective solution to his problem. She'd be there only to bolster the surveillance maintained by the hospital staff, not to apprehend Roz should she put in an appearance.

Laurenson was still debating what he should do as he dropped off to sleep about 1:00 in the morning.

Chapter Nine

By the time Laurenson went in to work the next day, the weather had turned bitterly cold. He hardly noticed. At long last he had something to act on, and act on it he would. By 8:05, a BOLF had been issued for Rozilind Smith, "present alias unknown." By 9:00 he'd talked with Smith's doctor, and had been assured that all unit staff would be reminded of the importance of monitoring Smith's visitors. By 10:00 he had several usable fingerprints from the coffee mugs and was running them through the computer in search of a match. He thought the chance of Roz's having been arrested at some point in the last five years was at least fair. Anyone who knew how to get hold of amphetamines stood an above average chance of being booked on drug-related charges at some point.

Roz hadn't ever been booked, but her fingerprints were on file, nevertheless. The prints taken from the coffee mug matched prints which had been lifted from the clutch purse in her closet and several bottles of nail polish in her drawer shortly after her disappearance. By 2:00 in the afternoon, Laurenson also had a match with a thumbprint from one of the Chinese food containers he'd taken from Smith's wastebasket. With a direct link between Roz and the amphetamines Smith had ingested, the Be On Lookout For was updated. Roz was no longer wanted to assist with inquiries; she was wanted on suspicion of attempted murder.

"Why would she do it?" Scott McVicar asked.

"We'll worry about 'why' later," Laurenson said. "Right now, I want to establish 'how.'"

By the end of the watch, they were beginning to get a handle on "how."

Dimas in Edmonton called to let Laurenson know that the five capsules he'd sent for analysis were dextroamphetamine sulfate.

"Is this, by any chance, related to the methamphetamines you brought in Friday?"

"Possibly. But these came in a Contac-C package."

"Contac-C? Not Contac?"

"Sorry, force of habit. The package says 'Contac 12 Hour Cold.'"

"White or blue background?"

"Blue. Different shades of blue. It's got to be new; the old Contac-C had a clock in the lower right hand corner. This has a capsule circling a globe."

"Yeah, that's Contac, all right. The new capsules don't look like the ones you sent me, but I think Smithkline Beecham may still be sending out old inventory in new packages."

"What the capsules should look like wouldn't make much difference to someone who never takes Contac-C. Hell, they weren't even on a blister strip but that didn't worry the old man who took them."

Right after work, Laurenson brought Smith the belongings he'd asked for. He chose to do this before 4:30, because he figured that the old man would probably talk with him more if he didn't encroach on the evening visiting hours.

Smith was happy to see Laurenson. He poked through his bag of belongings and slipped his watch onto his wrist. "Thanks a million. This is great! Wow, really cold."

"It's been in the trunk of my car."

They chatted about how cold the weather was getting, and Laurenson asked what temperature the house should be kept in order to keep the pipes from freezing. Smith reminisced about the winter sometime in the sixties when—with the wind chill—the temperature had bottomed out around minus seventy Fahrenheit.

Laurenson saw his opportunity. "Good thing you never get a cold," he said.

"I did that time. The minute I stepped outside to do my chores, I felt it in my nose. I knew I was in for a cold, and so I was. Practically the only cold I've ever had."

"So how come you keep cold medication under your pajamas? Is that just in case?"

Smith frowned.

"You did ask me to get you a pair of pajamas, you know."

"Yeah, I know. I'd forgotten about the pills, that's all."

"If you've had them that long, they're probably out of date and should be thrown away."

"Oh hell no. Someone gave them to me just the other day. You know how women can be, they'd have you medicating yourself 'just in case,' as you say. I mean, my voice was hoarse—that's more a smoking thing than anything—but this woman was worried about me. She thought I was coming down with a cold."

"So she gave you a package of Contac-C?"

"I thought it was really sweet of her."

"And so it was," Laurenson agreed affably. "Hope you didn't take any."

Smith looked at him sharply. "Why?"

"Just that, if I remember correctly, cold meds were something the doctors warned my dad to steer clear of. I think they contain high doses of caffeine."

"They do?"

"I'm pretty sure they do." Laurenson gave that a moment to sink in before going on. "You say this was recently? Maybe that's why you had an episode after doing so well for so long. Except, I guess you didn't take any."

Smith didn't answer for a minute. Laurenson waited patiently.

"I took a couple. Didn't want to hurt anybody's feelings."

"Only a couple?"

"Maybe I took three or four," Smith admitted grudgingly. "They gave me a boost. Made me feel better. Not that I'd been feeling sick;

just that they made me feel better than I had for a while, so after I took the first couple, I took another couple."

"Made you feel so good you went out and shoveled snow?"

Smith laughed. "No use denying it."

"Well, at least that explains why you got into trouble. It also holds out hope that you'll go back to the way you were, once you get over this. Assuming you steer clear of Contac-C."

"Of course I will. Will have to quit smoking again too, probably cut out the coffee, go easy on the physical—"

Laurenson raised an eyebrow. "*Probably* cut out the coffee?"

Smith laughed sheepishly. "Okay, no 'probably' about it. At least for a while."

Laurenson raised an eyebrow again.

"Well, hell, they're planning to put me on beta blockers. I'll be as good as new in no time."

Laurenson agreed, and turned the talk to other things.

After supper, Laurenson called several bookstores and the library, trying to track down a copy of *Grimms' Fairy Tales*. Unable to find anyone who had it presently available, he called Tasha Tavarov. Not only was he pretty sure she read her children fairy tales, he expected getting hold of the book could involve having a visit with her. He had always liked her and enjoyed talking with her, but after more than a week without Christie, he was beginning to feel he actually *needed* to talk with her.

"My goodness!" Tasha said. "Come right over. The children are in bed and Val's out running some errands. I'd love to have company."

"Have you, by any chance, a copy of *Grimms' Fairy Tales*?"

"I'll dig it out."

She opened the door to him with her three-month-old in her arms. "Rebecca needs her diaper changed. The book's on the coffee table. Get a beer out of the fridge and make yourself at home; I won't be more than a minute or two."

When she returned five or ten minutes later, Laurenson had already finished the short story.

Tasha glanced at the book still open in his hand. "'The Robber Bridegroom'? Now I'm intrigued."

"Why's that?"

"Because it's such a grisly tale, I'm inclined to think your interest in it must be professional. Surely there aren't such things happening around St. Michael?"

She settled herself in an armchair across from Laurenson and unselfconsciously began to nurse her baby. Laurenson felt he ought to look anywhere but at her—Lisa had always breast-fed behind closed doors—but he couldn't tear his eyes away from her freckled face, russet hair, and what little he could see of her alabaster breast. He wasn't sure whether he was held captive by what a comforting picture she made or by how disconcerting he found it to have her expose herself in front of him.

When the baby began to suck noisily, embarrassment superseded all else.

Tasha looked up at him and smiled mischievously. "Come on, you're a family man; you can take it."

"Now that's unfair. Women always expect men to forget *their* interest in breasts, just because they themselves have found another use for them."

Tasha laughed and the baby momentarily stopped sucking. "So what do you think of 'The Robber Bridegroom'?" she asked quickly.

Laurenson gratefully accepted the diversion. "I'm surprised," he said. "I thought it would be a kind of romantic, maybe Cinderella-like story, not one about men who dismember women, and a woman who's trying to escape marrying such a man."

"First trying to escape being dismembered herself," Tasha put in, "*then* trying to escape having to marry the killer. It's chilling, isn't it?"

"What would ever make a young girl read it over and over again?"

Tasha thought about that as she coaxed the baby into taking her breast again.

"Well," she said finally, "it *is* exciting. In the way thrillers are exciting, I mean. And it's rather clever how she gets out of the mess she finds herself in."

"You mean the story she tells at the wedding feast?"

"Exactly. How does it go? 'It's just a dream' she keeps saying to her bridegroom even as she proves to him beyond a doubt that she knows he commits atrocities. That, in particular, she knows every detail of his latest murder."

"And then she shows the wedding guests the severed finger, proving it's all true."

"He should have bolted a lot sooner. Though I guess it took him a while to realize she knew as much as she did."

"Why didn't she just tell her father and have the wedding cancelled?"

Tasha put Rebecca over her shoulder and tried to burp her. "I guess she wanted to nail the gang. It was quite a coup proving their guilt in front of a gathering of so many local people. And she managed to catch them by surprise…no manhunt, no trial. Weren't they all hung before the wedding dinner had a chance to get cold?"

"Well, in two sentences, at any rate," Laurenson said, looking down at the book.

"Good enough. Quite a tale of feminine derring-do."

"Turning the tables," Laurenson supplied after a moment's thought.

"Turning them dramatically. Actually, I rather like the story myself."

Laurenson had just been thinking that the dark story matched the grim picture of the dead tree under stormy skies that Roz had painted as a child. "Not *you!*" he objected. "I can't believe you're the type."

"What? The type to like a story like this? There's something very Victorian about that comment," Tasha warned him.

"Weren't Victorian stories about as lurid as they come?"

"I rest my case," she said smiling. "Victorians put everything dark and disturbing into their stories because they thought real life should be nothing but sweetness and light."

Just then, his arms full of groceries, Tavarov wrestled the front door open. "Thought it must be you when I saw the squad car," he said.

"Give us a minute, Val, would you?" Tasha said. "We've just begun to talk."

"Sure. As you wish," Tavarov said with exaggerated politeness.

He headed into the kitchen with his bags, and Laurenson called after him, "Feel free to eavesdrop, if you like."

Tavarov poked his head out of the kitchen and gave Laurenson the finger. "We'll talk later." He added with a grin, "About how often you commandeer my wife."

Laurenson turned back to Tasha.

"So," she said, "time is short. How's Christie?"

On the way over, Laurenson had been wondering just how much Val had told her about how things were going in that quarter. Tasha's question suggested he must have told her, at the very least, that all was not well.

"She's all tied up, these days, trying to deal with a pretty sticky situation involving her ex and her kids," he said.

"Not serious, I hope."

"Probably a blessing in disguise, though I doubt she sees it that way. In fact, I know she doesn't." He went on, sparing Tasha the necessity of offering any sympathy. "I'm a bit surprised at how philosophical *I've* become. After so many years of feeling it was up to me to fix everything around me that needed fixing, I've begun to rely quite a bit on things sorting themselves out, given a little time and patience."

"The Tao calls it order arising of its own accord," Tasha supplied promptly. "Why do you look so surprised?"

"You've never said anything before about eastern religion...or is it philosophy?"

"Philosophy," Tasha said without hesitation.

"Yeah, well, I just didn't know you were into that sort of thing."

"Nothing's as you thought it was," Tasha teased him. "These days, everybody reads *The Tao*. Except maybe cops," she added as an afterthought.

"I've heard of *The Tao of Pooh*," Laurenson said doubtfully.

Tasha's burst of laughter brought a growl from out of the kitchen. "Hey, keep it down out there."

"You know," she said to Laurenson, "it's a tenet of women's lib that patriarchy is a system designed to keep women down. "I'm beginning to think, however, that its primary purpose is the control of *men*. And the ace up its sleeve is restricting sex to marriage, which—while it worked—forced most of you testosterone-driven beings to yoke yourselves to a woman. That way you were obliged to live with a conscience, even if it wasn't your own; and you mellowed very nicely, I might add, under the influence of the supposedly brainless members of the 'weaker sex.'"

"Where'd you ever get an idea like that?" Laurenson asked in some amusement.

"From reading in one of Val's magazines that chemical castration works very well on serial rapists and killers," Tasha replied, placidly.

This time it was Laurenson's turn to burst out laughing.

"You can come in now," Tasha called out to her husband. "I need you to tell Dan about the serial killer who expressed gratitude for having his testosterone levels reduced. I don't think he'd believe me."

"I'll be damned if I'm going to come in to talk about *that!*"

"Aw com'on, Dan needs another beer."

"Oh well, then," Tavarov said, coming into the living room with a couple of beers in his hand. "How'd you get on to *that* topic?"

"Who knows?" Laurenson shrugged. "We started out talking about a fairy tale."

Tavarov glanced down at the book of fairy tales. "Not fit material to be reading kids, if you ask me. But then, we've argued about that for years. Tasha's dug up some psychological arguments in favour of it."

"Tasha was just accusing me of sounding Victorian, but then she came up with the top Victorian platitude of all times—that it's the influence of a civilized woman that saves any man lucky enough to marry one."

Tasha opened her mouth to say something, but ended up simply chuckling as, regarding her with a smile in his eyes, Tavarov said, "Well don't expect me to help you argue with her a mere hour away from *bedtime*."

Talk turned to general topics.

After Tasha had finally headed up to bed, Tavarov and Laurenson cracked open another beer each.

"Roz's favourite fairy tale was 'The Robber Bridegroom,'" Laurenson said.

Tavarov grunted.

"Read it when you get a chance."

"Still trying to figure out what makes her tick?"

"Having a lot of trouble figuring out how she could turn her hand to murder."

"You aren't buying Tasha's notion of women's moral superiority, are you? It's been *centuries* that poison's been known as the female's murder weapon of choice."

"I know. It's not women in general I'm thinking about here, just this particular woman...and this particular victim. He's a really nice person—"

"As though nice people never get murdered!"

"You didn't let me finish. It seems to me that Roz herself was a perfectionist. I've read through a list of New Year's resolutions she came up with after her mother died, and she was, if anything, heart-wrenchingly serious...to the point, I guess, of even being kind of prissy."

"People change."

"From all accounts, she became even more judgmental as time went by."

"Judgmental of other people. We tend to be more forgiving of ourselves."

"Yeah." Laurenson savoured a mouthful of beer. "You know what, though? In a way, something Tasha said might just make sense of 'The Robber Bridegroom' thing. And, if it does, Roz hasn't changed all that much."

"How do you figure that?"

"Well, bear with me, because I haven't even begun to think it through, but..." Laurenson took another long pull at his beer. "But 'The Robber Bridegroom' is about what Tasha calls a woman's feat of 'derring-do' and I can't help wondering if Roz hasn't come back to pull off some derring-do of her own. Or what she would maybe think of as derring-do."

"Killing her dad?"

"No, not that. Something to do with Lexilogic."

Tavarov shook his head. "Aw, com'on."

"No, but Smith once said, 'All her life she's been shafted. Even Heyden shafted her, the bastard.' Put that together with the fact that Heyden's been turning into a nervous wreck lately. Doesn't that make you wonder just a bit?"

"Sure it does. It makes me wonder what Heyden could ever possibly have done to Roz. From what I've heard, it was Roz who was shafting Heyden."

"I don't know what he did, or Smith thought he did. But if Roz thought he'd shafted her, and came back to get revenge—or justice, which is more likely how she'd think of it—then coming back on the sly starts to make some sense. So do a few other things too, like vandalizing the car of the woman who'd gotten her into trouble six years ago, *and Heyden's extreme nervousness when I came around because of that.*"

"Why Heyden's nervousness?"

"Because, as we've seen all too often, people with guilty secrets don't want the police digging into the past."

"Yeah, but don't forget," Tavarov said, "some victims are extremely leery about having the police poke their noses into their business. Companies that fall prey to fraud or embezzlement are notoriously close-mouthed about it. Having the fact that they've been victimized get out can do them more harm than the victimization itself."

"Yeah." After a moment's thought, however, Laurenson changed his mind. "No. I mean, not if it's a junior clerk who stole a few thousand dollars. That was a minor event that was dealt with very quickly; it shouldn't be a threat half a decade later."

"Well then," Tavarov replied promptly, "Maybe Roz's revenge involves some threat to the company that isn't minor and certainly isn't over."

"Fuck me blind!" Laurenson uttered under his breath.

Tavarov gave a sudden shout of laughter at the absolute unexpectedness of such an uncharacteristic expletive.

Laurenson was unaware of what he'd just said. "Who's more closed-mouthed than victims of extortion?" he demanded. "Ongoing extortion. It makes sense! Why are you laughing?"

"No 'fucking' reason," Tavarov said, continuing to laugh.

"Well, it does make sense. And one of his employees told me Heyden has some new products coming out in the spring. That would put his company in the spotlight; if not now, then soon. He's probably feeling extremely vulnerable."

"I have no problem seeing that. But haven't you just killed your own argument?" Tavarov asked, becoming serious again. "She *has* made an attempt on her father's life—two attempts—so how does that square with your view of her as a victim with the guts to come back and take revenge? Or at least, as nothing *but* a victim with the guts to come back and take revenge."

"Not very well, I admit. But, on the other hand, what reason could she have to kill her father? He's a genuinely nice person. Not only that but he's as poor as a church mouse and doesn't even have life insurance."

"Maybe he wasn't always so nice...or maybe he's one of those people who are nice with everyone but the members of their own family."

"He was overwhelmed when his wife died. He had a hard time dealing with his own grief and couldn't stand hearing Roz cry. But he was horrified when he hit her once because of it. He loves her. He's never given up hope she'd come back."

"Loves her how?"

Those three words stopped Laurenson in his tracks. "Oh Christ! *How naïve have I become in my old age?* he asked himself.

"I'm not saying he can't be everything you think he is," Tavarov went on. "All I'm wondering is how come she's so determined to put him six feet under if he is. Whether she's morally earnest or not, she didn't decide just on a whim to knock him off. In fact, if she's been around for a couple of months and Heyden is still sweating bricks but her old man is on life support at the hospital, I'd say it looks like you might have gotten her priorities backwards."

Laurenson wondered if his judgment had been thrown off by the fact that Smith reminded him of his own father. A moment later he brightened. "Maybe she's already done Heyden. I haven't seen him lately; I have no way of knowing if he's still sweating bricks."

"When was the last time anybody saw her on the cardiac unit?"

"Last Thursday. Since her picture went up on the bulletin board Friday, I think it's fairly safe to say she hasn't been back there since Thursday."

Tavarov grinned. "Who knows then? Who's to say Heyden hasn't dealt with Roz in the meanwhile?"

"Dealt with her how? Killed her?"

"'Had her killed' would seem more likely, wouldn't it?"

"This is St. Michael, Alberta," Laurenson objected. "And Heyden's a respectable businessman in the computer business in St. Michael, Alberta."

"Okay, best case scenario, maybe he got someone to put the boots to her and ended whatever threat she might have posed."

Laurenson shook his head. "Not unless he's as stupid as a shovel."

Tavarov raised his brows.

"Christ, Val. Would you want to put the boots to Roz Smith and leave her alive to come after you again?"

Tavarov thought about it. "No, I guess I wouldn't."

"You sound less than sure."

"No. Not if she turned truly nasty just because I wouldn't let her embezzle."

"She turned nasty with her boyfriend merely because his college prospects turned out to be better than hers."

Val rallied. "So admit it; she's not so nice after all."

"I never said she was nice. I don't think anyone has. But there's quite a difference between 'nice' and 'willing to murder in cold blood.'"

"It would be interesting to see how Heyden's looking these days, wouldn't it?"

Laurenson grinned. "I can hardly wait."

The offices at Lexilogic hadn't changed since the last time he'd been there but it was harder getting in to see Heyden.

"I'm sorry," Heyden's secretary said, emerging from his office. "Mr. Heyden is already late for a meeting."

Laurenson knew she was lying. He had already checked out the appointment diary on her desk.

"Then I'll keep my call as brief as I can," he said, walking past her. He felt like a bully doing that, but he wasn't about to be stopped by the imminent-meeting dodge.

And, indeed, Heyden wasn't going anywhere. When Laurenson opened the door to his office, he was engrossed in a screen full of text. So engrossed, in fact, that he didn't look up for more than a minute. Laurenson cleared his throat.

Startled when he finally registered another presence in the room, Heyden began to tremble. Laurenson watched with amazement as what he took at first as a startle reaction became a shivering fit that simply wouldn't go away.

"I'm sorry to disturb you," he said.

Heyden put a pair of very shaky hands under his desk. "I'm busy. My secretary must have told you. I'm too busy to talk to you." A moment later, as Laurenson walked closer, he banged his knuckles, hurriedly extricating his hands so he could clear his computer screen. "I said I'm busy. I'm too busy to talk to you today."

"I could wait here till your meeting is over," Laurenson suggested with unimpaired affability.

"This is—this is— What on earth do you *want*?"

Laurenson was already getting much of what he wanted out of Heyden's reaction to him. He was also noting with considerable interest how loose Heyden's suit had become, how dark the circles under his bloodshot eyes were, and what a yellow tinge his skin had taken on. "I want an appointment with you," he said calmly. "If not now, then after your meeting."

"You should have called."

"Apparently. Dropping in is, however, seldom this disturbing. I had no idea it would bother you so much."

"It hasn't! I'm not bothered, just amazed. That's all. I'm amazed that you wouldn't take no for an answer. I wonder if your commanding officer knows how you are with the public?"

"I *am* the commanding officer in St. Michael," Laurenson said softly. "And if this is your response to me, I'm glad I didn't send one of my men."

That appeared to take the wind out of Heyden's sails. There was no more mention made of a meeting that was already getting underway, no more blustering. "I'm a very busy man," he said, almost sadly.

"And, clearly, a man under great pressure," Laurenson replied with greater sympathy.

"No. No pressure. Just very busy. Never enough time. Never…" his voice trailed off. He sat staring into the middle distance so long that the ticking of his clock began to feel oppressive. Finally he roused himself. "I've had security beefed up, if that's what you're wondering about."

"I'm glad to hear it. What steps have you taken?"

A little pinkness came into Heyden's cheeks as he began to outline the surveillance equipment he had had installed since the vandalism to Chantelle Tilley's car.

"Is that all?" Laurenson asked when he was done.

"Isn't that enough?"

"If all you ever have to deal with is a passing vandal, yes, I suppose it's enough. But that isn't what you've got on your hands."

Heyden's head jerked up.

"Correct me if I'm wrong. That isn't what you've got on your hands, is it?"

"It is. It is."

"I wouldn't call Rozilind Smith a passing vandal," Laurenson said flatly.

Heyden's closed his eyes.

"Well, would you?"

"So you know."

"Of course I know. She's been seen in town."

"But…"

Laurenson finished Heyden's sentence for him. "But you haven't told me a thing. No. And that's not the first time you've obstructed justice." There was something about the man that made it hard to continue feeling sorry for him. In fact, the urge to make him suffer was becoming so strong that Laurenson began to suspect he possessed a sadistic streak he'd somehow overlooked until that moment. "And obstructing justice isn't the worst you've done, is it?"

Heyden looked dumbfounded.

"Where's Roz Smith?"

"How should I know?"

"Surely you're not pretending you haven't had dealings with her lately."

"No. Well, what do you mean by 'lately'?"

It was Laurenson's turn to be dumbfounded.

"Let's not play cat and mouse," he said harshly. "When, and how, were you last in contact with each other?"

"About a week before the big storm," Heyden answered promptly. "By phone."

"And before that?"

"Before that she'd call every day or two. Or I'd see her watching me. I don't get it."

"Don't get what?"

"Where is she? What's happened to her?"

Laurenson watched Heyden's face begin to break up. His features rearranged themselves into a grotesque smile, and finally he began to laugh a hard barking laugh. "I thought it was hell, when I kept seeing her. That was nothing compared to this."

"What's she after?"

"I wish I knew."

"You don't?"

"Well, she said she wanted $250,000, but I couldn't come up with that overnight; I've been sinking every penny I've got into the new products we're putting on the market in four months. So of course it took me some time. We agreed on installments. But, before I could make the first installment, she dropped all contact. Except, I guess, for the job she did on Chantelle Tilley's car, if you'd call that contact. And, of course, if you're sure that was her doing."

"We're sure."

"I was just days away from paying her 125 grand. Just days away."

Chapter Ten

Constable Genevieve Neve was waiting to talk with Laurenson when he returned to the detachment.

"Wait in my office," he said. "I'll be with you in just a minute." Tavarov looked up from his desk. "Well?"

"Extortion interruptus," Laurenson said with a grin. "It's driving him crazy."

"'Extortion interruptus'? What the hell's that?"

"That's when you start to extort a large sum of money from someone and, just when it looks like a done deal, you suddenly stop contacting them."

"Why?"

"That's what I'd like to find out."

"Extorting, how?"

Laurenson laughed. "If Heyden were half as afraid of me as he is of *her,* I'd know that. Unfortunately, I'm not terrifying enough, so I don't." He added as an afterthought, "He started to shake when he saw me, but I don't think that's because he finds me intimidating."

"No? If it wasn't fear of you, what do you think it was?"

"I think he's on the verge of a nervous breakdown, but still he won't tell me what she's done to make him willing to give her $250,000. He's still hoping to get a chance to give her the money."

"It ever occur to him that you might be able to save him a quarter of a million dollars?"

"I brought that up but it was a no go. Something will happen if he talks to the cops."

"What?"

"Damned if I know."

Tavarov mugged approval. "She's good at what she does."

"Genevieve's waiting for me. I'll keep you posted."

Genevieve was reading a report on his desk as Laurenson entered his office. He noted not only that she was adept at reading upside down (to judge from how far down the page she was) but also that she had excellent sight (to judge from how far from his desk she was). He walked up behind her, and she jumped a little, but only a very little. Nerves of steel.

"What can I do for you?" he asked.

"It's about Christie Devenish," she said. "She doesn't want me telling you, but I don't see how I could possibly, uh, avoid doing so."

Laurenson sat down at his desk, glancing at the report on it as he did so. If one of his officers had learned anything from papers he'd left lying around, he had better check out what it was before it slipped his mind.

She watched him apprise himself of the subject of the report, and flushed. "I think she realizes I'm talking to you about this in spite of her objections," she went on in a rush.

Laurenson smiled. "Probably. What's up?"

Neve sat back in her chair. "Christie has complained to the director of Family and Social Services about how she's been treated. I suspect Veronica Ralston is feeling some pressure, because she's contacted me about laying charges formally. I said we were not at all convinced there were grounds enough for laying charges, but that she'd better talk to you. As soon as Christie heard, she threatened to charge Veronica—and us—with harassment."

"Who told Christie what was going on?"

"I did, Staff."

"You told her without first telling me?"

"To be honest, I was trying to keep you out of it as much as possible."

"To please Christie?"

"Because she was dead set against involving you in any way. So dead set that I figured I'd lose all rapport with her if I didn't bend a little. And I didn't think it was right to leave her facing something like this totally alone."

"I gather she still holds me responsible."

"Not that so much—after all, you did tell her who to complain to—but she *was* humiliated, and I don't think she's going to forget that very soon."

"Yes, she was humiliated, but not by me!"

"No, not by you, but in front of you. Even though you weren't there, still she knows you were aware of everything that went on."

"Help me out here, Genevieve. I'm still having trouble seeing why it's humiliation that she's focusing on to the exclusion of everything else."

Genevieve stared at him. "But of course a charge like that is humiliating!"

"Well, it certainly isn't *pleasant*..."

She shook her head. "It's humiliating," she said with quiet emphasis. "And having you feel sorry for her was probably even harder to take than having an obnoxious stranger think she had actually done something like that."

Laurenson digested that for a moment. "In any case, it sounds as though there's a lot of sabre rattling going on. Ralston hopes to take the heat off by talking you into charging Christie, and Christie wants to turn the heat up by threatening legal action if you do. I suppose the one thing they agree on is that they don't want me involved."

"*They* don't, but Veronica's boss would be grateful. Beats me, though, what you could do."

"Do? Why, have everyone in for a nice long meeting to hash things out. Here, of course. It wouldn't do to give Social Services the home ice advantage."

"I have my doubts Christie would come here."

"Of course she'll come here. This is where it's going to be held."

"Then I don't think she'll come at all."

"She'll have to come. Tell her I'm going to do my utmost for her, but only if she comes to the meeting. She can bring a lawyer. In fact I think she should. But I'm not going out on a limb for someone who won't even show up because she'd feel sullied by entering my place of business."

"You wouldn't want to tell her, yourself, I suppose."

"No," Laurenson said smiling. "I know you'll do better than I could. So far, she hasn't pissed you off nearly as much as she has me."

Laurenson turned his attention next to the two questions most on his mind—why Roz wanted her father dead and what kind of extortion racket she had going with Lexilogic.

Talking with the old man was absolutely out of the question. Laurenson didn't even want to visit him just at present, considering how likely it was he'd bring a shadow into the sick room with him, along with his doubts and suspicions. Neither did he plan to talk again with Mary Grey. She'd convinced him she believed Michaelangelo Smith to be a good man. That being the case, clearly she didn't know anything about any abuse. It would be worse than useless to ask a lot of pointed questions that she couldn't answer in the first place.

Why risk hurting either the old man or his reputation when the original investigation into Roz's disappearance had already gone over the ground Laurenson wanted to cover? He spent three hours combing Roz's file for anything that could reasonably implicate Smith in any type of abuse. The investigation had been thorough, and yet there was nothing. That didn't mean he hadn't misjudged the old man, just that he'd come to a dead end with this line of inquiry. He decided to call John Bastian at the Integrated Technical Crime Unit, K Division Headquarters in Edmonton.

"I spend ninety percent of my time communicating only with a computer," Bastian said. "I'd love to talk with you about big business and extortion. Just give me a shove in the right direction, and we'll see what we can do."

Laurenson outlined what he saw as the pertinent facts. The target was a large computer software company. The payout was a quarter of a million dollars. The suspect was surprisingly young, a female who'd embezzled a little money from the company six years earlier and then disappeared. She was able to frighten her former boss to a surprising degree. And, by the way, she had suddenly dropped out of touch shortly before she was due to pick up the first installment of her payoff.

"You frightened her off," Bastian said.

"We weren't involved at the time she broke contact. Not with the company, anyway. I had been out to talk with her father a couple of times about an inquiry he'd made, but I can't imagine that scaring her."

"Why not?"

"At first I was just curious. And, anyway, I wasn't asking questions so much as answering a question of his that had been ignored for a couple of months."

"That's it from your point of view. Think it would look the same from the point of view of someone with a guilty conscience?"

"Maybe it wouldn't. But it sure didn't stop her from attempting something even riskier than extortion. Right under my nose, I might add."

Bastian didn't ask what that something riskier was; he'd been struck by another aspect of what Laurenson had just said. "Right under your nose? You mean she's in St. Michael?"

"I haven't been able to set eyes on her, but she's here. At least intermittently."

"You said she disappeared after the embezzlement."

"That's right. She's got a new identity and she's been as elusive as hell, but she *has* been seen."

"She's been seen in town since the extortion attempt began?"

"That's right."

"That's unusual."

"What is?"

"The up-close-and-personal part of all this. You have to go to a bank to rob it, but you sure as hell don't have to go to a victim to extort money from them. When was the last time you heard of a blackmailer or kidnapper who didn't try to keep as far away as possible from the vicinity of the victim?"

Laurenson thought of the only kidnapping case he'd ever worked on, and the hours of driving it had entailed, picking up instructions and trying to follow them. "I haven't had much experience with this sort of thing," he said. "You tell *me*. Do they all involve wild goose chases across hell's half acre?"

"They do," Bastian answered promptly. "And don't forget, in the most successful extortions—kidnappings, for example—it's not often anybody can put a face to the perpetrator. A former employee who disappeared under suspicious circumstances? I dunno, either you've got an adrenaline junkie, someone with a death wish, or...I dunno...a chick with all the balls in the world."

Laurenson scribbled himself a note. "Okay, I'll worry later about why she's in everybody's face. What else strikes you about this?"

"Sorry, I'm not quite ready to leave that," Bastian said. "This is a computer company, you said. Normal access would most definitely be by computer. Cyberspace is a wonderful wasteland where everybody's instantly accessible and the people who attack them can't easily be found. Think of it—hackers go after the Pentagon from their own cozy dens in Smallville and Outer Mongolia. Why isn't your chick with a past going after this company from Armpit, Saskatchewan?"

"Would she have to be a hacker to be able to bring a company like this to its knees?"

"It sure wouldn't hurt. There are other ways of terrorizing a business, of course—arson is one of the oldest—but the best extortions find the soft underbelly of the target. It's the company with flammable inventory that gets the arson threat, not computer companies but lumber yards and clothing manufacturers. It's a question of knowing where the company is most vulnerable."

"Computer companies would have reason to be afraid of hackers, wouldn't they?"

"You betcha."

"So she'd have to become a hacker."

"To some extent, at least. There are true hackers and then there are derivative hackers—lamers or script kiddies. Once hackers find a security hole they write programs that allow the hack to be automated and run by just about anyone."

"*They make hacking programs available?*"

"Of course they do. That's how they make their reputations, by issuing security advisories, publishing them in hacker journals or posting them on-line. Anyone—even you, if you like—can download cracking and hacking utilities from the Web."

"Allowing me to do what?"

"Gain access, interrupt service, flood a system with data, steal or contaminate files...the possibilities are endless."

"You don't sound particularly unhappy about it."

Bastian laughed. "I nail the little bastards every chance I get. If they ever stopped doing what they're doing, though, I'd probably be back writing traffic tickets and hauling in drunks. I'd rather be doing what I'm doing."

"You'd think a software company would be a tough nut to crack."

Bastian laughed.

"Well, you would, wouldn't you?"

"They can be as lax as anybody regarding security. Everybody's been relying for too long on what you might call 'security by obscurity.' You wouldn't believe the number of companies that instead of encrypting a password, will try to hide it in an obscure file, hoping no one is going to bother to look for it. That's ridiculous; already, hackers know all the best hiding places. And, anyway, they have a work ethic; they're willing to try the 432 most commonly used passwords and, if that doesn't work, move on to the 1,700 second-best bets. Hell, if necessary they'll try to log on using every damn word in the dictionary as a password, or they'll turn to social engineering."

"Social engineering? Does that mean some kind of con game?"

"Yeah, most often phoning a mark who has the required information and posing as a field service tech or a new employee with an urgent access problem."

"How would *you* go about extorting a lot of money from a software company?"

"I'd kidnap a program that'd take years to replicate or a system that's absolutely essential to their work. It's like grabbing the Rockefeller heir. The only difference is that there are no copies of the Rockefeller heir but there are of programs and systems. That means you have to be damned sure you've destroyed or fouled all available versions—except the one you're holding, of course—so the company that made it in the first place will now want to buy it from you."

"Could it be kept a secret within a company if this had been done? Wouldn't the staff quickly realize there's something wrong?"

"That would depend on the company and the attack made on it. You couldn't keep it a secret if it was a widely used system or database that was tampered with; but if it was something only a select few were working on…" Bastian fell silent a moment. "Come to think of it, that's the way to go whenever possible. Attack elite stuff. As elite as you can get."

"Why as elite as you can get?"

"If your victim can keep it a secret, they're going to want to keep it a secret. It stands to reason. Just as you won't last long if you're a mining company known for salting your ore samples, you won't last long if you're a software company known for having hackers ferreting through your files and tampering with your product. You're going to want to keep it a secret that they can breach your security, even though it's hard to carry on camping when everyone else thinks everything's all right, but you know the woods are burning."

Laurenson finished the thought. "And it goes without saying that having your target keep it a secret is the best thing that could happen to an extortionist."

"Yeah, all things being equal, I'd rather have as few people as possible know about it if I'm going to hold a gun to someone's head," Bastian said wryly. "Not to sound like a broken record, but I can't for the life of me imagine why she'd let her anonymity slip with her victim."

"She's got an axe to grind, and all the balls in the world."

It wasn't until he'd said it that Laurenson realized just how true it was.

"Would someone that ballsy drop out of sight?"

"One thing she should know, since she's been keeping an eye on him, is that her victim is scared shitless. He's not fighting back and he's certainly not thriving."

"Even less in her absence, I suppose."

"For sure."

"Well then, maybe that's the point of dropping out of sight for a while."

"There's such a thing as killing the goose that laid the golden egg," Laurenson replied tartly. But his mind was already on what to do next. "How do I go about catching her?"

"You don't. When your secretive computer mogul is tired of being screwed in the left ear, give him our number."

Laurenson said he would. But after putting down the phone, he sat for nearly an hour tapping his pen on his desk and staring unseeingly at the pile of papers in front of him. As he left for home at last, he chuckled to himself. Roz had him almost as well hooked as Heyden. Why else would he want so much to be the one to catch her?

Laurenson began the meeting by saying, "I stepped back from this investigation at the very beginning; I'm not going to apologize for stepping in now. If Constable Neve had felt there were grounds for laying charges, they would have been laid by now. If Family and Social Services had felt absolutely certain of their case, they would have proceeded without us."

Christie's lawyer tried to object at that point, and Laurenson silently cursed Christie for having no better sense than to hire this good-looking good-for-nothing with a reputation for using his legal practice as a source of quick lays.

"Mr. Annichiarico," Laurenson interrupted. "This isn't a court of law. You will have a chance to speak at length, but first we're going to hear Ms. Ralston out. This session is, as you know, being recorded so you needn't be concerned that anything will be lost or forgotten if you wait your turn."

Laurenson then introduced Val Tavarov and Genevieve Neve who, he said, would be the ones to decide if police action was warranted. He concluded with, "Naturally, Family and Social Services can always act independently if not satisfied that we are doing enough. Now, Ms. Ralston, if you would please begin at the beginning. We're all, I'm sure, anxious to hear in detail how you became aware of the Devenish family and what has convinced you that criminal charges should be laid against Christie Devenish."

Annichiarico objected again, but Christie laid her hand on his arm and shook her head. Laurenson had been battling an erection since first laying eyes on her this wintry Friday morning, but he found an antidote in the anger that stirred in him when counselor and client put their heads together and Annichiarico whispered in Christie's ear. The bastard's black hair touched Christie's honey-coloured hair. He put his hand over hers and kept it there as he whispered on and on. Finally Christie pulled back both her head and her hand.

Ms. Ralston had chosen to stand to outline her case. Laurenson tuned in to her just as she was saying, "That was when the call was put through to me. I asked the caller to repeat what he'd just told Intake and he said—and I quote—'I'm calling to report a case of child abuse. That's why Shaun Devenish ran away from home. His mother's been sexually onto him.' I asked him what he meant by 'sexually onto' and he said, 'Sexually abusing him. It's gotten so bad he can't take it anymore.'"

Annichiarico took an audible breath and Christie put a restraining hand on his arm again. This time, however, she removed it as soon as Ralston continued.

"I spoke with Staff Sergeant Laurenson, relaying the complaint to him and asking for his input. He said he didn't think Shaun was being abused by his mother. He did, reluctantly, agree to send Constable Neve out with me on the call I was duty bound to make in response to the complaint, and I took Virginia Polanica from our office with me. Virginia would be here today but, unfortunately, she's come down with the flu."

Laurenson, jotting down notes, raised his head as Ralston paused. She was watching him. He suspected she was half expecting him to raise an objection or two of his own.

"Go on," he said. "What happened then?"

"Well, Shaun's mother denied everything and became furious with me. I was grateful I had a police officer there to protect me."

This time Christie didn't try to restrain her lawyer, but Laurenson merely said, "Make a note of your objection, whatever it is. Your turn is next."

Ralston said, "In the end, she refused to talk with us any more without a lawyer. We weren't totally surprised. From a talk we'd had with Shaun's father and sister, who said they weren't aware of any abuse and expressed their shock and chagrin at what had been going on, it was plain she'd made her overtures in private. When a person always insures there'll be no witnesses, you can be certain they know what they're doing is wrong."

"Which, in this case, was?" Laurenson held his pen poised. "I'm still waiting to hear the specifics of the charge."

"The specifics of the charge are: that Shaun's mother was always parading herself in front of him in a lewd manner, often scantily clad and openly seductive. That she showed an unusual interest in his genitals and made an effort to see them every chance she got. And that she fondled him against his will." She looked Laurenson hard in the eye. "I believe you must be aware that unwanted touching is, by definition, sexual abuse."

Laurenson refused to rise to the bait. Instead he wrote on his notepad, *Unwanted touching. Of what nature?*

"Go on," he said. "Where did you get these specifics?"

"From the victim himself. Shaun Devenish came into our office the very next day."

Tears began to roll down Christie's cheeks. Laurenson wished she would control herself; crying now made her look guilty. Though, on second thought, there was no response an accused could make that couldn't be interpreted as proof of guilt by a person who already had their mind made up.

"So he's actually been in your custody for some time," Laurenson said.

"He's been in the custody of his father," Ralston corrected him.

"Without a word being said to his mother!" Annicchiarico exclaimed.

"We didn't want to make things more difficult for Mr. Devenish than they already were."

"Perhaps you wouldn't mind allowing us to make copies of Shaun's affidavit so we can pass them around."

"I'd rather not have my notes passed around, thank you very much."

"I didn't ask for your notes, just his statement."

"Shaun spoke with me, he didn't write a statement. He's only sixteen."

"Seventeen. Did you think him too young to affirm the truth of what he said?"

"He was very upset. It was plain to see he was telling the truth. Are you going to let me finish or not?"

"By all means, finish what you have to say."

"Well," she faltered, "that's pretty much it. Since his mother isn't really contesting his father's application for custody, the only question that remains is whether what she did to her son should be swept under the carpet or not."

"Thank you," Laurenson said. He turned to Annicchiarico. "Go ahead."

Like Ralston, Annicchiarico stood up. "It is our contention," he said, "that—one—Christie Devenish did not sexually, or in any other way, abuse her son, the minor Shaun Devenish, and that—two—if she did, it was unintentionally, inadvertently, and without malice aforethought."

Out of the corner of his eye, Laurenson caught Tavarov putting his hand over his mouth to hide a fit of unholy mirth. For his own part, he wanted to throttle the weasel whose slimy double talk had just put Christie in even greater jeopardy.

"That's not 'our' contention," Christie objected. "If Mr. Annricchiarico thinks it is, we need to talk before he goes on."

Good girl, Laurenson thought. "We'll take a short break," he said aloud.

Genevieve quickly slipped out of the room and Laurenson followed close behind, directing Christie and her lawyer to an interview room. He watched the altercation between them from the viewing room, pleased to see Christie was angry and became angrier the more Annicchiarico tried to soothe her. Of course, Laurenson thought with a grin, it didn't exactly help his cause that he tried to offer her a shoulder to cry on.

Finally, she turned to the camera. "Damn you, Dan Laurenson, come in here."

Thirty seconds later Laurenson stepped into the room.

"Can you do better than this useless tit?"

A vein in Annicchiarico's forehead stood up at attention.

"Without a doubt. Her case has more holes than a fishing net."

"What should I do?"

"Go back. Have him state that you categorically deny the charges." He turned to the lawyer, whose face was beginning to acquire a tinge of magenta. "And, you, ask to defer your comments until a few details have been clarified. I'll step in, requesting clarification. When I'm done," he turned back to Christie, "you can decide how you want to go from there."

In short order he found himself back before Ralston, framing his first question. He started by asking who she thought had called in the anonymous tip. They discussed briefly the reliability of hearsay and, in particular, of hearsay offered by anonymous informants.

Laurenson accepted her avowal that she had complete confidence in the veracity of the caller. These calls were recorded, weren't they? He wanted to hear the call. Ralston objected that that would serve no purpose.

"If nothing else, it would help establish whether the call was made by Shaun himself."

Ralston called this a groundless allegation and, seeing she had clearly lost points with her boss, Laurenson was content to go on to their own initial conversation about the case. There, too, he wanted the tape or, at the very least, an opportunity to compare their respective notes on the conversation. Ultimately, her notes didn't differ much from his and he was quick to point out that they didn't support her claim that he'd been reluctant to send an officer out with her. Nor did they show her as having fairly represented what his response had been when told of the accusations.

He asked Genevieve, who had long since returned to the room, to describe the interview between Devenish and Ralston as it had appeared to her. He watched as Ralston's superior took copious notes at a furious pace. And then, gathering steam as Ralston lost hers, he went into the details of Shaun's accusations. What was lewd about Christie's behaviour? What constituted being scantily clad? Touched Shaun how? How did she try to catch glimpses of his genitals?

It turned out that lewd was being seductive and being seductive was being playful; being scantily clad was going to the bathroom in a negligee; and trying to catch glimpses of Shaun's genitals was teasing him once that he didn't have anything she hadn't already seen. As for the touching, Laurenson made mincemeat of the claim that Shaun hadn't liked his mother putting her arm around him as she read to him before bed, and that she should have known he didn't like this though he never actually told her. The alleged incidents, which had at first appeared bizarre, began to look innocuous once it was established that Shaun was five at the time they occurred.

Ralston became increasingly angry as she insisted that it didn't matter if Shaun had complained to his mother or not...he was complaining now. Laurenson responded with a few words on the importance of being able to test a complaint by examining the complainant.

Finally, he called into question the wisdom and the humanity, if not the legality, of failing to notify a custodial parent that a runaway was safe and sound and had been put into the care of the non-custodial parent. It was simply icing on the cake when Annicchiarico was able to establish with a question of his own that Shaun had been taken out of province, to Toronto, several days earlier.

Ralston complained that her word as a professional counted for nothing.

"Ms. Ralston," Laurenson said with weary patience. "There's very little about your handling of this case that meets the normal standards of professionalism."

A throat was cleared, and everyone turned to the Director of Family and Social Services, who had almost escaped notice thus far. "I believe Ms. Ralston has the best of intentions," she said. "And that she'll be a credit to our department. All the more so for learning from this case, the importance of corroboration, documentation, and caution regarding complaints."

She stood up and walked over to Christie, holding out her hand as she got closer. "I'm very sorry, Mrs. Devenish, that you've had so much to deal with, and that we've unwittingly added to your troubles."

She shook Christie's somewhat unwilling hand.

"I hope you'll forgive us."

"I will if you'll send me a letter saying what you just said."

Ralston headed abruptly for the door. She was, however, still on the premises talking to Constable Ross Waring when Laurenson headed back toward his office a few minutes later.

Genevieve came up behind Laurenson. "I ran all the markers in the parking lot," she said *sotto voce*. "Just in case."

Laurenson stared at her uncomprehendingly.

"A list of unpaid tickets as long as your arm," Genevieve said nodding toward Ralston with obvious glee.

Just then, Christie walked away from her lawyer. "Excuse me, could I have a word with you?"

"With me?" Laurenson asked.

"Would you mind?"

"Not at all."

He put his hand on the small of her back and steered her toward an interview room. "Just a moment," he said.

"Going to start the camera?" Christie asked with asperity.

"Are you kidding? I'm going to make sure it's turned off."

She looked down when he returned. "I think I owe you an apology," she said carefully.

He gathered her into his arms. "You most certainly do."

She gave him a little shove. "Then let me say what I have to say."

"Not a chance," he murmured, bending down to kiss her.

Chapter Eleven

At some point in the weekend that followed, Laurenson was able to let knowing Christie in the biblical sense give way to coming to know more about her in the ordinary sense. As they lay naked and tangled in each other's arms, he asked her how Angie had ended up leaving with her father, instead of staying until the custody hearing.

"I realized how angry I was with her, and I thought some 'time out' wouldn't be such a bad idea, after all."

"How angry you were with *her*?"

Christie turned to look into his face. "Didn't it ever strike you that you were bearing the brunt of some anger that should have been directed at someone else?"

"That *I* was?"

She laughed. "I guess not. But you were, you know. I was somehow excusing Shaun, imagining he'd been traumatized by finding out you'd stayed over that night last June. I figured finding out I was—as he put it—'a whore' was such a shock, he began to think I was so obsessed with sex that I must be after him. That was easier to take than finding out when it was Social Services first talked with Angie. Something she let slip made me realize she talked to them even before Shaun did. Suddenly she was not only someone who knew there was an investigation underway and didn't tell me about it—someone other than *you*—but, unlike you, who might well have been trying to appear fair in a tough conflict-of-interest situation, she was working against me, acting as a go-between.

"Not only that, she didn't tell me Shaun was safe with his father. Neither did his father, of course, but it was Angie I expected loyalty from, not Justin. I had no way of knowing Shaun wasn't on the streets, and she didn't spare me even one moment of worry about that."

"So you're saying you were angry at her but you were taking it out on me?"

"That's an oversimplification. I mean that wasn't the only reason I was angry at you. But it probably helps explain why I went absolutely ballistic. Only I didn't realize how little of it was your fault until you came by that night to give me the name of Veronica Ralston's supervisor. That is why you came by, isn't it? The question was just an excuse."

"The question was genuine enough, but I suppose I could have taken it to someone else. Or maybe even have waited. I later found proof that 'Neither of you get it' *was* a slip of the tongue, and the person I was wondering about *had* returned."

"Well, knowing you, I should have known it wasn't totally manipulation. I did figure, though, that you thought maybe I'd be so grateful at receiving the contact information—which you could have sent in the mail, you know—that you had an ulterior motive for coming by. Anyway, the more I tried to hate you for being selfish and manipulative, the more I realized I was working at being angry. Finally it hit me and I felt like such a fool!"

"What hit you?"

"That Ange had been so phony for so long. That she'd been dodging me when I needed her. I mean, it came as a shock that what I was really mad about was the way she'd been pretending to sympathize but avoiding me for weeks. And here I was thinking you were awful because you wanted to talk, but I'd have given anything if only *she* wanted to talk with me half as much as you obviously did. Isn't it weird? I was getting angry at you for doing what I wanted her to do!"

"Whew!" Laurenson said with a laugh. "I'm glad we finally got that worked out."

Christie gave him a smack on the arm. "Don't you dare make fun of me! I've been to hell and back."

"I'm so glad you're back," Laurenson murmured, giving her a hug.

She gave him a quick kiss on the lips. "You won't believe what else happened," she said impishly. "It—it was the weirdest thing, and it put Shaun in a whole new light."

"I'll believe it when I see it."

"Okay, picture this. I'm walking down Jasper Avenue in Edmonton, where all the panhandlers and people who are off their meds seem to be gathering these days, when a severe-looking woman with a guitar catches my eye." Christie gave Laurenson a whack on the arm. "What are you doing?"

Laurenson, who had closed his eyes and scrunched up his face, opened one eye just a little. "Hey, don't hit me. I'm picturing it."

"Stop goofing around. This is a moment of enlightenment I'm trying to convey. There were little notes pasted all over her guitar and I was curious because she didn't seem like the guitar type, if you know what I mean. And she wasn't! The notes all said things like, 'The end is coming' and 'Prepare to meet your Maker.'"

Laurenson chuckled. "Let me guess—one said, 'Spare the rod and spoil the child.'"

Christie gave him a scathing look. "One probably did. The thing is, I stepped closer to read the notes and the woman said in a very loud voice, 'YOU'RE NOT A VIRGIN!' I realized she was staring at my red blouse. She was talking to me! She started shouting 'IT'S PLAIN TO SEE YOU'RE NOT A VIRGIN!' and everyone was turning around and staring at me. I think I must have turned the colour of my blouse. I tried to hurry away, but the sidewalk was jammed. It was noon and we were in the middle of a huge crowd. But then suddenly it hit me; why was I embarrassed? I'm forty-two and the mother of two children. Who said I was supposed to be a virgin?" She laughed happily. "I mean, give me a break! Where did Shaun get the idea I had no right to be sexual? I won't say I suddenly got mad at him, but I finally admitted my sex life was his problem, not mine."

"Ah, Christie," Laurenson said, giving her a hug. "You're one in a thousand. I'm so glad I met you."

"Hey, what do you mean by that?"

"I love you. What did you think I meant? *I love you.*"

"I know. But why so much suddenly *now?*"

Laurenson smiled happily, "Because you're the only woman I've even known who'd take an incident like that and somehow use it to save yourself."

The return to work Monday morning brought a raft of less pleasant thoughts. Smith was being discharged from the hospital soon, and he remained adamant about returning to his own home. The burning question now was how to protect him. Or, rather, how to apprehend his daughter before she could harm him. How much should they tell someone his age who had just been very sick? It went without saying that they'd have to post a watch—not an easy thing in the country in the winter—but there were other complications, as well. Smith might notice the absence of the mugs and the Contac package. They could be put back before he ever got home, but that would eliminate their usefulness as evidence. They might be needed as evidence.

"Damn it," Laurenson complained to Tavarov. "This is the first time I've had to keep a potential victim from finding out they're in danger."

"What makes you so sure you have to?"

Laurenson was unable to provide a quick answer.

"Exactly," Tavarov said triumphantly. "It would be nice not to have to tell him, but I doubt it's essential. After all, he's suffered the stress of—what is it?—more than a week of not seeing his daughter, and maybe even imagining that all sorts of horrible things have happened to her. It might even be a relief to him to find out why she's been away. If, that is, he hasn't already figured it out."

"How would he figure it out?"

"Come on, he could've overheard the staff talking. He could've just put two and two together…the way she's dropped out of sight and you've been avoiding him yourself. He could've himself begun to wonder at some of the recent coincidences, like getting sick right after taking the pills she gave him and eating the food she brought him. Let's face it, he might have been able to read you like a book, catching on to what you suspected, ages ago."

"Okay, okay, I get your point."

"Don't you think it's time you had a talk with him? Isn't even the worst news better than no news at all?"

Laurenson thought about it and then headed over to the hospital.

Outside the door to Smith's new room, a semi-private down the hall from intensive care, Laurenson steeled himself for the task ahead. Almost as soon as he stepped into the room, Smith turned to a middle-aged man in the bed by the window.

"Would you mind giving us a few minutes, Morgan?"

"Not at all, Michaelangelo," the roommate said, pulling on a dressing gown. He cast a curious look at Laurenson, and hurried out.

"What was that all about?"

"Never mind that. What did you come to tell me?"

"Nothing—"

"Don't bullshit me. She's dead, isn't she?"

"No. I can't say for sure but, if she is, I haven't heard about it."

"Then why the face of doom?"

Laurenson was irritated. "I think you're mistaking duty for doom. It's important we have a talk before they send you home."

Smith made an expansive gesture. "Go ahead. I'm all ears."

"No, that's not the way it's going to be this time. I have some important information to give you, but I'm not going to do that until you've answered a few questions."

"I haven't done anything. Why should I have to answer questions?"

"Because I want to know to what extent you're aware of just what you *have* done."

"Which is?"

"Uh uh. That's not how it goes. I'm the one asking the questions here."

"You're in a pretty nasty mood," Smith remarked mildly.

"It's the kid gloves you're missing. Sorry, they have to stay off for a while. When did you see Roz? It was on your stakeout, wasn't it? When?"

"You're pretty damn sure I saw her."

"I have been for a long time. You were surprisingly uninterested in the report on the body that was found near the Devonian Gardens. Though you tried, you weren't a good enough actor to convince me you were interested."

Smith gave a meagre shrug. "Yeah, well, I did catch a glimpse of her, it's true."

"If it had been just a glimpse, you'd have kept up your stakeout."

"What you don't seem to understand is that a man's got to keep his word. I gave my word not to tell anyone. I take that seriously."

"You've kept your word. You haven't told me squat. But I don't see what good it does her or anyone else for you to refuse to tell me anything now that I already know so much. What harm could it possibly do for you to satisfy my curiosity on one or two points?"

"Points like what?"

"Why would she want you to keep it a secret that she'd returned?"

"Someone who owes her a lot of money will stop at nothing to avoid giving it to her."

"It's hard to imagine who could owe her so much money after so much time."

"Someone who stole an idea of hers."

"An idea? From a girl fresh out of high school? Or was she still in high school?"

"From a smart girl who knew more than you seem to want to give her credit for."

Laurenson ran his mind's eye back over the room Roz had left just as it was, a testament to her interests as well as her personality. There were books on drama but none on computer technology. If she had come up with a concept worth selling to Heyden, surely it would have been in the field of computer technology.

"What?" Smith asked sharply. "You don't think she could have an idea worth selling?"

Laurenson didn't think it likely, but didn't want to argue the point. "Are you afraid the 'stopping at nothing' includes killing her or having her killed?"

"Not really. I think it's a whole lot more likely they'd try to smear her...come up with some trumped-up charges to get her arrested and locked away for years."

"Admittedly that would be hard on a young woman in the prime of her life."

"Even more so when it's a young woman who hasn't been able to enjoy the prime of her life because of what they...this person...did to her years ago."

"You mean stealing her idea. Or was there something else involved?"

"If there was, I don't know about it. She's willing to settle for the money owed, so I figure that's the extent of what she thinks she has coming to her."

"Any idea how she hopes to get it?"

Smith shook his head.

"Obviously she doesn't feel she can sue for it."

"No. And I admit I'm at a loss when it comes to figuring out what she *could* do. But, as I said, she's a smart girl, and a determined one. And she's been planning to go after this money ever since she was forced to hightail it out of here."

"Her disappearance was connected to the stealing of her idea?"

"Of course. If she hadn't disappeared, he'd have gotten her then. He had it all set up. She worked in billing. He cooked the books and made it look like she was stealing from the company. At the very first indication she wouldn't let him steal from her, he turned it around so it would look like *she* was stealing from *him*."

Realizing how great a victory it was to have induced the old man to say this much and what damage a careless word could still do, Laurenson was careful not to name names. "He never said a word to us about her stealing from the company. Not even when we were knocking on his door looking for a possible reason for her to have run away."

"Yeah, I know. I figure there's a spark of decency buried somewhere deep inside that black-hearted bastard. She was his daughter's friend, after all; it must have bothered him to some extent that he was shafting her. But not enough, obviously, to make him do the right thing."

Laurenson let that go without comment. "When was the last time you saw her?"

"Almost two weeks ago. She warned me that she'd be coming and going without a word, but I wish her timing had been just a bit better. I could have done with her around when I got sick again. And it's felt like forever since I last saw her."

"Have you been worried about her?"

"Of course I've been worried about her. I wish she had let me know she was going away for a while; I wouldn't be lying here imagining her lying in a coma down the hall or something. To make matters worse, I don't even know her new name, so if she turned up in an obituary I wouldn't have any way of knowing it was her unless there was a picture included."

"She didn't even give you a phone number where she could be reached?"

"No. I told you she thought I was an idiot."

Idiot. The first time Smith had used that word, the day he was taken to the hospital, he'd bemoaned having been one of the idiots who'd made Roz's life hell.

Apparently in response to whatever he read on Laurenson's face, Smith explained himself. "After all, you can't trust an idiot with sensitive information, can you?"

"You're not an idiot," Laurenson snapped. "Do you really think she thought you were?"

"I don't just think she did, I know she did."

Laurenson grinned suddenly.

"What's so funny?"

"Nothing." He wasn't about to start trying to explain why that one word had taken such a load off his mind that he couldn't help smiling.

"Nothing, my eye! You obviously think I'm an idiot too."

"Bear with me," Laurenson said, casting about for something to say that would distract the old man and be useful as well. "Maybe that's why she insisted you take the cold capsules. She thought you were such an idiot you couldn't tell if you were getting sick or not."

Smith snorted. "Fat lot you know! For one thing, she didn't insist—"

"Okay, let me put it another way—she *made* you take the cold capsules."

"If you'd just listen! No, she didn't make me take them; she didn't even insist I take them. She just left them with me. In fact, she said to think it over. I'd have taken them right then and there just to please her, but she said she wanted me to have them because she thought they'd do me a lot of good, but she didn't want to pressure me into doing anything I didn't feel like doing."

Smith laughed at the look he saw on Laurenson's face. "Now what's there in that to make you look so knocked for a loop?"

"What did he say when you told him?" Tavarov asked the next morning.

Laurenson swore under his breath.

"You didn't tell him," Tavarov guessed.

"No. But not for the reason you think."

"This I've got to hear."

"Well then, let's get ourselves a cup of coffee. This is going to take a while."

They settled into the coffee room, which was empty but freshly stocked with donuts.

"He'd have laughed his head off," Laurenson said, as he snagged himself a maple nut, after a moment's indecision.

"What makes you so sure?"

"It was his choice to take the supposed cold capsules. As it turns out, she wasn't even there when he took them. Now how likely do you think it was that she had any certainty at all that her father, who prided himself on never getting colds, would take the medication she left with him?"

"He did take it."

"Yes. But how likely do you think it was that she thought he would?"

"What about the Chinese food? It had amphetamines mixed right into it."

"True. The Chinese food incident was handled so completely differently, you'd think there could be no connection. But let's not worry about that, just yet. I'd like to know how I was supposed to tell the old man his daughter tried to kill him by giving him amphetamines disguised as cold medication when she wasn't even there when he decided to take them."

"Son of a bitch! Okay, so he'd have laughed his head off. Does that mean you don't think she was trying to kill him?"

Laurenson raised his hands to run them through his hair, remembered the maple nut donut, and went over to the sink to wash. "Yeah, well, funny you should ask that."

"Don't tell me, something's happened to that theory too."

"Just before we talked about the supposed cold medication," Laurenson said. "Admittedly, we can't assume there wasn't any abuse just because the investigation into her disappearance couldn't find evidence of any, but… "

Tavarov groaned. "I know you like the old man."

"It's not that. It's not *just* that. Girls caught in abusive relationships with their fathers…what do you think, Val? Do they tend to think of them as monsters, creeps, bastards, or idiots?"

"What are you getting at?"

"Would Roz have thought of her father as an idiot if he'd been terrorizing her in some way? It doesn't make sense to me that she would, but I'm damned if I can come up with a reason for her to kill him unless he did something at some point that was worth killing him for."

Tavarov sighed. "Love or money—the two great motives. If she didn't hate him, maybe you overlooked some financial profit to killing him."

"No insurance, a thousand dollars in the bank, and no investments anywhere. He doesn't even have a vehicle."

"What about the house he's living in?"

"An old clapboard two-bedroom shack—" Suddenly Laurenson groaned. "God, it was right under my nose. How'd I ever miss it?"

"The house?"

"No, it's worth maybe five thousand. Ten thousand in an inflated market. *The land.* He told me once he's got a few acres he's living on and a couple of quarters he's rented out. He must have at least a half section."

"So he's not totally broke after all."

"Val, it's three kilometres from the city limits. It could be worth a million, maybe more. Not only that, but Roz was recently talking to him about selling it. *This is it; this is the motive.* And I knew…or should have known that was what he was talking about when he said, 'Neither of you get it.' He was talking about why he didn't want to leave the land. Roz must have nearly choked when she saw how close the city had come since she left home and realized how much a half section so close to town would be worth. She must have started urging him to sell off and move into town. That's why he had no patience with me when I broached the subject; he was tired of arguing with her about it."

Tavarov laughed. "So here we find a strong financial motive just as it begins to look like she was awfully hit-or-miss about administering the first dose." He shrugged. "Aw, what the heck; I don't care. I'll go with motive any time. Maybe she knew her father would balk at medicating himself if she urged him, so she used reverse psychology."

"Too damned hit-and-miss for me. He said he was willing to take it right away because he was touched by the fact that she cared. It's not reverse psychology when you stop someone from doing what you want them to do. It's something else. Hell if I know what."

"Ever been so torn between two alternatives that you flipped a coin?"

Laurenson immediately saw the point of this prosaic-sounding question. "You think that was what it was? Son of a bitch! It makes sense."

"Of course it makes sense. I thought of it."

Laurenson ignored that. "Hell, it ties together the fact that he was—is—a good man, that she is—was—someone with moral standards, and that she's fast losing what moral standards she once had."

"How so? I mean, how's giving him a chance show she's losing her morals?"

"Not giving him a chance, but failing to give him a chance a little bit later. It could be she's become someone who's willing to do almost anything to the jerks and idiots of this world."

"So there's two sides to her."

"More like two stages. Stage one, she had qualms about harming her father because, whatever his failings, he *is* a decent man; and she saw herself as someone turning the tables on bad guys, not as a bad guy, herself. Stage two—"

"Whoa. Stop right there! Someone who embezzles and extorts doesn't make it to my list of good guys. Are you saying you think

Heyden did something so bad to Roz that he deserved anything she cared to dish out?"

"No, though maybe that's how she started out, feeling he'd been cheap, he'd reneged on a promise, and he would never miss a few thousand dollars that he should have given her in any case. I don't believe she had an idea that he stole from her. That's just a story made up to explain things to her father. I think when it comes right down to it, Roz has spent so many years being mad at this idiot and that jerk and the other creep that she's come to believe they all deserve what they get."

"That they deserve what she dishes out, you mean."

"Exactly. And it only makes sense that what she's willing to dish out would have escalated. I don't think resentment improves a person."

"Escalated between the cold medication and the Chinese food?" Tavarov sounded incredulous.

"That's something I'd like to talk to her about. If you're right about this flipping a coin thing, it might be that when her dad did take the amphetamines, she figured that was it—the coin had come up heads—and all her qualms went out the window. Or maybe, because he came so close to dying when he took them, she got a taste of being within an ace of inheriting a fortune and she was hooked. The land must be worth a fortune, maybe not a million dollars if sold to a developer, but close to that or even more, if this smart young woman became its developer herself."

Tavarov was shaking his head. "Hold it a minute. She assumed a new identity six years ago."

"So? What's to stop her from coming home, inheriting, and turning her inheritance into a fortune?" Laurenson grinned. "That is, *as long as it's safe to come back as Rozilind Smith.*"

Tavarov began to grin, too. "Extortion interruptus! Of course!"

Laurenson's grin faded. "Good news for Heyden, but the worst possible news for her father. And I doubt he'll ever believe it, so it means a long hard haul for us."

"Rather more serving and protecting than most police forces are set up to deliver," Tavarov said. "Good thing our motto is only 'Maintain the right.'"

"If you can tell me how to do that in this case, I'll be everlastingly grateful."

"Maybe it's not as bad as you think," Tavarov said. "Maybe, for all we know, Roz has had a change of heart. Or maybe she ended up scared shitless when her second attempt led to her picture being posted in intensive care. She might have seen it. That could be why she dropped out of sight. She saw it on the bulletin board and got the hell out of there before anyone saw *her*."

Laurenson mulled it over. "Could be, I guess. If so, I hope to God she goes after Heyden again."

Tavarov raised his eyebrows questioningly.

"We won't know that she's not planning another attempt on her father's life unless she does go after Heyden again. And I'm damned if I know how we're to protect her father over the course of months, or even years, if her intentions remain unclear."

"Frankly, I could care less about her intentions. Those could change at any time. What would make me feel better is a good solid charge against her...an outstanding warrant, for something we can prove. This attempted murder thing just isn't good enough. No offence, Staff, but you've Sherlock Holmes'd yourself to a charge of attempted murder. Juries aren't that smart. Not smart enough to follow your reasoning on this. You and I may know she's got it in for her dad, but it won't do us a bit of good until we can prove it."

"We've got fingerprints and lab reports..." Laurenson ground to a halt. It was no use. If she'd played Russian roulette with her father's life to the extent it looked like she had—hell! one bullet, not even two—there'd always be a reasonable doubt in any ordinary citizen's mind. The fact that she'd given her father a chance to refuse the amphetamines wouldn't, of course, be likely to become common knowledge. Certainly not if she actually succeeded in killing him. But Laurenson knew he couldn't suppress evidence, not even to "maintain the right."

"I agree," he said to Tavarov. "We need to catch her. That's the only thing that'll work."

"And maybe not even that will work," Tavarov said. "Unless, of course, you can get a confession out of her."

"Just let me get my hands on her and I'll get a confession out of her," Laurenson replied, grimly.

Tavarov considered that for a moment. "I wouldn't want to bet on it, but there's a chance you might be able to pull it off. The thing is, Staff, she's as elusive as hell. She was, even before we got serious—and official—about looking for her. She's not going to be easier to find now that things have come to this point."

"I know, damn it. I know."

"So, any ideas?"

Laurenson sighed. "Maybe Mary Grey remembers the particulars on the car Roz was standing behind when they saw each other."

"Months and months ago," Tavarov put in. "And then what? Check DMV records for any such vehicle owned by any twenty-something female? Wouldn't it be easier to just canvas all hotels, motels and campgrounds in the area?"

"It goes without saying that we'll check out the local accommodations. If that doesn't work, we may have to start tracing credit card activity at gas stations. She probably started buying gas in the area some time in August, and chances are good she used a credit card to do so."

Tavarov made a show of shuddering. "If that's what it could come to, I, for one, am hoping she'll come after her father with an axe ASAP."

Chapter Twelve

The canvassing of local tourist accommodations slowly ground on without generating any leads. It was, comparatively speaking, a success. That is, it was more of a success than Laurenson's attempt at getting clearance for a wiretap on Michaelangelo Smith's phone from Judge R. Randolf Northumberland.

"Damned old coot has run out of powdered elk horn, or whatever it is makes it possible for him to get it up," he fumed to Tavarov. "Turned me down flat. Turned me down with *pleasure*."

"Sure he did," Tavarov affirmed. "Haven't you heard? He was charged with driving without due care and attention last week. Thinks all police are the Gestapo now. Wrong time to go to him for a wiretap."

Laurenson pondered this for a moment.

"I'd have warned you if I'd known what you were planning to do."

With a bit of luck, the wiretap would have been a relatively easy means of tracing a heretofore frustratingly invisible suspect. Without it, or even a present alias, or the cooperation of the would-be victim... Laurenson brought the flat of his hand down hard on his desk.

"It was a long shot at best," Tavarov said quietly. "She's not taking any chances."

"No, thank God. She's careful. I doubt that she trusts a soul."

"That makes you *happy*?"

Laurenson shrugged. "Well it doesn't make me *un*happy. If it will keep her from making another attempt on her father's life, it actually suits me very well."

"You want this case sitting open another ten years?"

"Maybe it won't take that long. She's got a source of big bucks tearing his hair out because she's backed off from taking them from him. How long do you think she'll let that ride?"

"I wish I knew what's running through her mind," Tavarov said. "There's more money to inherit than extort, and usually money is *the* great motivator but…"

"But there's also revenge to be taken," Laurenson finished for him, "and in the case of Rozilind Smith that may just be the greatest motivator of all."

"Yeah. I wish I knew which way she's leaning."

"I'm putting a lot of stock in the fact that she gave her father a chance once…that she made a point of not pressuring him to take the pills."

"She wasn't so obliging the second time around."

"No. I guess seeing how close he came to dying had its effect. But then look what happened after the second attempt—her picture went up on the bulletin board of the cardiac unit."

"She may be unaware of that."

"I know. But the longer she stays away from the old man, the more I'm inclined to believe she saw it *and got the scare of her life.*"

"Figure it could have made her think twice?"

"More than twice. Since she was a bit reluctant to begin with, it might have made her grateful to have a reason not to go through with it."

Tavarov nodded. "So the more she realizes we've got our eye on the old man, the better it'll be for him."

"She's a smart girl," Laurenson said more to himself than Tavarov. "I'm sure she's capable of finding out there's a Be On Lookout For her. What I need is to make sure all the attention seems to be focused on her father and none of it on Lexilogic. I want her to get back to revenging herself on Heyden."

"How much of a push would it take? It's what she's been dreaming of for six years."

"But she must know that there'll be no coming back to inherit once she's extorted such a large sum of money out of a local business. If apprehending her is out of the question for now—damn that officious, inept, stupid old bastard!—then I'd like to find a way of making the extortion irresistible. Otherwise, she might have the patience to wait, to put off—or forgo—the actual criminal act that could make it too costly to ever come back as Rozilind Smith."

"Hey, since when is a life sentence nothing? She's already attempted murder."

That was the moment at which a new scenario played itself out before Laurenson's eyes. It was over in a flash, but after it was over, he sat bemused for more than a minute.

"I know I said it could be tough making the charge stick—" Tavarov began.

Laurenson nodded absently.

"What the hell's worrying you now?" Tavarov asked.

"The possibility that she may be smart enough to think of a way out of this mess."

"What way out of it? You think there's a way out of it?"

"She could return as Rozilind Smith *now*." Laurenson watched Tavarov's face closely. "What better way to scotch the charge of attempted murder? If she returned now, while her father is still alive, he would be the trump up her sleeve. He could tip the scales in her favour just by telling how she urged him to think twice about taking the pills." Tavarov opened his mouth to speak and Laurenson added quickly, "Yeah, she left a fingerprint on the Chinese food container but...so did I."

"I take it you figure the money could outweigh the revenge, even with her."

"Heyden has played into her hands so far. He's been a piece of cake. She may figure she'll be able to get him later, another day in another way. Or maybe, having put him through so much already, she's satisfied for the moment." Laurenson rubbed his jaw. "Hell, returning to live in close proximity to him, without doing anything further to him, could be the perfect revenge if only she knew it...mental torture of the highest degree, without the slightest vulnerability. She may already have thought of it. Val, the possibilities are endless. Don't they worry you just a little? They scare the hell out of me."

"But you figure she's got something that belongs to him, right? Surely Heyden's not such a wimp that he's going to let her move back to town totally scot-free."

"Whatever she's got, she could give it back. She could say she was doing him a favour, testing his security. Or she could rely on the story she told her father about being owed money. Hell, she could probably even convince a jury she'd been under extreme provocation but was too nice a person to actually *do* anything criminal to the nasty man who—take your choice—framed her, broke his promise, destroyed her innocence, or stole her idea for the software she later stole back from him. Whatever she might say—whatever lie she might tell—would probably make a crown prosecutor think twice about wasting time on her unless she had made a profit from her actions or, at the very least, had done some damage to some property."

"Okay, okay. Spare me the details. You've made your point."

"That's not what I wanted to hear."

Further reflection on what he knew of revenge made it a toss-up for Laurenson which would be worse—no progress on the case or the kind of development in it that Rozilind Smith might be capable of generating. He was alert, unusually so, to the phone ringing or the static that preceded a radio communication. Alert as he was, he heard every detail of Todd Rainier's call to report the fatality on Highway 16X, the afternoon of November 30th.

"Officer down, officer down," Rainier said.

Laurenson was out of his office and beside the radio transmitter before Rainier could name the officer who was down.

The static and a woman's prolonged keening drowned out his next words.

Miranda tried to make herself heard. "Ten-9, ten-9, say again."

"It's Dayandan. There are no vital signs. I repeat, no vital signs."

Miranda looked toward Tavarov. Her eyes were stricken as they met his, but her voice was strong and steady as she asked Rainier for his location.

While waiting to hear more, Laurenson saw before his mind's eye flashes of Keith Dayandan, the quiet man who looked more like a librarian than a cop. *"Maybe we should define our terms," Laurenson had said to a room full of officers being briefed on a serial rapist. "If memory serves me, necking can be carried out almost anywhere." "What a memory!" Dayandan had responded with faked awe. "I can't even remember that far back and I've only been married eight years."*

That brought back an image of Dayandan poking his head into Laurenson's office, offering to work late on a canvas that was getting no results. *"Go home," Laurenson had said with some exasperation. "You've a wife and family, you lucky bugger. Go home."*

As soon as he heard where Rainier was, Laurenson headed out in a squad car, flashers and siren clearing the way for him. Under a lowering sky, he found traffic creeping at a funereal pace past two squad cars and two late model sedans. Rainier was at one of the cars trying to calm a hyperventilating woman; a man sat slumped forward behind the wheel of the other car, clutching his head in both hands. Dayandan lay two metres in front of the woman's car, ten metres behind the man's, at the side of the highway in brown slush that was rapidly turning red. No ambulance had arrived yet. When he saw that, Laurenson realized just how much he had wanted to get there in time to prove Rainier wrong and prevent some over-hasty EMR personnel from mistakenly declaring Dayandan dead. Well, he'd been quick, but dead is dead for all that.

The sun momentarily broke through the clouds, laying a narrow band of bright light across the figure sprawled across the shoulder of the road and into the ditch. Before it withdrew again, it highlighted such massive injuries that Laurenson found it hard to begrudge Dayandan his death. Still, he wouldn't give up until he had himself checked for pulse, respiration, and heart beat. He did this though Dayandan's brown eyes stared vacantly at the top of a tree throughout the procedure.

It was only after an ambulance had taken the body away that Laurenson left. He left because it fell to him to go now to Ramona Dayandan and break the news to her as gently as he could.

She answered the door, smiling; but a moment later, her smile faded and her face turned white. "What is it?" she asked, taking an involuntary step back.

"I have some bad news, I'm afraid," Laurenson said. "Can I come in?"

"It's Keith," she said, her hand flying to her throat.

"It is. He's been in an accident."

"Is it bad?"

"I'm afraid so."

"How bad?"

"Very bad. He was patrolling Highway 16X and stopped a vehicle. He was hit by another as he stood checking out the driver's registration."

"He'll need me. I'll have to go to him." She looked around her distractedly. "The children are napping… I–I don't know what to do."

"I'll find someone to stay with the children," Laurenson said. "But, Ramona, I haven't told you everything yet. Can we go inside and talk for a minute?"

Her hand dropped from her throat. "There's no hurry? Is that what you're trying to tell me? Is it too late?"

With the utmost reluctance, Laurenson nodded. "He died instantly. He never knew what hit him or felt a moment's pain."

She tottered, and he put his arms around her. "I'm sorry. I'm so sorry."

They stood like this in the open doorway oblivious to the cold pouring into the house.

It was Christie who stayed with the little Dayandans, it was Christie who held Laurenson that night and the nights that followed, and it was Christie who helped Ramona get through the days leading up to the funeral; but it was Laurenson who planned the funeral and saw to the myriad of official details that constituted the aftermath of such a death.

The funeral itself was an official event. Part of Laurenson hated how official such events were—circuses, really—but part of him was determined that there would be no stinting this man who had fallen in the line of duty…that he would be honoured as he deserved to be.

All Saints Anglican Church was only a kilometre from Fountain Gardens Funeral Home, so Dayandan had gone to Fountain Gardens, thus making possible a procession from where he lay in state to the church where his funeral would be held. A kilometre would accommodate the pipe band, the honour guard, and the hundreds of uniformed officers who would escort him to church. It would give people of the community an opportunity to pay their respects without actually trying to crowd into All Saints. There were many such people because Dayandan had worked with Tough Love and a variety of school programs.

The day of the funeral was cold, too cold for walking a kilometre in a red serge uniform, but there was never any question of doing anything else. Though the Calgary city police and Ontario provincial police wore their winter jackets, members of many other forces wore only their dress uniforms, as did every Mountie in attendance. Laurenson had taken mercy on his staff to the extent, at least, of forming the procession within doors as much as was feasible. There was nothing that could be done, however, about the long slow walk down Fallhaven Boulevard; it simply had to be endured. For the bagpipers in kilts it must have been much worse.

For Laurenson, a pallbearer, the cold assuaged a little the guilt he couldn't escape at still being alive. It tore him apart to be carrying a man who had once been so vigorous but now could not move even a millimetre under his own power. That this man was only thirty-two made it even worse. That he had been run down like a dog on the highway made it almost unbearable.

He felt for the officers behind him. He, at least, was able to enter the church without delay; many of the hundreds trying to squeeze into first the church and then the church hall and corridors were forced to stand outside for another half hour. At least a hundred would stand throughout the entire church service. Seating had been reserved only for family, close friends, and dignitaries; but there were plenty of those. Among the dignitaries who would speak at the celebration of Keith's life, there was a commissioner and assistant commissioner of the RCMP, the deputy prime minister, a solicitor general, and a lieutenant-governor.

Laurenson looked across the aisle at Keith's widow, but looked away quickly. He wouldn't torture himself. Once *Bridge Over Troubled Waters* was over, he figured the worst was over; and, indeed, it was— among the many tributes paid to Keith there were ones that made everyone laugh. Even Ramona had risen to the occasion with a eulogy, read by her brother, which dared a little affectionate humour. She had, according to the eulogy, often teased Keith that she had married him only for his red serge, to which Keith had just as often replied that he had married her only for something *she* wore. Her brother conveyed with a cupping of his hands what it was that Ramona wore, and the rafters rang with masculine laughter.

It was during the Prayer for the RCMP—the part that goes *Endue them with loyalty and courage, and grant that wherever they may be called to duty or danger they may be under your protection*—that Laurenson noticed a woman in a pew to the right of the altar. She was smiling at him. Smiling at him? Was that possible? His head had just been bowed, surely she couldn't have been smiling *at* him. And, in any case, this was hardly a moment for smiling.

Bowed heads were lifted throughout the church, and there was a general shifting of position, a kind of universal shuffling. It was time for the pallbearers to go to the flag-draped casket. Laurenson looked once more at the woman. She was still smiling in his direction. He took a step toward the casket and then turned in utter disbelief back toward the woman. It was Rozilind Smith!

He told himself he was crazy, but her smile had grown bigger and brighter now that he had recognized her. He wasn't crazy, *she* was. She had been waiting for him to recognize her. Lord only knew how long she'd been watching him, perhaps trying to draw his attention, sitting in a pew that put her face to face with him, though at a distance.

There were five hundred law enforcement officers surrounding them, not counting special constables and by-law enforcement personnel. There was no lack of police presence. Roz Smith raised her eyebrows. Here she was, would he take her? But he was a pallbearer with one duty still remaining, carrying the casket out to the hearse that would take Keith to the crematorium. It would be unseemly to disrupt the funeral, even by raising his voice and gesturing.

He took another step toward the casket. He was torn as he had never been before between duty and propriety. Suddenly he realized how large both these imperatives had loomed in his life. Which took precedence? They seemed to be equally important—doing the "right" thing and "maintaining the right." Antagonistic though they were at this moment, they hung before him, perfectly balanced.

If respect for the dead hadn't called for solemnity at a time like this, if the media and the commissioner hadn't been there to interpret anything he might do as either grandstanding or—worse yet—as being more important than Keith's death, if he hadn't felt he ought to be able to count on apprehending Roz without interrupting the funeral, he would not have felt so torn between diametrically opposed possibilities. After all, for him, doing his duty had always been first, last, and everything in between.

Would she be smiling like that if she had the slightest doubt she had him between a rock and a hard place?

Whereas she seemed to be sure she knew what he would do, he wasn't willing to stake anybody's life that he could return the compliment. For all he knew, she planned to turn herself in within five minutes. But, alternatively, she might have a sure means of disappearing forever which she would use so this tantalizing glimpse of her would be his only one.

He thought of the ancient tradition whereby churches were off limits to the authorities…places where fugitives could, and often did, seek sanctuary from the law. Shit, who today remembered that? And Keith himself would want him to arrest her…even here and now.

These were only the thoughts he later remembered having. Time seemed to expand to accommodate them, a host of others, and the one final thought that put an end to thinking. He knew this audience better than she did. There need not be a disturbance.

He turned to the totally unknown man behind him and whispered, "Take my place."

He then began to walk quietly toward Rozilind Smith.

For a moment she stood frozen, perhaps not believing her eyes, perhaps trying to decide what to do. Now she was the one who had to deal with the possibility of all eyes being on her. It wasn't a possibility only; it was a fact as soon as she stepped out into the aisle. As soon as Laurenson began to walk more quickly toward her, hundreds of police officers came to the same conclusion about why she'd done so. Halfway up the aisle toward the door, she found her way blocked by a cop from Montreal, one from Winnipeg, and one from Toronto.

It took only a word from Laurenson before he was free to go and Roz was not. Seeing that none of the pallbearers had moved, he returned to the casket and took his place once again. Without so much as a glance back at Roz, he tenderly carried his subordinate outside, and surrendered him to the hearse.

Val Tavarov, also a pallbearer, turned to Laurenson. "I'll take care of it if you like."

"Thanks, Val. I'd appreciate that."

As Laurenson stood in line to offer condolences to the family, a television reporter asked for a minute of his time.

"Tomorrow, if you like," he said.

"Perhaps you could just confirm whether or not a woman has been arrested."

"I'll gladly give you an interview on Constable Dayandan, the carnage on our roads, or both, but you'll have to see me tomorrow if you want me to talk about anything else."

Knowing something about television's perspective on time, he wasn't the least bit surprised to see the reporter hurrying off…no doubt in search of Tavarov or one of the three out-of-province officers instrumental in holding Roz till after the funeral. A short sound bite today was worth more to such a person than an in-depth interview tomorrow.

With Christie having taken care of Keith's children during the funeral, it was only to be expected that Laurenson would find himself eating sandwiches and drinking tea with Keith's parents and giving his children piggyback rides, as well as swapping shop talk with friends Keith had made while posted in Nova Scotia.

Finally, Christie came and tucked her arm quietly into his as he stood momentarily alone.

"Willing to come home with me?" she asked smilingly. "I've about had the biscuit."

"So have I," he admitted. "But I should stop by the detachment for a few minutes."

"You've got to be kidding."

He considered that. "Yeah. What could possibly be so important it couldn't wait for tomorrow?" He gave her hand a squeeze, and they took their leave.

Since, however, Christie had her truck and he had his car, their leaving together didn't mean they drove home together. Under the circumstances, it was, if not inevitable, at least understandable that he ended up taking a short detour to the office.

Darin Childe was working the front desk.

"Hey, Staff, you've just missed Val by about five minutes," the young Blackfoot officer said. "Congratulations. He told me about you spotting Roz Smith. During a prayer, with your head bowed, if he's to be believed. I wouldn't mind a tip or two on how to do that!"

Laurenson laughed. "I've no doubt you could already do it. Probably better than me, from what I know of your interest in pretty girls and prayer."

"Pretty! Well," he added grudgingly, "yes, I suppose she might be easy on the eyes under the right circumstances. Being dragged in here by Val didn't do much for her looks."

"*Dragged* in?"

Childe grinned. "According to him, it wasn't until it came to the point of actually having to walk inside that she realized he wasn't going to let her go. When it hit her that he wasn't, she went for his balls. The wonder is he could even drag her in. She caught him a good one."

"Really! So you came to the rescue, I suppose."

"Best exercise I've had in a week. What is it with women, they think they can take their best punches and nobody's going to mind?"

"The wonder of it is, they think nobody's going to charge them with resisting arrest. Though, come to think of it, they're not so far off the mark there. Memories being what they are, and male egos."

"Well, if she'd canned me, I'd have done it, but Val put it down to hysteria. Wouldn't leave her alone till the matron got here. In fact, he thought she might be suicidal."

"Did you?"

"Think she might be suicidal?" Childe considered this. "Homicidal would be more like it."

"I don't think you're quite as chivalrous as Val."

Childe laughed. "She's my generation, I've seen her type before."

"What type would that be?" Laurenson came behind the counter and planted his weary bones in Tavarov's chair.

"Warrior women," Childe said readily. "But you don't want to get me going on this subject."

"Oh but I do," Laurenson said. "I have the opinion of a little old lady, now I'd like the opinion of a strapping young man. It's a balance thing, you know."

Childe looked as though he knew nothing of the sort. If anything, he "knew" his leg was being pulled. "Well," he said, with the ghost of a smile, "I doubt your little old lady has been cruising the bars lately, so I may know a thing or two she doesn't."

Laurenson considered that the understatement of the year. "I don't doubt that for a minute," he said. "Warrior women are plentiful on the bars scene?"

"They're not in short supply anywhere. They're really easy to spot in a bar. They're not the ones looking around, people-watching, enjoying the company; they're looking for someone. The guy, *person*, I mean—these days, it could be a girl—who'll give them the perfect orgasm. They're not itching to dance; they're showing off their perfect or as-perfect-as-they-can-make-it body. If they danced, they might sweat and then their make-up would run. They're not laughing, or if they are, it's not for the fun of it; they're too focused on the job at hand. You have to let go to laugh."

"I can think of several possible jobs they might have on their minds."

"Don't be distracted by details; there's just one job—counting coup."

"Taking scalps?" Laurenson asked with surprise.

Childe made a face. "When was the last time you said, 'that was quite a scalp!'?"

It took a moment. "Oh," Laurenson said, "as in 'that was quite a coup!' I stand corrected."

Childe grinned. "Well," he said, "that's about it."

"Not so fast," Laurenson protested. "Are you saying the job is winning?"

"I guess. But, of course, not in the sense of 'he who dies with the most toys wins.'"

Laurenson thought back over the women he'd known. Some had wanted a husband who would be a good provider, some had wanted equality of one sort or other, one would have given anything for a successful conclusion to her psychiatric treatment… "It's too broad," he complained. "Anything can be dubbed winning. Even—for a masochist—losing."

"That's why I don't specify the job. Hell, it's not what a woman thinks will make her life perfect that matters, it's how she goes about living her life. That's why a woman on a barstool is so easy to read. I don't guess their dream; I don't have to."

"What did you read in Rozilind Smith?"

"Fury. The hell-hath-no-fury-like-a-woman-scorned kind."

"Fury? That doesn't make sense."

"Exactly. What did she have to be furious about, right? She goes to a cop's funeral and parks herself facing the man who's put a Be On Lookout For out on her…what did she expect would happen?"

"Not what happened, apparently."

"Apparently. She lost control of the situation. Now, I don't know about you, but I sure as hell wouldn't be seeking out the company of upwards of a thousand cops if there was an alert out on me. And I think, if I did, I'd be just a mite philosophical about things turning out badly."

"I once said she's got all the balls in the world," Laurenson said. "Little did I know."

"There's balls and then there's balls. In my book, it's not balls if you can't take the consequences. I'm not even sure it's balls if you haven't got a handle on what the risk factor is."

"So what is it if it isn't balls?"

"Hell if I know. Mental illness?"

"How do we know she didn't have the perfect orgasm sitting there risking everything?"

"Are you going to ask her?"

Laurenson laughed. Inwardly, however, he was wondering about the interview. To say it wouldn't be easy was to err on the side of optimism. The woman, the possible charges, what he knew balanced against what he was willing to reveal he knew, and her options in responding to the situation were too complex for effective pre-planning.

He hated like hell to go after someone like her flying by the seat of his pants. That wasn't just tidiness of mind, he wanted to count coup.

"It's the old control thing," he said, more in response to his thoughts than to what Childe had just said. "I think I may learn more about how a woman like her sets about controlling a man like me than I ever dreamed possible."

"Or wanted," Childe put in. "Well, not to worry. You're the one with a set of keys."

"Hardware!" Laurenson was dismissive. "She can get out of this. She may not have realized she can. In fact, it looks a lot like she hasn't. But all it would take is a little thought and she could be thanking her lucky stars we've got her behind bars tonight."

"Yeah, right," Childe said chuckling.

"She seemed to be hysterical, you said. At least that was what Val thought. Has she been seen by a doctor?"

"No. Believe me, she's not hysterical, she's mad."

"We'll see about that," Laurenson said. A monitor above his head showed Roz sitting on the cot in her cell, staring at the floor. "I know she doesn't look to be in a bad way," he added, nodding toward the monitor, "but appearances can be deceiving."

He called Christie to apologize for having taken a detour that had turned out to be longer than intended, then went down to the holding cells. Both Roz and the matron who was watching her looked up, the matron with pleasure.

"Hi, Annie," Laurenson said. "She giving you any problems?"

"No no, none at all."

Laurenson stepped closer to the bars and stared, rather as people at zoos stare at the animals. Roz pointedly turned her back to him. A mild response, he thought, considering how the tables had been turned. He ambled back to the matron's desk and checked the paperwork.

"What's this?" he asked. "There's been no body cavity search done?"

Annie hesitated. "Corporal Tavarov thought—"

"I know what Corporal Tavarov thought. But a prisoner who may be suicidal is the *last* one you want to lock up for the night without taking every precaution."

He strode back toward the cell and stared again. "Looks to me like she's drugged."

Roz turned two glittering eyes toward him.

"Yes, she's on something all right. Better call Dr. Ramsaran."
"*I'm not on anything,*" Roz said between clenched teeth.
"Like you'd tell me if you were!" Laurenson laughed.

It took a while, but before Laurenson left, Rozilind Smith lay on her cot, heavily sedated.
"You're sure she'll sleep through the night," he asked Dr. Ramsaran as they walked out together.
"Without a doubt. A woman in the state she was in… I wasn't about to under-medicate. If anything, I may have been a bit heavy-handed."
"You were doing her a kindness," Laurenson reassured him. "A woman in her frame of mind would have been up all night thinking."
Dr. Ramsaran snorted. "Thinking! She'd have been up all night banging her head against the walls."
That, Laurenson feared, was destined to be *his* fate. He had half a mind to envy Roz her solid night's sleep, but he didn't for a minute regret having ensured she'd get it.

Chapter Thirteen

The next morning, Laurenson put his staff to work on running markers for all vehicles parked within three blocks of All Saints. By the time Roz was awake, he had two possible names which could be hers—Dawn Forsythe and Carmela Sanabria. Naturally, the former struck him as more likely than the latter, but he knew he couldn't count on either being right. Realizing there would be a considerable psychological advantage to knowing Roz's present name right from the start of the interview with her, Laurenson kept her waiting a little. He took Polaroid pictures of both the vehicles which had drawn attention through being registered to women in their twenties, and then lifted latent prints from the trunk of one and the driver's side door of the other.

Next he called Lexilogic. The secretary who had merely said, "just a moment," when Laurenson first asked for Heyden, came back on the line rather abruptly. "I'm afraid Mr. Heyden has just stepped out of the office. If you will leave your number, I'll have him call."

Mary Grey was rather more available. She agreed to try to identify the car near which she'd seen Roz standing. While Laurenson paid her a quick visit, Makarian checked the prints for a match with Roz's, and Glendinning ran both possible aliases through CPIC.

"Lord love a duck!" Mary Grey exclaimed. "I do believe that's the car! If it isn't, it's certainly the right colour."

Good enough.

When Laurenson went back to the office he found a printout from CPIC on his desk. Dawn Forsythe had been questioned six months earlier, after stopping to talk with a known drug dealer for a suspiciously long time. No exchange had been made; neither had drugs been found on her person or in her car. There was nothing conclusive about the entry, but, of course, Laurenson found it hopeful. He had expected that at some time or another, a person who knew where to get amphetamines had probably had some kind of a brush with the law.

Makarian came in at about that time, smiling broadly and holding two fingerprint cards in his hand.

When finally Laurenson took a seat opposite Roz in an interrogation room, he greeted her with studied equanimity. "Good afternoon, Dawn, I'm sorry to have kept you waiting."

"If my father only knew how you've treated me," Roz said.

"Yes?"

But by then the "Dawn" had registered and she had lost a lot of her interest in Laurenson's treatment of her. She tried to take up where she'd left off, but her heart wasn't really in it.

"He'd see you for what you are," she said rather flatly.

"I think he already does," Laurenson responded smoothly. "Now, before we get started, I think you should know this interview is being taped. You've been arrested on the charge of attempted homicide. You're entitled to a lawyer and, if not able to afford one, one will be provided for you. You are not required to speak with me. Anything you may decide to tell me could be used against you at your trial. Do you understand?"

"What is my name?" she asked.

"I was about to get to that. Do you understand that you have the right to remain silent?"

"Yes."

"That if you choose not to exercise that right—"

"Yes. Yes. Yes. Everybody knows this stuff. What's my name?"

"Rozilind Claire Smith," he said. "Also known as Dawn Renata Forsythe. What would you like me to call you?"

"You think I give a damn?"

"Don't you? Well then, let's stick to Roz. It's how I've come to think of you."

"Oh it is, is it?" Her tone was parental or, at the very least, school-marmish.

"Am I being a bad boy?" Laurenson asked. Contrary to all expectations, he was beginning to enjoy himself.

"You're being insufferable," she responded in a suffocated voice.

"Overly familiar? I'm sorry, it's just that I feel as though I know you. You, I realize, can't be expected to return the sentiment."

"Oh I feel like I know you. Don't think I don't. You're the cop my father calls a Nosey Parker. You've been making a nuisance of yourself for over a month now."

"More like two months," Laurenson supplied helpfully.

"Two months then," she snapped. "The bloody son he never had. You two hit it off. How nice for you."

"Well thank you, but I'm afraid we're getting off topic."

"The topic's supposed to be me, right? What a rotter I am, right? What am I doing back here, right?"

"Well, two out of three's not bad," Laurenson said. "Let's start with a little of your history starting in late 1989."

"Because you know everything about me, up to that time. Or at least you think you do."

"Right. So tell me the things I don't know. Tell me why you left St. Michael so suddenly."

He could see this gave her some hope. She was probably cautiously optimistic that he didn't yet know about the extortion attempt. Damn Heyden for dodging his call that morning. Damn him for not returning it yet. An update from that quarter could make the world of difference.

Roz started off like a little girl doing a school recitation. "I worked for a software company here in town. I got an idea for some office software. I told my boss about it and he got excited. But then he passed it off as his idea and, when I objected, he made it look as though I was stealing from the company. I left quickly and quietly. I wasn't sure how far he'd go with his threats. It sure didn't look as though he was bluffing."

"Where did you go?"

"What does that matter?"

"Did you go directly to Calgary, or did you get there by stages?" She deflated a little. "I went directly there."

"That's where you found your new identity?"

"Yes."

"How?"

"I reminded someone of her granddaughter. Her granddaughter had died. I looked up the obituary and, well, I guess you know the drill. It wasn't hard."

"What about the grandmother? She wasn't a problem?"

It took Roz a moment to catch his meaning. "Oh. No. I never saw her again; she was just someone I met while I was looking for a job."

Laurenson read out an address. "Yours?"

"Yup."

"Still single?"

"Why?"

"Perhaps you'd rather just give me your social insurance number and let me find these things out for myself."

"How *do* you know so much?" she asked, suddenly. "Even my own father doesn't know as much as you do. How could you put a name to me when I wasn't carrying ID and I've never been fingerprinted? Until last night, that is."

"Interested in taking up police work?" Laurenson asked ironically.

"You think I'm a joke? Well, a fat lot *you* know, you arrogant prick!"

Laurenson shrugged. "I certainly don't think you're a joke. I haven't totally made up my mind about you, but I have noticed you haven't asked me a single thing about the charges against you. Doesn't that suggest you know you've committed a serious crime?"

"To you, obviously. All it really means is that I don't give a shit about your charges. I know I haven't done anything." His expression must have changed, though he was unaware of it, for she said, "What?"

"Whatever you know, apparently you *don't* know the justice system. It *is* flawed. Mistakes *do* get made. So it's incumbent on you to take all this supposed nonsense seriously and defend yourself as well as you can, so it won't take a bite out of you while you're busy laughing at it." He added as an afterthought, "Do it without resorting to lies, though. Lies are fatal."

"Is that how I'm supposed to have attempted homicide? With lies?"

"Your lies—like disappearing just before Christmas—don't fall under the Criminal Code. I told you it was a flawed system. Noxious substances that are likely, or are thought to be likely to cause death, *do*. Taking into account your father's heart condition, amphetamines are, in his case, a noxious substance."

She paused to reflect. Laurenson gave her time. The last thing he wanted to do was create another diversion, or give her an excuse for creating another diversion, by prodding her.

She didn't need his help with creating diversions. "I love my father," she said a moment later, dissolving into tears.

As someone who had seen many displays of grief in his time, Laurenson studied hers with interest.

"What the fuck are you staring at?"

Convincing tears, but ruined by the anger, he thought. He pushed toward her the box of tissue they always had handy for such occasions.

"Yeah," she said bitterly, "you've made lots of people cry. Give 'em a Kleenex and move on; that's what you do, isn't it?"

"We seem to spend an inordinate amount of time talking about me," Laurenson pointed out. "I've yet to hear from you why you don't consider giving your father amphetamines as *doing* anything."

This was it, the moment at which she'd have to choose which way her defense would go.

"I offered him some pick-me-ups I had," she said. "He was complaining about having no energy. We'd been out of touch so long, I didn't even remember the heart condition."

Not bad. Though it would have been better if she'd said, "I didn't even remember the heart condition, such as it was." Laurenson was startled to find himself critiquing her reply. Aloud, he said, "And when the first 'pick-me-ups' only landed him in intensive care, you decided he needed some more?"

Her eyes opened wide. "What other amphetamines are you talking about?"

Clearly the drama lessons weren't wasted. "Our case rests largely on the amphetamines in the Chinese food," he said. He was deliberately giving her the least amount of information he could, so, if she got at all careless, she would divulge knowledge of something she could know only if she was the perpetrator.

"I brought my father food from the Golden Dragon," she said promptly. "Is that the Chinese food you're talking about?"

"Chicken, noodles, and stir-fried vegetables? Yes," Laurenson said. He thought, *Fuck, there goes the fingerprint as damning evidence.*

"Well," she said, "there were no amphetamines in the food *I* brought him. How could there be? The only time I let it out of my sight, before giving it to Dad, was when I went into the washroom at the restaurant."

Laurenson's heart sank. All it took, as any airline passenger knew these days, was time out of sight. It wouldn't save a person from a charge of smuggling drugs, because you were warned never to leave your bags unattended, but no one warned people not to leave their takeout orders on the counter while nipping into a toilet stall in a public washroom.

Not that he believed Roz had done such a thing, just that no lawyer worth his salt would fail to raise some doubt of guilt by claiming she had.

"You're saying there were other people in the washroom?"

"Several. I didn't pay any attention. I certainly couldn't give you particulars on them."

"Where in the washroom did you leave your order?"

"On one of the sinks. I don't remember which one. Does it matter?"

"How long were you in the stall?"

"I don't know. Anywhere from two to five minutes." Roz smiled suddenly. "You know how it is, what takes a man a couple of minutes, or less, takes a woman at least twice the time."

Laurenson knew that smile; he'd seen it on the face of more people than he cared to remember. The bit about how long it took women to use the washroom was the sort of flourish that went with just such a smile. Seeing safety within reach and feeling relieved, many suspects became friendly, even jocular, and relatively talkative. Roz was beginning to feel safe.

Laurenson pushed a piece of paper towards her and handed her a pen. "Sketch me the floor plan," he said, "indicating where you were, and where you left the bag."

"I can't draw," Roz said, pulling back as though the paper were a pan of red-hot coals.

"Anyone can render a floor plan. It's a diagram, not a picture."

"Well, even so, I wasn't paying attention. There's lots I can't remember."

It was Laurenson's turn to smile, but he wasn't so careless as to do so. "I'll give you a few minutes to think about this and to draw whatever you do remember. Obviously, unless you were unconscious at the time you entered the washroom, there are some details you'll be able to recall. There'll be *something* to indicate you were in the washroom as you said."

He left her then, ostensibly to give her time to remember, but actually to speak to Val Tavarov in the observation room.

Tavarov had the phone cradled between his shoulder and his ear. "I've got Genevieve on the line. She says 'no problem.' Do you want to speak to her?" When Laurenson shook his head, Tavarov said. "Thanks, Gen. Don't forget to get lots of pictures. See you back here in five minutes." He laughed. "Okay, ten minutes then. You're a sweetheart." He hung up. "Well, looks like we've finally gotten a break."

"Glad to hear you say that. I'd hate to think I was only imagining we had."

"You kidding? If she'd ever been in that washroom, you think she'd be looking like that?" He indicated Roz through the observation window. She sat no longer facing it but with every line of her motionless body so filled with tension that her panic was palpable.

"She should have thunk," Laurenson said.

"She was doing quite well. Better than you, if you don't mind my saying so, Staff. How was she to know you were such a stickler for details?"

"I wonder how much of that hostility is just an act," Laurenson mused aloud.

"None," Tavarov responded promptly. "And there's more where that came from. I can see why my dad used to always say, 'If you're going to go after revenge, you'd better dig two graves.'"

"Any idea what he meant by that?"

"Isn't it obvious? You think she's going to live to a ripe old age, full of years and grace?"

"Full of years and grace?"

"That's how I remember it. Haven't you ever read the Bible?" Laurenson groaned.

"I bet you go over well with the Jehovah's Witnesses when they come to call."

Laurenson continued to watch Roz. "I wonder how she is with her father. If deep down he knows that his wounded little girl, so serious, smart, so disappointed in everybody, has ended up just plain..." He searched for the right word but couldn't find it.

Just then, Roz picked up the pen and began drawing something on the paper—large squares and small ones inside the largest square of all. Slowly, methodically, she drew.

"*No!* She's been in the Golden Dragon's ladies' room. Some time or other, she has." Laurenson turned to Tavarov. "Why am I so surprised? As a high school student she must have gone out for Chinese food with her friends."

"On to Plan B, whatever the hell that is," Tavarov said.

No one knew better than Laurenson that there was no Plan B. Just more of the plan that Roz was bringing crashing down around their ears.

"It's time we went over her car with a fine tooth comb," he said. "If Ident can't get out here this afternoon, we'll do it ourselves." He looked into the interrogation room with little enthusiasm. "Well, back to the salt mines." At the door, he paused. "One other thing. Send a car out to pick up Heyden. Bring him in. I'm done waiting to hear from him."

Back in the interrogation room, Laurenson noted with relief that Roz had not regained her earlier air of confidence. On the contrary, she had just erased part of her drawing.

"Time's up," he said.

"You know, shock can do a real number on a person," she responded. "If you think someone who's just been traumatized by arrest on serious charges is going to be able to th—remember clearly, you're living on another planet."

"Oh, I know what shock can do," Laurenson said. "I avoid interviews with traumatized suspects. But, of course, when a suspect says they don't give a shit about the charges, I'm reasonably sure they haven't been traumatized by being arrested on them."

She said a lot about this, the gist of which Laurenson was willing to retrieve from the tape later; he had become so intrigued by the mechanics of her approach to setbacks, that what she was saying amounted to a mere distraction. She was like a huge castle under siege, with just a lone defender, running from balustrade to balustrade, turret to turret, and window to window. No wonder she sometimes ran to the wrong turret or brought the wrong weapon.

"You know," he said in a surprisingly gentle voice, "not every attack requires a response."

She must have been attacking him in her rant, for this inspired her to try to bring the art of sarcasm to new heights. He smiled, and she took this as a put-down.

Laurenson unconsciously started to reach out to her. "Roz. I didn't mean anything by it."

She snatched her hand out of his vicinity. "Don't you dare touch me!"

He sighed. "Has it ever occurred to you that you were never further ahead than you were at the very moment you decided to 'get even'?"

She stared at him as though she thought he must be losing his mind.

"Think about it. Aren't you getting further and further behind?"

For once she was speechless. Ironically, considering the circumstances, Laurenson liked her better that way. There was something pitiful about his tiny impulse of kindness having made her more afraid, something pathetic about her seeming helplessness when not under attack.

"I don't expect you to let down your guard," he said. "Of course, you see me as the enemy. I'm holding you here against your will; I have no right to expect you to see me in any other light." Wherever he'd been intending to go with this, he lost his train of thought as her smile at the funeral flashed before his mind's eye. "I imagine you've disliked me for quite some time. It took guts to get yourself a front row seat at the funeral and wait for me to recognize you."

She stirred.

"In fact," he went on, "'dislike' is too small a word, isn't it? You risked your freedom. Who risks their freedom out of dislike?"

"Not me," she said.

"What made you hate me so much?"

He'd expected her to enjoy telling him, to savour the terms of abuse she'd already used to describe him. When she remained stubbornly silent, he realized that, of course, it was impossible for her to tell him. To do so would be to incriminate herself. Her answer was likely some version of, "You made it impossible for me to get my rightful inheritance." To say that was tantamount to saying, "You came between me and my plan to kill my father."

"Were you really willing to let Heyden off the hook? Or were you just putting him off till later?" He didn't expect an answer; it was just that his one remaining question kept demanding to be asked.

"Heyden is scum," she said. "My dad is—"

She stopped. Laurenson assumed she was pulling herself together for a really good piece of acting. He began to wonder what she was up to, however, when she remained silent and he saw how white her knuckles had become.

"He's *royalty*, compared to Heyden," she finished in a rush.

Still waiting, he watched her swallow, take a breath, and set her jaw. So, since when did she try to minimize her feelings? Why wasn't she letting—or making—the tears come?

"He's always felt he let you down."

She turned her head away a little.

"He never stopped believing you'd come back some day."

"I'm *glad* he recovered. I want him to end his days happy."

"What do you think the chances are of that?"

She didn't answer.

"How do you think he'll take the news?"

"Of my arrest?"

"Of your arrest, and for what."

"There's something I just don't get," she said, turning to Laurenson suddenly. "He doesn't know anything about you looking for me, or why. You've been sparing him. I don't understand why you've been sparing him."

"I didn't want to break his heart. I still don't."

Laurenson looked at where he knew Tavarov was watching, no doubt shaking his head and making derisive comments about Roz. He was glad he couldn't hear them. He needed to keep straight about a few things—about the fact that he didn't have Roz...not by a long shot, nor was he at all certain she could ever be successfully prosecuted for attempted homicide. He also needed to remember that he didn't, in fact, have the power to decide what to do with her. Once she'd been arrested, she'd become part of a process that was public enough that there'd be hell to pay if he overstepped the bounds of his authority. On the other hand, it was also a fact that he couldn't protect the old man over the course of months or years, but that a confession from Roz at this juncture would virtually hold her hostage as a warrant for his safety. Indeed, if Roz should prove willing to confess, that would be compelling evidence of what? Of a change of heart? A return to comparative sanity? Laurenson shook his head. What were the chances she, Castle Indomitable, would consider for a moment, putting herself into his hands by admitting to anything? They were zip, zilch, zero.

Roz raised her head. "I know," she said.

Laurenson was startled. "What do you know?"

"I know how hard it must be for you to believe I'm glad my father is all right."

"That's easy for you to say," Laurenson said. "It's not so easy for me to believe."

"No. I guess it wouldn't be."

"The hell of it is, I do believe you."

"Yeah, I'll bet." At first she sounded cynical, but then her tone changed. "Why?"

"Because I know you didn't push him to take the fake Contac. Still, I don't see how I can rest assured he's safe, unless you admit to the second attempt."

"So you can lock me up and throw away the key?"

"You're too smart to think that's the only way I have of protecting your dad. Or maybe you just don't know how practical public prosecutors tend to be."

Roz thought for a moment. "They don't prosecute unless they think they can win?"

"Exactly."

"A person would be a fool to confess to one, then, in order to try to spare her father from having to learn she'd—" She steeled herself. "That she'd ever wished him dead."

"A confession wouldn't necessarily make it possible to prosecute the case successfully. It would depend on what was said in it, and how. Unless, of course, your father ended up dead of anything but natural causes; in which case, it would almost certainly put an end to life as you know it."

"My father is safe...from me, at any rate. That's more than I'd be if I listened to you."

Laurenson went on anyway. "A person would have to be damned careful about how they negotiated and just what they admitted to. There'd be no doing it without a good lawyer."

She cast him a quick look. "Who's good these days?"

"I don't know if there's anyone in St. Michael I'd recommend. There is someone in Edmonton who's had his name taken in vain by every cop within fifty kilometres. The wonder of it is that he's not sleazy; in fact, he's got a good reputation."

"What's his name?"

"Are you sure you'd want to consult someone I'd recommend?"

"If other people endorsed him too; sure, why not?" She laughed. "Let's face it, you don't like me, but you do like Dad. That counts for a lot." She assumed a business-like mien. "And now, Staff Sergeant Laurenson, I'm about to invoke my right to remain silent. I want to hire a lawyer, and I don't want to answer any more questions without my lawyer present."

"*'I don't know if there's anyone in St. Michael I would recommend,'*" Tavarov expostulated. "*'There is someone in Edmonton,'*" he continued on a rising note of incredulity. "What the hell were you *thinking*, Staff?"

"Jesus, Val, aren't you the one who's always trying to keep our stats looking good by cutting loose the lame ducks and the dogs? Well this one was a dog *with a grenade up its ass*. And I didn't even cut it loose...technically."

"You *want* her out on the streets again?"

"Show me where in the tape I steered her toward some clever ways of dodging extortion charges."

Tavarov thought about that and seemed mollified. "Ident called a few minutes ago. They'll be here within the hour."

"Good. What about Heyden?"

"He's on his way too."

Laurenson smiled.

Heyden was hustled in, not fast, but against his will. He was muttering under his breath, "You'll regret this. You'll pay. You'll wish you'd never been born."

Under the circumstances, Laurenson had him brought to his office rather than an interrogation room. For the moment, he wanted neither Heyden nor Roz to know the other was in the building.

"What's this nonsense?" Laurenson asked sharply. Constable Tony Kostyshyn brought detainee and chair together by a feat of legerdemain.

"My God, my God," Heyden said, "you don't know what you're doing. This is fatal. The worst possible thing you could have done."

"Perhaps you'll explain why that is. I'd appreciate it if you would start by explaining why you didn't return my call."

"Your call. I couldn't!"

"You were there."

"But, you see, I couldn't. I really couldn't. Oh, why are you harassing me like this? I need this like a hole in the head."

Kostyshyn, standing at ease beside Heyden's chair, grinned and rolled his eyes.

"What you need is to calm down and begin to act more rationally," Laurenson said, dampeningly. "Unless, that is, your primary objective is to obtain a free psychiatric assessment."

Heyden's mouth made a large round O, rather wet and trembly. Looking at it, Laurenson hoped Roz had had the good sense to keep the free samples to a minimum if her evil genius had, indeed, induced her to provide free samples at all.

"I'm a law-abiding citizen. You can't talk to me like that."

"It's not law-abiding to obstruct justice."

"But don't you see?" Tears filled Heyden's eyes. "It's *you* who're obstructing."

"Justice?" Laurenson asked. "This I've got to hear. How am I obstructing justice?"

"By forcing yourself on me."

"By *what*?"

Kostyshyn tried manfully, but couldn't suppress a sound like air escaping a balloon. He went off into a fit of coughing.

"And your timing is incredibly bad...incredibly."

"My timing of *what* is incredibly bad?"

"Of this concern, of course. This misguided meddlesome concern about what is absolutely none of your business."

"You think I called you out of concern?"

"I don't care what you call it. It doesn't make a particle of difference to me whether you're worried or..." The reply fizzled out unexpectedly under Laurenson's unresponsive scrutiny.

"I'm not concerned," Laurenson said evenly, "and I'm certainly not worried. I do, however, need some information from you."

Heyden's reply dripped sarcasm. "Sure, sure. Ruin me. Who cares as long as—"

"Ruin you? What *are* you talking about?"

"If I should be seen talking to you...if it should become known that I've been here, no matter for how short a time—"

"Don't count on it being for a short time," Laurenson interjected curtly.

"I may never— They may— All that money for *nothing*!"

"Don't tell me you paid her," Laurenson said, eliciting another whoosh of suppressed mirth from Kostyshyn.

"But I did. I did."

"How much did you give her?"

Heyden's eyes opened wide. "All of it. *That* isn't why she did it."

"Did what?"

"Kept the copies."

"How long ago did you pay her off?"

"Two days ago."

Two days, Laurenson thought. *So she opted days ago for a small fortune from her old enemy rather than a large one from her father.* He felt a weight lift from his shoulders. He hadn't misjudged her.

"There was an exchange?" he asked, turning back to the matter at hand.

"Yes. Only she gave me blank diskettes."

"Blank, you say."

"That's right. Well, not totally blank. Each directory had the right file names in it, but the files themselves were empty."

"You didn't open one at random, just to check before you paid her off?"

"Who'd ever have dreamt she wouldn't keep her end of the bargain? I mean, I kept mine; it only made sense that she'd keep hers. Unless she thought it was a trap. But, if that's what she thought, she's had time to put them in the mail or something. I don't want to piss her off before I receive them."

"Mr. Heyden," Laurenson said firmly, "her not keeping her end of the bargain is precisely what you should have expected."

"But that's crazy; she got the money."

"Obviously the money wasn't enough."

"It was exactly the amount she asked for."

"That being the case, you've got to ask yourself why this smart young woman would be so dumb as to leave you in a position where you have nothing to lose by going to us with a complaint against her."

Heyden seemed struck by the thought. He stopped fidgeting. Laurenson watched him pull himself together and try to focus.

"I dunno. It doesn't make sense. Could it have been just plain meanness?"

Laurenson crossed his arms on his chest. "That's a phenomenal amount of meanness for someone to be feeling with regard to her best friend's father, a man who gave her a job, always liked her, and didn't said a word against her even when she embezzled from him."

Heyden shifted in his seat. "I was good to her, and she's been nothing but trouble to me. But even putting that aside, I gave her all the money she asked for and she kicked me when I was down. That's meanness I can't even begin to understand."

"Meanness...you bet. But what strikes me is how angry a person would have to be to do that. Who wouldn't take the money and run? Who would put themselves at risk when they've won? I'd say she's more angry than mean. In fact, not just angry...furious."

"I'm the one who should be angry."

"So it would appear. It's interesting—the person who should be afraid is angry, and the person who should be angry is afraid. Why is that?" Heyden remained silent and eventually Laurenson went on. "Well, whatever is between you is between just the two of you. My business isn't what happened six years ago, but what's happening now. There's a crime in progress *now*, but I need your cooperation if I'm going to do anything about it."

"Nothing happened six years ago, except maybe that she flirted outrageously with me, the little slut."

"I found it thought-provoking when you said you'd kept your end of the bargain so it only made sense that she would keep hers. Put that way, it made me wonder if that wasn't the point of giving you blank diskettes. Kind of like saying 'That's what it feels like to be shafted. That's what it feels like when the other person doesn't keep their part of the bargain.'"

For once Heyden didn't fuss or bluster. He became still and thoughtful.

"As I just said, what's done is done. The extortion, on the other hand, can be dealt with if you'll just cooperate with us."

"I kept my half of any bargains," Heyden interjected. "Maybe she hoped—"

"She wasn't a hopeful person."

"Well, then, she misunderstood."

"Someone once put it to me that she wasn't the sort to depend overly much on words alone, not even a promise." Laurenson felt a twinge of annoyance at finding himself again wasting time on one of Heyden's self-justifications. "Mr. Heyden," he said with quiet emphasis, "we shouldn't let ourselves get side-tracked by past history. We need to stop talking about the past and start talking about what to do about her now."

"She may yet return the diskettes."

Laurenson doubted she would unless forced to, but he didn't say that. "Even if she did, that's not good enough."

"You just don't understand."

"Oh, but I do. There's a price to be paid for refusing to keep silent any longer, but believe me, it's a small price compared to the alternative. Bullies rely on their victims' silence. They couldn't do what they do if their victims refused to keep quiet about it any longer."

"The software can be recreated, given time. I can absorb the financial loss. I've been doing extremely well; it's not that big a deal."

"It is a big deal. It's leaving a clever, bitter woman out on the street, after she's tasted success as a criminal. It's her against the world, and she's learned a few good tricks about preying on big business. You don't want her out there. It's not in anyone's best interests for her to be out there."

"You think I care about that? I just don't want her coming after me again."

"We've got her in custody. It's not totally out of the realm of possibility that she could be induced to return your software to you. Your money, too, for that matter."

Heyden hesitated. It was plain to see that the idea appealed to him. But then a shadow crossed his face and he shook his head. Laurenson would have given a lot to find out what had just run through his mind. Did he have good reason to fear further revenge, or was he simply a coward?

Heyden sat up straighter in his chair. "It's my understanding that unless I lay a complaint, you have no authority to act in this matter."

"Beats me why you wouldn't lay a complaint."

"My losses are my losses. This is none of your business unless I ask you to make it your business."

"It might be therapeutic to confront her."

"I haven't been well. Enough's enough."

To judge by Heyden's face, his mind was made up. Even a rookie like Tony could see that. Laurenson exchanged glances with his constable and then stood up.

"Well, think about it. If you ever change your mind—"

"Thank you," Heyden said. "Thank you, I'll keep that in mind." He was halfway out the door before he finished the sentence.

"Man," Kostyshyn said. "What a loser!"

Laurenson rubbed his weary eyes. "Don't be fooled by the state he's in. He's a smart professional and a successful businessman."

"But he's letting her get away with it."

"Yeah. Being smart isn't everything."

Laurenson left the office soon after that, heading off into the woods behind the detachment, going for a long walk through gusts of sleet as he dealt with the distinct possibility that Roz would go scot-free in spite of having committed two serious crimes. He wrestled with guilt because he had valued Michaelangelo Smith's peace of mind more than he had valued getting a conviction. True, at the time he'd tipped Roz off to the possibility of cutting a deal, he'd been sure they'd nail her for the extortion. Even now, he couldn't totally blame himself for what he'd done. If his suggestion worked, there'd be no need to worry about her harming her father any time in the foreseeable future. Unfortunately, the same couldn't be said about her pursuing a career of white-collar crime.

Still, he'd done his best with Heyden. Was there a tactic he'd overlooked? Aw, to hell with it, he'd tried his damnedest. What was it with that man? Laurenson suspected there was more to it than just fear—the risks had been lessened by having Roz in custody—so what was it?. Could it be a tinge of guilt?

When he headed back to the office, he was not necessarily feeling less guilty, but he was definitely feeling much better.

Miranda, in the middle of a call, waved Laurenson over. "I'm sorry," she was saying, "I can't give you that kind of information over the phone. If you'd like to come into the office, though, I'm sure one of the officers would be willing to talk with you.... No. No." She grabbed a pen and scribbled *Ident is here. Val wants to talk to you.* "No," she went on. "If you're that anxious to check it out, you'll have to come in to make your inquiries in person."

She dropped the receiver into its cradle.

"They hung up on you?"

"Yeah."

"What did they want?"

"To find out if a car someone's trying to sell has been reported stolen."

Laurenson saluted her. "Miranda, they don't come any better than you."

She laughed. "Well, they don't come any older than me, at any rate." She waved him on towards the back. "If you liked that, just wait till you talk to Val."

"Where is he?"

"Downstairs with the car they brought in this morning. Ident's been working on it for the last half hour."

Val was hunkered down on his heels by Rozilind Smith's little brown Honda watching a technician at work. He uncoiled as Laurenson walked over.

"Good news, Staff."

The technician poked his head out from under the car. "I say we split it fifty-fifty and head for Costa Rica."

"Dewy Jones! How the hell are you?"

"Same old, same old. I see you've been busy as usual."

"Well, yeah. This hasn't been a bad posting...always something going on. So I gather you've found some money. Have you found any diskettes?"

"Sure have. Would you prefer the diskettes to the money?"

Laughing, Laurenson turned to Tavarov. "Lots of money?"

"As long as we strip search Dewy before he leaves."

"How much?"

"Two hundred thou. We may yet find the rest, or it could be she's been making a series of bank deposits. Too soon to tell which yet."

Laurenson grinned happily. "In any case, it sounds like enough to make Heyden think twice about his decision not to cooperate."

EPILOGUE

Laurenson awoke and glanced at the clock. 7:00 am. Too early. He and Christie had a canyon crawl booked for eleven, but it would be a shame to wake her too soon; she'd started to nod off before the fire countless times last night before finally admitting she couldn't stay awake another moment. It was the fresh mountain air and all that cross-country skiing.

Imagine that, he thought with delight, *I've finally made it to Jasper. What took me so long?*

He'd been asking himself that ever since carrying their suitcases into one of the loft units at the Jasper Inn. He'd shared the question with Christie in the steam room down by the pool before supper. It had been the subject of his last thought as he'd looked through the skylight last night.

He loved the mountains in their mantle of snow. He loved the tiny kitchenette where Christie had heated chili and toasted garlic bread while he got a fire going. He loved the pine tree that sheltered their tiny balcony. Thank God he'd booked a full five nights.

He'd done that so this would be Christie's best Christmas ever, even without her kids and in the wake of so much trauma. This could well be as good as it would get; Shaun and Angela might even now be regretting having gone to live with their father. Laurenson gave himself a mental shake—where was it carved in stone that there couldn't some day be good relations between them and these kids? He would, married or not, be with Christie for a long, long time. Marriage? He thought he'd better talk Christie into it...he could protect her better as her husband than he ever could as an interested other. He wanted to stand between her and whatever harm might yet come her way.

Too damned pessimistic, he told himself. *Things work out. It's amazing how they work out. For the best,* he added, snuggling up against Christie. There'd been a time when he'd thought he knew how things should be, and it was up to him to make them be that way. He'd confessed that to Christie the day of Keith's funeral and she had quoted him a Taoist saying, "If you try to grab hold of the world and do what you want with it, you won't succeed. The world is a vessel for spirit; it wasn't made to be manipulated. Tamper with it, and you'll spoil it. Hold it, and you'll lose it."

He'd come a long way since he first got up on his high horse and rode off to save the world. With a smile, he relived what, as a rookie, he had considered the epitome of what police work was all about. He could still see the six squad cars drawn up around a country crossroads, their flashers surrealistically strobing the dark. He'd been one of the cops sheltering behind the hood of his car with his gun drawn as a police dog confronted a young man in a beat-up old truck.

"Come out with your hands up." The order, delivered through a megaphone, had sliced through a background chorus of country sounds, mainly the songs of crickets and frogs. "Leave the truck. Bring the child with you, but keep your hands in the air."

In the end, no charges had been laid. The tip had either been made in error or motivated by malice. Though they searched both the vehicle and the road it had come down, they were unable to find the illegal firearm the suspect was alleged to have in his possession.

That, and who knew how much other police work he'd prided himself on, was the other side of the universe from "order arising of its own accord." Now it looked to him like excess, like playing cops and robbers.

Jeez, he thought. *The Tao of Pooh! More like, the Tao of Laurenson! She wasn't just an extortionist; she tried to kill her own father.*

He remembered having said once to Christie, "There are some things I would never do."

She had responded without hesitation, "Well, there aren't many I can think of that I would *never* do. Because, given the right incentive, feeling angry enough or frustrated enough, or confident enough that there'd be no consequences...well, how do I know for sure what I would do?"

He'd pressed her with, "Would you commit murder? Would you torture a child?"

But she hadn't backed down. "I've got to believe it's possible, or I might one day get taken by surprise and simply lose it—my head, my self-control or whatever—to my everlasting remorse and unending regret."

He now regretted, come to think of it, the murderous rage he'd felt when the crown prosecutor chose to plea bargain with Rozilind. Although Heyden had agreed to cooperate, he had quickly emerged as the weak spot in their extortion case.

"Christ, Laurenson!" Vincent Takahashi had said, "If he's this evasive about their past dealings now, how's he going to answer her lawyer's questions on the witness stand? The defense will make mincemeat out of him."

"Still, there's no question that she actually took a quarter of a million dollars from him."

"Of course not, but if they keep raising the question of why she did, and he continues to look furtive...well, juries are only human."

"But to trade attempted murder for extortion without so much as a statement from her!"

"There isn't a hope in hell of getting her for attempted murder."

"You don't need to. The threat of trying her for it would be enough. She doesn't want her father to know. When it hit her that what she'd done in private would become public, would be hashed out in every despicable detail before her father's eyes—"

Takahashi had chortled. "You mean she was willing to kill him, just not to have him know she was willing to kill him. Yeah, right."

"You've never resisted a temptation solely because it occurred to you that someone might find out?"

"Are you suggesting that the only thing that's preventing me from doing what Rozilind Smith did is the thought of getting caught?"

He'd come within a whisker of retorting, *No, I'm suggesting there are a lot of things you've done that you wouldn't have done if you'd thought anybody would ever find out.* Instead, he'd said with faint hope of being heard, "She's built her life on always being right and everyone else being all too often wrong."

"Stick to the policing and leave the lawyering to us," Takahashi had said. "She'll go to prison for extortion. If we don't plea bargain, she'll go free."

It had taken time for him to become reconciled to that decision. Only gradually did it occur to him that justice might still be served. Mug shots and fingerprinting are humiliating for most people. Living in a cage with only a pony wall to provide a scrap of privacy while using the toilet is demeaning, even for less private and fastidious women than Roz. For that matter, gloves-off interrogations are brutal for all but hardened criminals; the ones Roz underwent were harsh in their unrelenting accusations, implied judgements, and subtle shaming.

He'd finally realized that there was no saying for sure who had won and who had lost. The process Roz was undergoing was bringing a whole wall of her castle tumbling down. Taking away her sense of being right, they'd taken away her sense of safety.

He'd paid her a visit in lock-up one night when he couldn't sleep. From all reports, for two nights she hadn't been able to sleep either. When she'd looked up at him that night, he'd felt the full force of what was torturing her. He would never know for sure, but he had a strong suspicion that, like so many other lost souls, she'd grown up believing she had to be perfect to be loved. He'd recalled then that she hadn't even waited to see if her diagram of the washroom was good enough to get her off the hook; she had begun to cave in when the realization hit her that her father couldn't, in the normal course of events, fail to learn what she had done to him.

"He's behind you a hundred percent," he'd said quietly.

Her voice was husky. "He'll worry himself sick. You've got to tell him I did it."

"I already have. In his view, anyone you'd go after deserves what they get."

"Could you arrange for me to see him?"

"Let's give him a little time to get back on his feet."

Laurenson suddenly remembered it was December 23rd, the anniversary of the day Roz had left her father to get through Christmas without knowing whether she was alive or dead. He thought, *It took her a long time to acquire a little basic human decency.*

Christie turned, eyes still shut, and wrapped her arms around him. What a long way they had come this past year! He kissed her eyes and whispered in her ear, "What's your idea of the perfect orgasm?"

"Whaat?"

"Darin Childe gave me a little lecture once on warrior women out to count coup. It popped into my mind just now. Apparently one of the ways of counting coup, is having 'the perfect orgasm.' So...what's the perfect orgasm for you?"

She laughed. "One *I* have."

"That goes without saying."

"So does sex."

"Yeah but..." He got distracted by a glimpse of white breast where her pajama top gaped a little around a button that had come undone.

She watched him let go of the threads of his inquiry in favour of going for her breast.

"Good choice, Dick Tracy," she said.

"*Dick Tracy! You'll pay for that!*"

But not just yet. As so often happened at times like this, the urge to come home to her took precedence over everything else.

The End